D0359511

ADMISSION

ADMISSION

TRAVIS THRASHER

Northern Plains Public Library
Ault Colorado

MOODY PUBLISHERS
CHICAGO

© 2006 by
TRAVIS THRASHER

All rights reserved. No part of this book may be reproduced in any form without permission in writing from the publisher, except in the case of brief quotations embodied in critical articles or reviews.

Cover Design: LeVan Fisher Design
Cover Photo: Andrew Kolb/Masterfile
Editor: LB Norton

Library of Congress Cataloging-in-Publication Data

Thrasher, Travis, 1971-
    Admission / by Travis Thrasher.
      p. cm.
    ISBN-13: 978-0-8024-8671-4
      1. College students—Alcohol use—Fiction. 2. Missing persons—
Fiction. 3. Roommates—Fiction. I. Title.

PS3570.H6925A66 2006
813'.6—dc22

                                                            2005023641

ISBN: 0-8024-8671-1
ISBN-13: 978-0-8024-8671-4

We hope you enjoy this book from Moody Publishers. Our goal is to provide high-quality, thought-provoking books and products that connect truth to your real needs and challenges. For more information on other books and products written and produced from a biblical perspective, go to www.moodypublishers.com or write to:

Moody Publishers
820 N. LaSalle Boulevard
Chicago, IL 60610

1 3 5 7 9 10 8 6 4 2

Printed in the United States of America

For Andy, Lane, Scott, Westra, Chris, & Corey
They know why.

April 1994

SOMETHING DEEP and terrifying jerked him awake. Even before he opened his eyes, Jake knew he was confined, his head lodged against something unmovable. He couldn't feel his arm tangled underneath him. His dry tongue rolled against cracked lips as he tried to clear his ragged throat. The first thing he saw was the tan faux-leather back of the car seat. Then, looking down on the floor, he saw a handgun wrapped in a muddy towel.

He sat up in the big backseat, the scent of reefer undeniable. The smell alone identified the car as Bruce's tattered Chevy Monte Carlo, but there was no sign of his friend. The keys were still in the ignition.

Moving brought a wave of nausea and pain. His back was drenched in sweat. Rolling down the window, Jake breathed in and felt a throbbing in his left side. Like an air bubble, but far worse. It felt like the time he'd been beaten to a pulp, the time he lost consciousness just a month ago. But judging by the way he felt, and his total ignorance of where he was or what had happened to him in the last twelve or twenty-four or God knows how many hours, he realized this time could be worse.

He opened the car door and stumbled out, falling over and feeling the sting of blood rushing back into his legs. For a moment he lay there breathing, the morning sun making him perspire more.

The sky and the clouds above looked peaceful, and he wished it could be like this, staring at the heavens with no worries or fears. But something nagged at him. Something awful.

Finally sitting up, Jake looked around. He sat on a patch of gravel off a rocky unnamed road. A cornfield fenced him in on one side, a forest on the other.

He stood up and looked around. Then he stared down at his shirt, his jeans, his shoes.

All were covered in blood. The crusted red on his white T-shirt—the dark smudges on his jeans—the specks on his shoes, even his shoelaces—Jake absorbed all this with a slow-burning hysteria.

He'd come out here with his friends for the last few days of spring break. To camp out and drink and have fun. The last thing he remembered was sitting around the fire last night. Or maybe the night before.

Jake didn't know.

A feeling of guilt and dread began to fill his mind. The scary thing was that he had no idea why.

January 2005

I CAN'T REMEMBER a New Year's Eve that ever lived up to the hype. Even during my wild days of college, I found typical weeknights more exciting than the inevitable bust of December 31. But on the first day of 2005, after toasting in the New Year amidst friends and colleagues, I came home to my silent condo in Colorado Springs at 2:45 a.m. and got the surprise call of the decade.

"Hey, Jake—long time, huh? It's Alec. You're probably out celebrating. I would be too. In fact, that's why I'm calling. I'm getting ready to go out, permanently. To just get away. And I thought I should finally call."

Something crashed in the background, as if he had knocked over a table or a lamp.

"Things are sorta hairy, and I just wanted to—well, I guess I've always needed to tell you this. I bailed after all the craziness at college. But I promised Carnie and wanted to finally call. . . ."

The rambling message stopped for a second.

"Carnie wanted you to know he was sorry it all happened. It was his fault, and he felt guilty. He didn't—he couldn't—tell you, even in those last few days. I think he might have tried. Maybe none of us wanted to listen.

"I never thought—no, I never believed it could happen. Not that way. I heard about it, you know. I should've come back. I know. I should've been there. But I couldn't."

Alec let go with a long curse.

"I just never thought he'd do it, you know? But there's lots I never knew. . . . I just wanted you to know in case . . . in case whatever. In case you don't hear from me again."

There was a click. No good-bye.

Not a call, a card, or a sign of life. There had been silence for eleven years. Even after letting it all go, I'd thought about Alec. A lot. I often wondered how he was doing, how he was coping, how he was living.

These could be the delirious words of a drunk, as far as I knew. I didn't take them seriously. I put the call out of my mind and went on with my regular business, assuming I wouldn't hear from Alec or any of the guys again.

Just six months later I would find out how very wrong I was.

THREE

December 1993

THE PARTY THAT officially started at 7:17 p.m. on New Year's Eve at Four-leaf Clover sports bar would not be over for another six months. The spark of violence ignited that night would take eleven long years to burn out.

Jake wasn't thinking about where he would be in a decade, much less in ten hours. He lived in the moment, and the moment meant potato skins and beer, a little pool with his big roommate, Carnie, then eventually heading over to Franklin's house in the suburbs. There would be over a hundred students at the party, which Franklin had been planning since Halloween. It would be a great way to celebrate the New Year and the last semester of his college experience.

The last semester. It had a nice ring to it. One more semester, then freedom.

Jake leaned back in the plastic chair and drained another cup of Lite. He had programmed an hour's worth of music on the jukebox, and the howling vocals of Kurt Cobain filled the bar.

"All right," Jake said to his roommate of three years. "What gives?"

"With what?"

Jake nodded at the backpack on the chair beside Carnie. "Late night studying?"

Carnie didn't smile but looked around the room. There were a few people at the bar. "Take a look," he said.

Jake took the backpack and placed it in his lap. He unzipped the top and saw the black metal butt of a handgun wedged between a couple of shirts. "No way. That real?"

Carnie nodded and adjusted his Tennessee Vols cap.

"You planning a hit?" Jake joked.

"I told you I was going to buy one."

"That looks like a cannon."

Carnie took the backpack from Jake and zipped it back up. "It's a .45 automatic." He described the make and model and weight and other information Jake didn't pay attention to.

"So what's all that mean?" Jake finally asked, amused at the long explanation by his usually tight-lipped friend.

"It'll do its job."

"You know—you might be able to fire this off in your backyard down there in the Tennessee hills, but around here people might take exception."

"I've got a membership at the range."

"How much that gun cost?"

Carnie glanced at him. "Enough."

"I'm sure it wasn't cheap."

"Yeah, but it was *my* money. Your parents approve of your spending habits?" Carnie looked at the empty cup in Jake's hand.

"Got me there," Jake said with a smile. "Next round's on me." He went to the bar and came back with another pitcher.

"How much is cover tonight?" Carnie asked.

Jake laughed. "Come on. Franklin's covering us."

"You sure?"

"He'd better. The guy's loaded. He drives a BMW."

"He's a tightwad."

"Whose parents have gone to the Caribbean for the holidays."

"Who goes to the Caribbean for the holidays?" Carnie asked with an amused look.

"I guess Chicago snow and cold get pretty old. If you can, why not?"

"Why didn't he go with them?"

"You know Franklin. Mr. Independent."

Snow fell outside, continuing the trend of the last week. None of them liked to drive when they were going out, but all of them got behind the wheel without thought. It was part of the game, part of the life. Carnie was driving tonight, having lost the best of three rock-paper-scissors.

"Think we can spend the night at Franklin's?"

Jake shrugged. "You can have his parents' king."

"Can you imagine Alec sleeping in their bed?"

They both laughed.

"He wouldn't care whose bed it was," Jake said.

"He had a problem."

"Yeah, it was a big problem. He just didn't care."

Carnie laughed. "A man has big problems when he can't get up to go to the bathroom."

"Like I said, Alec just didn't care."

"Where do you think he is?"

"Who knows? Maybe he's in a prison somewhere."

"Think we'll ever see him again?"

"Probably not," Jake said, then added, "I kinda hope we don't."

"Why's that?"

"I want to finish out college alive."

As Pearl Jam began to blare over the bar speakers, Carnie lit up a cigarette, then paused, anticipating Jake's outstretched hand.

"Why don't you get your own?"

"I don't smoke," Jake said.

"Only when you drink."

"That's right."

"That's every day."

"Are you saying I have a problem?" Jake asked.

"My name is Jake, and I'm an alcoholic," Carnie answered.

"My name is Carnie, and tonight I'm going to pass out in Franklin's living room."

"My name is Franklin, and I dry-clean my shirts."

"My name is Bruce, and I smoke weed for medicinal purposes."

They both laughed and lit up smokes and drank their beers.

The night would be long, and it had just started.

➤➤ ◄◄

A crowd had already gathered at Franklin's mansion in Burr Ridge when they arrived around ten. The swooping arch of the driveway was littered with cars.

Bruce Atkinson, another of their roommates, greeted Jake and Carnie near the door. He was already pretty lit and was stepping outside for a smoke.

If Carnie was the redneck in their group, Bruce was the surfer dude. Born in Illinois but raised in California, he was the one most often found wandering off to smoke pot and zone out. He wasn't the smartest of the lot, but he had a big heart. Sort of like Ethan Hawke in *Reality Bites,* in both looks and character.

David Kirby completed the foursome that shared an armpit of an apartment ten minutes away from Providence College. Compared to Franklin's home, their place was a bomb shelter. Initially they were going to have the New Year's party at their apartment, but Franklin got permission from his traveling parents to bring in kegs and liquor and live it up for the night.

Jake led the others inside, feeling like a rock star coming onstage. He was the life of the party. It used to be the tag team of Jake and Alec. People watched to see what the two of them would do next. So maybe it was for the same reason that people liked watching a train wreck, but they watched. At a small college like Providence, most people sat on the sidelines. Some out of fear. Some, supposedly, out of faith, whatever that meant. But Jake and Alec weren't afraid to be on the field, front and center. They loved to laugh, loved to have fun, and loved to drink.

Now that Alec was gone, Jake had to stand alone. And that was okay with him.

Franklin, Mr. Preppy himself, was wandering around in his turtleneck sweater with a glass of Coke. Carnie found Kirby and settled into conversation. Bruce went over to the stereo and selected "Breaking the Girl" off Red Hot Chili Peppers' latest album. An assortment of students from nervous freshmen to aloof seniors mingled in the open, high-roofed living room and kitchen.

In the blur of people and music and motion, even before he could get a beer in his hand, Jake saw her across the room, talking to some Jim-Bob sports dude he didn't know.

Alec used to say she was Jake's evil desire. Carnie called her "the princess," not sarcastically but with genuine regard. Bruce called her untouchable.

Her name was Alyssa Roberts.

What's she doing here?

Jake had stumbled on to Alyssa two years before, when she was a freshman working in the Dean of Students office. He'd been enamored from the first, for reasons that were long but not complicated. She was beautiful and innocent and wanted nothing to do with him.

Well, not exactly *nothing*. There was a connection, one that both fascinated and frustrated him at the same time. Alec once said she was screwing with his head, and Jake said he didn't care and she could continue messing around with it all she wanted.

Jake got a plastic cup of beer and went over to talk with her over the wailing funk of the Chili Peppers.

"I knew you'd be here," Alyssa said with a smile.

Jake looked at the cup in her hand.

"Sprite," she said, answering the question that probably worked itself over his face.

"O'doul's," he said, making a joke that was lost on her.

The guy at her side had momentarily disappeared.

"Have a good Christmas?" she asked him.

"Yeah. You?"

"It was wonderful. My entire family came in for the holidays."

"Get any nice gifts?"

"I'll be going to Europe this summer."

Jake raised his eyebrows. "I'm talking about going to Europe with some of the guys. Maybe we'll follow you."

"I'll probably be hanging out in different places from you."

He smiled. "You know, one of these days, you're going to realize that you have me all wrong."

"I do?"

"At the core, I'm a gentleman. I don't know why you can't see that."

"I see more than you think," Alyssa said, her dark flowing hair and deep brown eyes entrancing him in that single moment just like a thousand times before.

Then Jim-Bob came alongside and interrupted them, and for a moment Jake wanted to take the guy's perfectly white teeth and make them eat his fist.

Jake nodded and went on to enjoy the party and do what he did best: mingle and drink. It took his mind off Alyssa and off the fact that he would never be a smiley-teeth sports dude.

➤➤ ◄◄

Around eleven-thirty a dozen seniors arrived, taking Jake and his buddies by surprise. The newcomers were part of the illustrious jock crowd, a pack of basketball and baseball players and their dippy girlfriends. Jake had told Franklin not to invite them, but for parties like this, you didn't send out invitations. The buzz got around and people came, even people you hated.

The dominos started falling when Jake saw the hulking six-foot-four figure of Brian Erwin with his close-cropped military haircut. They had a history.

"I see you're in typical form tonight," Brian said with a condescending laugh.

Jake thought of a few choice adjectives to describe what he thought of Brian, but decided not to voice them.

Brian had Laila Henson at his side, which only made Jake realize how pathetic the college sports god was. He knew he hated the guy and that it was partly out of jealousy. If you could admit why you hated a guy, that made it okay. But

Laila—she was "boil the rabbit" material, and everyone except Brian knew it. She was good-looking in a cheap, scary way, but that was it.

Laila and Jake had a history too.

Around midnight, as the television and radio and the crowd all did the countdown, Jake frantically searched for Alyssa, first inside and then out in the driveway. But she was nowhere to be found, so all he could do was toast himself and finish his beer as the snow continued to fall and the sweat on the back of his neck dried to a chill.

⇥ ⇤

An hour later, in a haze of blurred emotion, Jake seized onto Brian's throat after the big guy shoved him into a wall. The fight, over something stupid—and wasn't it always over something stupid—ended up with Brian clocking him in the forehead before Bruce and Franklin intervened.

Jake barely felt the blow, even though he stumbled and fell to the ground. He continued to rail curses and insults at Brian. Jake didn't even know what he was saying, but Brian knew and would remember. And in the middle of the whole scene hovered Laila, the blonde-haired temptress who had caused the confrontation.

⇥ ⇤

When Jake woke up the next morning, he remembered none of this. He looked in the mirror and saw his nice shiner and had to ask where it had come from.

His last memory was of standing in the snow longing for Alyssa and wishing he could give her a New Year's greeting.

FOUR

June 2005

THE FIRST THING I NOTICED about the chalet was a large family photo that could be spotted a mile away if the front door was open. It featured a picture-perfect family: aristocratic-looking father, pampered wife adorned in jewelry, perfect blonde daughter.

I walked into the main room and turned my head to take in the immense ceiling that curved down toward the deck. The open family room centered around a stone fireplace half the size of my apartment bedroom. The big man I followed waved me toward the L-shaped sofa as he asked if I wanted anything to drink. I told him a soda would be fine.

From where I sat I could see the tops of surrounding mountains waiting for winter to cap them and keep them busy. The cabin felt homey but not quite lived in, a bit too immaculate. It almost seemed as though it should give off a new-car scent.

"Nice getaway, huh?" the host said as he handed me a glass with ice and cola.

"Very nice."

It had taken me a couple hours to get to this cabin in Breckenridge from my apartment in Colorado Springs. I had declined to answer the first few voice mails from a woman working for Mr. Jelen, then had spoken to her in person but had still decided not to meet with him. Jelen had personally gotten ahold of me at home a week ago. He was used to getting his way.

But it wasn't his negotiating skills or business bullying that got me standing in his Colorado getaway. It was his dropping the name Alec Tristam.

Gregory Jelen sipped something other than soda and glanced around the cabin, as if just getting acquainted with it himself.

"Do you know the first weekend after they finished building this, my daughter had a party here without my consent? That's my Claire."

"Your only daughter?" I asked the obvious.

"My only child. She just turned twenty-one. Supposed to be a senior at the University of Colorado."

"Good school."

"A party school for dopeheads and liberals. It wasn't my choice."

"My parents didn't think much of my choice either."

"Did it work out for you?"

"Not exactly," I told him with a smile, thinking about the disaster of my freshman year at University of Southern Cal.

Gregory Jelen crossed his leg and rubbed his chin, studying me for a moment. I knew the basic reason why I was here, but I hadn't agreed to anything. Jelen's assistant hadn't given many details.

What I did know was that Mr. Jelen was a wealthy businessman who got his name mentioned in the Forbes 500 list every year. He had begun a technology company that started out making chips and now made parts for everything—PDAs, Ipods, cell phones. I read an article about his blue-collar roots and how he had made himself a multimillionaire. He lived most of the year in New York City, but he owned this chalet and also a beachfront property in Miami.

"So you own your own business?" Jelen asked.

"Yeah. Outdoor Excursions. I started it five years ago."

"I read on your Web site that you've climbed Mount Everest three times."

I nodded, thinking of my big claim to fame. I wondered how much he had heard. "We've taken one expedition up there. The first two times were just for myself."

"What's it like standing on top of the world?"

I laughed. "Honestly, the first time I almost couldn't make it. You can be in the best physical condition of your life and still get beaten up on a climb like that. The first time I didn't even appreciate it. But it looks good on a résumé."

"It certainly does. How is business?"

"It's fair," I said, not being fully honest.

Business in the last year had tapered off, and bills had risen. After the accident a year ago, it was easy to understand why. That was why I was in this room and not on the side of a mountain or taking a trek in the jungle.

"Well, look, let me get down to the reason you're here. Thanks for driving, by the way. How long did it take you?"

"Couple hours. No big deal."

Mr. Jelen looked serious, his strong jawline tightening as he sat silently for a moment. He was one of those men who thought before he spoke, a trait nobody would ever accuse me of.

"As you know, my daughter disappeared in January. She should have graduated by now, but instead she vanished. At first we thought she was a missing person, but investigators discovered she had disappeared with a guy named Alec Tristam. For months we've tried to find her."

"You involve the cops?"

"We've involved everyone we possibly could. She's an adult; she can do what she wants. Of course we were relieved to hear that nothing had happened to her—but we still want to know where she is."

"And you have no leads?"

"We know that Claire met Alec last summer while she spent time at our place in Miami. She went back there over winter break and never came back."

"Alec was in Miami?" I asked.

"You didn't know that?"

I chuckled. "Mr. Jelen, I haven't seen Alec since college."

"Yes, I'm aware of that. But you said you had heard from him a couple times since graduation."

"Just once. He left me a message earlier this year."

This piqued Jelen's interest. "What'd he say?"

"Nothing, really. Just called to say hi."

I wasn't about to mention Carnie, especially to a stranger.

"You never knew where he was living?"

"No," I said. "It doesn't surprise me that he was living in Miami. Nothing would surprise me about Alec."

"What was he like?"

I shrugged and took a sip of my soda. "He was fun. Crazy. A bad influence. But I was a lot different back then."

"How so?"

"I just needed to grow up," I said, a simple answer that didn't begin to sum up the truth.

"He's your age, right?"

"Yeah. Thirty-four."

"Why did Alec leave college a week before graduation?"

I looked at Mr. Jelen to see if this was an honest question or if he was trying to bait me. He probably knew more about Alec's history than I did. But I was sure there were a few details he didn't know.

"He wouldn't have graduated anyway," I said.

"But he disappeared, right?"

"Alec was good at disappearing. He'd done it once before that year. Have you checked with his family?"

His nod said *Of course we did.* And if he was talking with me now, they had surely exhausted most of their resources.

"I don't know anything more than what I initially told your assistant. Alec's father lives somewhere around the Indiana-Illinois border. His mother lives—or used to live—somewhere in Florida. That's probably what he was doing in Miami."

"That's correct."

"I'm sure you know tons more than I do, Mr. Jelen. I haven't seen him in eleven years."

"I believe you can help me."

"How? What do you want me to do?"

"I would like for you to find him," Mr. Jelen said with eyes that didn't blink and didn't move off mine. "I will pay you to find Alec. And my daughter."

"You're sure they're together?"

The man, dressed in khaki dress pants and a light blue button-down shirt that probably cost more than my last month's earnings, nodded again.

"If you haven't been able to find him, why do you think I can?"

"You're his friend. You can talk to some of your other college buddies."

"It's been a long time since I've seen any of them."

"This could be a reunion. I hear you didn't go to the ten-year anniversary last year."

I was beginning to get annoyed at how much this guy knew.

"I don't think many people went."

"We spoke with a few of your friends, but they were resistant to help at all."

"Really? Like who?"

"Bruce Atkinson. Franklin Gotthard. Mike Fennimore."

"You talked to all of them?"

"Someone did."

It didn't surprise me that none of them wanted to help this guy. If they didn't know where Alec was, then what else were they going to do? What else could they say?

College was eleven years ago. We had left those times and memories behind. At least I had.

"Mr. Jelen—if I knew anything more about Alec, I'd help you, but—"

"This is my offer. Go see all of your college friends. Ask them about any details related to Alec—if they've seen him in the last few years, what they know about him, anything. Be an investigator for a few weeks. Give me whatever information you learn."

"I can't just take off a few weeks."

Mr. Jelen nodded, and I suddenly realized he probably knew how business had been going for me.

"How does fifty thousand dollars sound?"

I let out a laugh. "Uh, great."

"I'll give you that up front to work for me."

"You serious? For how long?" I asked, suddenly numb at this offer. I hadn't made fifty thousand dollars last *year.*

"I want you to turn up every lead possible."

"But if I don't find him—"

"I'll give you the money up front. And will pay for all travel expenses."

"Just to—just to go see my old buddies?"

Mr. Jelen bent over and picked up a leather book from the table between us. He handed it to me.

"These are photos of Claire," he told me as I began looking through it.

His daughter was a pretty blonde who looked as if she had taken after him in height. She had a defined jawline and could be a model. I thumbed through the photos.

"I just want to find my daughter again and know that she's safe. You're one of my last resorts."

I put the album down. "I just—I don't want to take this job—and your money—only to tell you I still don't have a clue."

"Your friends know more than they're telling," Mr. Jelen said. "I know that. I think you know that too."

"And you think they'll tell me?"

"I know they will. You were the one everybody talked about. The one they asked about. Jake Rivers. The infamous Jake Rivers."

"I don't buy that."

"Yes, you do. You and Alec were close. You two were the ringleaders."

"That doesn't mean I'll find him."

"If anybody can, it's you."

I put my glass down on the table and stood up. "Look, I appreciate this . . . this offer. Really. But I just . . . I can't."

"Jake, please," Jelen began to say before I interrupted him.

"I can't. Not now, not after all this time."

There are certain things you don't know and will never know.

"I don't know where else to turn."

23

"If you haven't found him, I have no idea how I will be able to."

Mr. Jelen stood and faced me with an intense stare. "I think you should really consider this opportunity," he said, his tone suddenly different.

"Meaning what?"

"Meaning there was a lot I learned about Alec and his friends during college. A lot of very interesting information."

I stared at him. "What are you saying?"

"I know what happened to Paul Carnigan. What happened before you graduated. Why the police were so interested in all of you."

I stood, momentarily frozen, looking at him, waiting to hear what else he would say.

"There were some interesting things I discovered, stuff people might be interested in. You see—I don't believe people just 'disappear.'"

I knew exactly what he was saying. What he was *really* saying. This was no longer a simple request. It was blackmail.

"If I try to find your daughter and can't, do I know if—"

"Then at least I'll know we tried. You'll still have your money. And I won't ask anything of you."

"There's a lot you probably don't know about college," I said.

"I'm sure there is. And I don't care about any of that. Jake—listen to me. I just want to know where my daughter and *your friend* disappeared to. That's all I want."

I nodded and said I would get back to him in a day or two with an answer.

But he had already made my decision for me. It was that simple.

January 1994

THE SNOWFLAKES ON the sidewalk were light enough to brush aside with an errant swoop of the leg. Jake was heading across the courtyard to return an overdue book he had found just yesterday under his bed. It was only a month overdue. It gave him a reason to visit the campus and check his mailbox, along with other things.

One of those other things, perhaps the only other thing that really mattered, he found in the library. It was a lucky guess. He saw her sitting at a table reading, of all things.

"Please tell me you're not doing homework," he said.

The deliberate eyes regarded him for a moment "Please tell me you're not actually checking out a book."

"And if I were?"

"The universe as I know it might be in serious jeopardy."

"No need to fear," he said. "Just returning a book."

"I like the eye," Alyssa noted. "Very macho."

"I did that for the yearbook photo. When are those again?"

"They were in November."

Jake feigned disappointment as he nodded and tightened his lips. "Working over the holidays?" he asked.

"Not till next semester."

He looked at the book sitting open on the table. *"Middle-march?"*

"Reading can be fun."

"May I?" he asked, gesturing to the chair facing her.

"No, thanks."

"No, thanks? You make it sound like I'm selling some-thing."

"It's that big grin on your face. I don't trust grins like that."

He laughed. Even after all these years and all these conver-sations and even that one memorable date, he still couldn't figure this girl out. Every time he thought there might be some-thing, anything, between the two of them, the door would shut and he would get a comment like *No, thanks*.

Jake sat down anyway. "We don't have to be quiet, do we?"

"It's a library."

"We're on winter break."

"Aren't you *always* on a break?"

Jake laughed again and admired her flawless complexion. Alyssa was one of those girls who simply never got a pimple, period. He looked scraggly with several days' worth of beard and unruly hair and that nice, attractive shiner to gaze at.

"I remember the day I first met you."

"The driving-on-the-soccer-field incident?"

"Oh, come on. How could you forget?"

"That's right. The panther." She rolled her eyes.

"People don't give me enough credit for taking a five hundred-pound cement panther."

"I think that makes you so very cool."

She picked up her book to resume reading.

"I only got suspended for a week."

"Only?"

"It was worth it."

"Taking the heat for your friends," Alyssa said, her soft voice so articulate and formal. "Such nobility."

"It was destiny, you know."

"What?"

"My running into you."

"That sounds like such a romantic notion," Alyssa said.

26

"Well, if you say so . . ."

"I would say it was inevitable. Working in the dean's office, meeting a fine, reputable student such as yourself."

Jake shook his head as she started reading again. "What is it about me that you hate so much?"

Alyssa's dark eyes darted back to him. A slight smile wrinkled her lips. "Hate is a strong word."

"Okay, dislike then."

"That black eye, for one thing."

"I know—it's pretty ugly."

"It's something drunken frat boys get on the weekends."

"Providence doesn't allow fraternities."

"Oh, really?" she asked, raising her eyebrows. "I thought that's what your apartment was."

"You know, you only have one more semester left to mock me."

"But you have the rest of your life to live with yourself."

"I'm pretty happy with myself," Jake said.

"Bravo for you."

He held back his retort.

Deep down, he knew something was there. That was what the college experience was like, why it differed from everything else he had known and might ever know. You spent so much time with classmates and roommates that relationships inevitably grew beyond simple friendship or acquaintance. Deep in the heart of night in a popcorn-smelling study room—or the smoky recesses of a loud bar—truths came out. And he remembered the time Alyssa almost admitted to something being there.

Jake decided to call a truce. For today. "As always, it was a pleasure, Miss Roberts."

"Stay away from big jocks," Alyssa said as he walked away from the table.

When he got back to his car, he realized he still had the library book in his hand.

➤➤ ◄◄

On the drive back home, snow falling steadier now, he recalled their first meeting.

Jake had walked into the office of the Dean of Students fully expecting to be kicked out of college.

"I'm here to see Ms. Peterson," he told the longhaired brunette behind the desk.

She gave him a knowing, courteous smile and looked down at the planner on the desk. "She's with another appointment. You're down for 10:45."

Jake was fifteen minutes early, a first so far for anything at Providence College.

"I can wait." He gestured toward the closed door to the office. "Anybody I know?"

She smiled politely but didn't answer.

"Do you go here?" he asked.

She nodded again, still smiling. Her red sweater looked striking with her dark hair and eyes.

"What year are you?" Jake asked.

"I'm a freshman."

"Sophomore."

She nodded. "You were in my accounting class last semester."

He thought for a moment, trying to place her.

"I don't think you came very often," she said.

"Maybe that's why I got a D." He laughed. "You can't wing accounting."

She looked so young, like a high school kid, with thin eyebrows and a small nose. She didn't appear to have suffered from the dreaded "freshman fifteen" that came from a nice cafeteria and freedom.

"I'm Jake," he said.

"I know." She pointed to the appointment book.

He nodded. "You know, where I come from, people usually say *their* name when I give mine."

"Alyssa Roberts," she said as if reading off a report.

"Pleasure to meet you, *Alyssa Roberts*."

"Are you sure?"

"What?"

28

"That this is a pleasure?"

He chuckled. "Well, no, I've been dreading it ever since I got caught. But now, I'm thinking maybe it was fate."

"I don't think stealing a school mascot had anything to do with fate."

"One never knows."

"One bit of advice. Don't tell her that."

The door opened, and a young woman Jake didn't recognize walked out. Ms. Peterson followed her, then saw Jake waiting.

"I guess you can come on in and get this over with."

"I don't have to," he said. "I can stay and talk with, uh, Alyssa for a while."

Ms. Peterson gave him a cute-now-get-your-tail-over-here look.

Jake smiled at the beautiful girl at the desk. Suddenly he didn't want to get kicked out of Providence after all.

June 2005

IT HAD BEEN ELEVEN YEARS since I set foot on the campus of Providence College. I honestly thought I'd never be back.

"This place has changed," I told David Kirby as we shook hands.

"It's doubled since we graduated."

In the center of the college stood an ivy-covered structure that had once been a church years ago.

"I forgot how impressive that looks."

"That's Vermuelen Chapel," Kirby said with a grin. "I'm sure you attended every week."

"Ah, yes. You know me—never missed one."

Kirby laughed. He didn't look much different from when he was my roommate in college—still skinny, but more balding. "So how're you doing?"

"Can't complain," I said. "Thanks for seeing me on such short notice."

"Come on," he said.

"What?"

"I've been trying to get you here for, what?"

"A while," I said with a nod.

"Try years," Kirby said.

Kirby had been Director of Alumni Relations at Providence

for the past four or five years. Every so often I'd get a letter or a voice mail from him asking if I would like to come to Providence and speak in chapel.

"Not every Providence graduate goes on to climb Mount Everest. It'd be great for the students to hear about that."

"You know, there have been tougher climbs than that," I acknowledged.

"If you came and spoke in chapel, we'd hear all about it."

"Before last summer, I wouldn't have had much to say. Nothing uplifting, that is."

"You'll always have enough to say. It's getting you here that's the problem."

"Ever since my parents moved to Colorado and I followed —there haven't been a lot of reasons to come back."

We sat on a cement bench located close to the middle of the courtyard. Three sidewalks converged to this area in the midst of the chapel, the new science building, and the older classroom buildings that were there when both of us attended college.

"Where's your office?" I asked him.

"In what used to be called Dykstra Hall."

I could see the old two-story building from here.

"Remember when Alec tried to climb up to the balcony?"

Kirby thought for a moment but shook his head.

"That was the first time I ever went out with him," I said. "Actually, the first time he was ever on campus. It was January, and he was locked out of his dorm. I told him to climb up and get us in. He ended up slipping on ice and fell back and hit his butt on the air conditioner sticking out of the building. The air conditioner ripped out of the building. He went to bed all bloodied."

"Alec," Kirby said, shaking his head. "That guy was crazy."

"*That guy* is actually why I'm here." I told him about my meeting with Mr. Jelen and his request.

"So you agreed to help him?"

"It was hard to turn down."

Kirby looked at me with curiosity. "So how can I help?"

"Remember that e-mail I sent you awhile ago?"

He nodded.

"There's a part of me that's wanted to bury Providence and every memory about it."

"That's impossible."

"I know. But—it's like this is some golden opportunity that I've been given. Maybe God is handing this over to me on a silver plate, you know? And when I say silver, I mean silver."

"What do you mean?"

"This guy wrote me out a nice hefty check—just to try to find his daughter and Alec. Isn't that insane?"

"I'd worry too, if my daughter ended up missing with Alec."

I laughed. "Yeah, I guess you're right."

"You want me to tell you if it's a good idea?"

"No. I just—you know, out of all of us, you were the only one who had his head screwed on right."

"I don't know about that," Kirby said with a smile. "I was friends with you guys. I actually agreed to be your roommate two years in a row."

"That's right. What were you smoking?"

This prompted a genuine laugh. It was refreshing to hear it, a reminder of something good from the past.

"Sometimes I'll see a group of students and think back on all of us," Kirby said. "It doesn't seem like it was that long ago."

"For me it does. And there are things I've chosen to—well, I guess the only word is ignore. Going back to rekindle memories with our old college buddies might dredge up some pretty ugly stuff."

"Especially when those buddies include people like Alec," Kirby said with a solemn look.

"Have you heard from him at all?"

Kirby shook his head. I could see the sun shining down on his scalp.

"I think someone was trying to track Alec down not long ago," he said. "The last known address I had for him was somewhere in Florida. Miami, I think."

"But you haven't heard from him since graduation?"

Kirby shook his head. "He wouldn't come around here. Most of the guys wouldn't."

"You see any of them? Mike? Franklin? Shane?"

"Shane lives in Jacksonville, actually. Let's see. Mike lives downtown. I've seen him a few times. Franklin lives in the northern suburbs. He's a tremendous supporter of the school. I run into him sometimes at college functions. And Bruce—last I knew he was living in California."

"Probably on a pot farm."

Kirby laughed. "I can't give you any more on Alec than you already know. I was always more of the outsider anyway."

I looked at Kirby for a moment before responding. "You bailed us out of a lot of things."

"It didn't end up helping in the end, did it?"

I knew what he was referring to. I'd always wondered how much Kirby knew about everything, especially about our last spring break.

We quickly changed the subject, spending the next few minutes talking about his wife and two children.

"So what about you? Ever think about marriage?"

"From a distance," I said. "I think it's probably not for me."

"You just have to meet that right person."

"Yeah, probably."

I asked if I could get all of the known addresses he had on the guys. Mr. Jelen's folder had all that information, and it was probably more up-to-date than Kirby's files, but I figured I'd make sure since I'd come all this way.

"What's it like working here?" I asked as we entered the old Dykstra Hall.

"It's an entirely different college, to be honest. President Bramson left a year after we graduated."

"President Bramson," I said, not hiding my contempt. "He was a real winner."

"Yeah—he loved you too. No—everything's different. The students. The teachers. Some are still here. Remember Dr. Schilling?"

"The English prof?"

"Still here. Still looks the same. Things are just—I mean, the students, for one thing. They're so different from us."

"How so?"

"We were the poster children for Generation X. These new students—I'm telling you. They're different. They work together. They're not so full of—"

"Angst?" I interrupted with a smile.

"Angst. Rebelliousness. Attitude. It's just a whole different group."

"Then you had our class."

"Yeah. I don't think there'll be another class like ours. At least not at a college like Providence."

I spent an hour in David's office as he looked up and wrote out information on the guys and then showed off various items from over the years—photos, plans for new buildings, stuff that occupied his time every day. He eventually picked up a framed picture that sat on a desk full of shots of his family and handed it to me. I was surprised to see what it was.

The photo was taken in the apartment our senior year, back when it was Bruce, Carnie, Kirby, and I living together. Mike and Franklin were in it too.

"Look at that. Look at all of us." I hadn't seen a photo of Carnie for a while. Seeing him again—the meaty face peppered with several days' worth of beard, the contagious grin and good-natured eyes—it actually hurt a little. It stung, simply because I hadn't been expecting it. "Wow. I've never seen this."

"I think Shane must have taken it. The only other one not in the picture is Alec."

"Remember—he took off for a semester. Or a couple of semesters. Then showed up again in the middle of our senior year?"

"That's right. Practically lived with us until graduation."

I couldn't stop looking at the smiling face.

"Ever think about Carnie?" I asked him.

Kirby nodded and looked at me. For a moment there was nothing else to say.

"Sometimes I wonder what would have happened if Alec hadn't come back," I said.

"I still wonder what happened that spring. People still ask about the disappearance. It's become Providence lore."

"What do you say?"

"I tell them the truth: I don't know. I wasn't there. And I

was out of the loop, especially in those final few weeks. I've always figured you guys knew more. Not you—but Alec probably. And Carnie. Especially Carnie."

I nodded and thought of his words. *Those final few weeks.*

"It seems like that was a movie I watched years ago," I said. "Some movie I only vaguely remember."

"What sort of movie?" Kirby asked me.

I stared at the picture of Carnie and remembered the last time I saw him, on the morning of our graduation.

"A horror movie. One I don't want to watch again."

"I think you've got a great opportunity."

"To what?"

"To make peace with your past," Kirby said.

"What if I can't find Alec? And what about the others—they might not be thrilled to see me."

"Then at least you tried, right?"

I nodded. "I would love just to find Alec and ask him about those final days, you know. There was a lot he never told us."

"The only thing . . ." Kirby's voice trailed off. "If you do decide to, to seek him out, just . . ."

"Just what?"

"Just be careful."

"Of what?" I asked, half laughing at his earnestness.

"I don't know. A lot can change in a decade. You might not be the only one who wants to keep that stuff in the past."

SEVEN

January 1994

THE RULES PROHIBITED IT and the campus pharisees judged him for it, but they didn't know how *good* it was to feel so alive and real in the moment. And sometimes, as Jake sat on a stool at Shaughnessy's ten minutes from Providence, drinking bottles that cost $2.50 and listening to Stone Temple Pilots, he knew that this was temporary, that it was not necessarily even real, that tomorrow he would feel the staggering effects from drinking all evening through late night to early morning. But he loved losing himself in the moment, the music and the friends surrounding him and the memories he was building, and in some way it made him feel better. Perhaps a decade from now he'd look back on this time with fondness and a tinge of longing.

They were all out tonight, the night before D-day, before registration and before the official start of their last semester. Tonight was a time to reminisce about days past and brag about the months ahead. They were all drunk and having a good ole time. People said drunkenness was bad, but when you didn't drive and didn't harm anybody and didn't develop bad habits, what was wrong with it? So what if the college rules said you couldn't drink?

Carnie sat across from Jake, his big eyes occasionally drooping, tired from the beers and from the endless banter he usually stayed out of. Jake noticed that his Ford Trucks T-shirt was a couple sizes too small and a couple washes too faded. Carnie enjoyed listening and smoking and just sucking down the beers one after another. He was part of the audience, never a contestant and never the game show host. Carnie liked it that way.

Bruce brought them another round, dropping the bottles on the table and laughing at the warm reception fifteen bucks could get him. His long, layered hair needed a haircut that would probably expose good looks and a boyish charm. A slight goatee was all he could muster, and you had to be close to really notice it. His eyes would grow tinier as the night went on.

David Kirby moved at an offbeat to the music, trying his best to look cool. David Kirby was never going to look cool no matter how many beers he might have or how hard he might try. At this point in his college career, Kirby had grown out of nights like this. But tonight he was one of them, and they all accepted him regardless of his offbeat vibrations or the way he nursed his one beer.

Shane talked the most, saying things like "—and everywhere she went, I'm serious, they're all looking at her like *who is this chick* and all I'm doing is just hanging on saying sure, acting like we're all a couple—" and waving his hands and showing his square jaw and grunge hair. Shane and his stories could go on forever, with Jake usually ribbing him and getting him riled up.

Franklin sat next to Carnie, and this sort of made Jake feel all warm and cozy, the reality of a guy like Carnie hanging out with Franklin. The redneck from Tennessee hanging out with moneybags from suburbia.

Then there was Michael Fennimore, the kid everybody was still growing used to—too young to shave, a fake ID in his wallet. Jake started hanging out with Michael when he met the freshman last year. At first everybody wondered who the underage kid was. Alec especially hadn't liked Mike at first. But it didn't matter. Jake could have brought Ms. Peterson in and the guys would have shrugged, had a beer, and gone on with things.

They talked about women and the world and jobs and the

next semester and classes and professors and the girl at the edge of the bar who looked like she could be a working girl but one never knew and the soccer season and Alec and the New Year's Eve party and Brian Erwin and the fight. The conversation just kept going, and an hour passed like recess in grade school.

And as they spoke about graduation day, he appeared.

The man, the myth, the legend.

"Alec!"

A chorus of howls and curses greeted the short figure with spiked hair and devilish eyes that reeked of mischief.

Alec seemed embarrassed at the spectacle and went immediately to the loudest, Shane, who gave him a bear hug and asked in less-than-delicate words where he had been.

"Oh, here and there."

"Well, it's about time you're back!" Shane said, handing him a beer.

Franklin came to Alec's other side and asked if he was back for good. Bruce chimed in as Carnie simply smiled and lit up a smoke.

"The soccer team went downhill this year—"

"Are you registering tomorrow?"

"You know we got an apartment?"

"So what's the scoop, man?"

And as the conversation flowed, the mood suddenly subsided for Jake. He remained silent, watching Alec and his wry grin and his downplay of everybody's actions. He never did say where he'd been since disappearing almost a year ago.

Alec looked over at Jake and briefly nodded. "What's up?" he said, smiling.

And at that moment, Jake knew it was going to be an out-of-control semester. Just like that.

Jake didn't say anything. He was still pricked by Alec's simply taking off the middle of their junior year. He might have died for all they knew. Now he came sauntering back the triumphant hero to a bunch of drunken guys ready to finish out their school year. Alec the hero, conqueror of who knows what and back for only God knows why.

Jake felt a chill and drank to get rid of it.

➤➤ ◄◄

Jake looked over at Alec and saw the mischievous grin that made him think of a young Dustin Hoffman.

"The note you left was touching," Jake said. "I appreciate you letting me know where you were going."

"Did you like my phone message?"

"What message?"

"The one I left next to the note."

"Right." They were driving home, heading down back streets in Alec's Jeep. Even though Alec didn't slur and acted fine, Jake knew a Breathalyzer would give him away.

"I thought you'd be a little more thrilled that I'm back."

"I bet you only came back for the free drinks. Where will you head off to tomorrow?"

"I was thinking of going tonight," Alec said. "Vegas? Or Milwaukee? I'm having a hard time deciding."

"How about jail? Or AA?"

"You are funny. Anybody ever tell you that?"

"All the time."

Alec turned up the radio and blasted the Soundgarden song. The heat didn't seem to be working in the Jeep. Its rag-top, more suitable to summertime, leaked in the outside chill. But the speakers sounded brand-new.

"Still driving the CRX?" Alec asked after a couple of minutes of cranking the song.

"Ten months and four thousand dollars later. Yeah."

"I thought it might be totaled. It took a beating that night."

"So did we."

Alec looked at Jake and smiled. They drove for a while and passed an empty grocery store parking lot. Alec pulled in and parked the car on the edge, facing the unlit building with the deserted parking lot stretched out in front of them.

"Is this where you confess your deep-rooted love for me?"

Alec laughed. "Now *that's* funny. Sorry, I'll always be Carnie's man."

"That's 'cause he bought you beers all night long."

"He knows how to show his appreciation."

"I'm sorry, but I already went shopping for the month."

"Really?" Alec said, his eyes looking reckless and amused. "But have you gone hunting?"

Jake looked at him and tried not to smile. "No."

"Oh, yes."

"No, not tonight."

"And why not?"

"Bad idea."

"There's no such thing as a bad idea. A simple notion or conviction can't ever be bad. When was the last time you went shopping-cart hunting?"

"It's been awhile." Jake turned his head around to look around the empty lot. "The moron who taught me how suddenly disappeared off the face of this earth."

"But you're not bitter about that, are you?"

"Go ahead," Jake said, daring him as he lit up a cigarette off the pack of smokes he had bummed off Carnie.

"Got one for me?"

"You're going to get pulled over."

"I wonder what they'll say about me not having a driver's license?" Alec laughed, then floored the gas.

The Jeep raced over the yellow lines of the parking spaces toward the one lone shopping cart resting dead center in the middle of the lot. Jake started laughing before they reached it. Then, as the bumper of the Jeep slammed into the cart and sent it careening upwards and outwards, amazingly without effort and without slowing the Jeep's 70 mph, the two of them laughed uncontrollably.

"You're an idiot," Jake screamed above the screeching voice of Kurt Cobain, Alec's hero, who had suddenly begun singing as if on cue.

"Such a best friend."

"Best?"

Alec sucked in his cigarette and drove out to the street. He looked over at Jake and only laughed.

"You can fool all the others, but you'll never fool me. I know you're glad I'm back."

A block down the street, stereo speakers thumping with angry rock, the Jeep driving steadily, the two of them passed a policeman driving the opposite way.

Jake looked at Alec. His friend—okay, maybe his best friend, if he really wanted to be honest—raised his eyebrows and laughed.

"It's all about timing, Jakester," he said. "All about timing. And some of us are just born lucky."

EIGHT

June 2005

IT WAS NINE O'CLOCK, and I was staying at a Fairfield Inn close to campus. Kirby had asked several times if I wanted to have dinner with him and his family, and after the tenth or eleventh time I finally said okay. I had just gotten back to the hotel, about ten minutes away from Providence, and was sprawled across the bed watching ESPN when the phone rang.

I assumed it was Kirby. Who else knew where I was? I never expected the voice on the line.

"This is Alyssa," the voice said, sounding the same way she did a decade ago.

"Alyssa? As in Providence College's Alyssa Roberts?" I said, trying to be funny but probably not succeeding.

"The one and the only."

"How'd you know—" I began.

"One guess."

"Did Kirby call you?"

"He might have possibly said something about you being in the area."

"I just had dinner with him."

"Yeah, I know."

I had asked about Alyssa during dinner and hadn't gotten a

lot of information. But Kirby had smiled, as if he found my interest in her surprising after all these years.

"Are you— Where are you calling from?"

"I live in Orland Park."

"Still close by, huh? So—how are you?"

"Wide awake," she said, surprising me. "Any chance you'd want to get a cup of coffee?"

I had just had maybe four cups back at Kirby's house. "Sure, I'd love some."

"David told me you would be leaving tomorrow, and I thought—well, it's been awhile."

My mind had finally caught up with my adrenaline, and I had to ask. "Are, uh—does tonight work? I mean, if tomorrow worked better—I don't want to take you from, you know—"

"It's just me, Jake," Alyssa said. "You won't be having coffee with a married woman, if that's what you're worried about."

"No, I wasn't worried. I just—I thought—"

"It'd be nice to get you up-to-date on my life. I keep reading about yours in the alumni news."

"I can't help any of that."

"Let's talk at Starbucks. You remember where the old Bakers Square used to be? Still is? It's across the street."

"Is there anything closer to you?"

"I'm calling on a cell," she said. "I'm actually already here."

It's seldom that I'm so utterly and completely surprised.

"See you soon," I said.

➤ ◄

The years had been kind to Alyssa Roberts. Extremely kind.

I opened the door to Starbucks and immediately spotted her at a small table, a tall cup in her hand, her friendly eyes finding mine and lighting up. A controlled smile curled at her lips as she stood. She seemed taller than in college, but that was probably just my imagination. Her hair was shorter but still fell to her shoulders. It was pulled half-back and held with a barrette. She put down her coffee cup and stood there, waiting for me.

43

I had imagined this scene many times before. The dramatic meeting again. I had seen it in my mind, but seeing her in person, all intentions and plans suddenly seemed inept. I walked toward her with a smile and eyes that didn't blink and knew the one and only thing I could do was hug her.

For a brief second or two, I amazingly found myself back in the arms of Alyssa Roberts. Her hair was soft against my cheek, her body slight. A slight scent of citrus covered her. I moved away and saw her staring at me, studying me without realizing she was doing it.

"Good to see you," I said.

"Thanks for coming."

"I had a lot of other plans, I hope you know."

"I'm sure."

"Would you like anything else?"

She shook her head and sat back down as I got myself coffee. I sat down across from her, studying the young girl who had grown into the woman across from me. She wore jeans and a white button-down shirt, untucked. She still could pose as a college student, even though she was probably thirty-two.

"It's good to see you," I said.

"You already said that." She grinned.

"I'm still in shock. I don't know what to say."

"We never did have a proper farewell," Alyssa said.

"I'm used to doing improper things."

"You look well."

"Is that 'well' as in healthy, or is that a pause, as in, 'well . . .'?"

"I see your sarcasm is still alive and kicking."

I chuckled. "I do that when I get nervous."

"Jake Rivers, nervous?"

"I can jump out of a plane, no problem. But this—well . . ."

"Well," Alyssa repeated with a smile.

There was a decent crowd in the Starbucks at this time of night, but we ignored them. It felt surprisingly natural, sitting across from Alyssa and sipping on my latte.

"So you own your own company?" she asked.

"That makes it sound glamorous. The overhead is mine too."

"Do you enjoy it?"

"Yeah, very much. It's great to see something you've wanted to do slowly build into something halfway decent."

"Are you growing?"

"Trying to."

"That's good to hear."

The confidence in Alyssa was still there, along with her gentle nature. She had always carried a great mystery about her—this disciplined and controlled young woman who seemed like she had a huge heart. I had always wanted to see more of that heart. I was just too stupid and immature to get the chance.

"Are you still teaching?" I asked.

She nodded. "Just finished my ninth year."

"Must be going well."

"I never thought I'd be teaching for this long—but life can sometimes throw you a curveball."

I didn't want to ask, because really, it was none of my business. But her unexpected call, her dramatic declaration that "it's just me," the lack of a wedding ring—they all said the same thing.

And the awful thing was, I couldn't help but be elated.

"What grade do you teach?"

"Third, which I love."

She looked more mature than the girl I remembered. But the beauty, the softness, and the lack of ego or edge all remained. I found myself staring at her, studying her I tried to remember when I first heard about Alyssa Roberts getting married. It was a few years after college, to some guy whose name sounded vaguely familiar. The news hadn't shocked me. Seeing Alyssa without a ring did.

"What?" she asked, breaking my silence.

I hadn't even noticed my sigh until it was all the way out.

"Just—being here—around college. Time can be a strange thing."

"It doesn't feel like ten years."

"Eleven," I said.

"Kirby said you're looking for Alec."

"Yeah. Trying to see if he's still alive."

"I'm surprised you guys didn't stay in touch."

"With Alec?" I shook my head. "It doesn't surprise me. Then again, there was a lot of cleaning up I needed to do after college. One was my choice of friends. It was easy with Alec. He just disappeared."

"Do you ever think about those days?"

I didn't want to tell Alyssa the truth. "The more time goes by, the less I find to look back on."

"I think of the person I used to be," Alyssa said in earnest. "This little prim and proper girl working for the dean of students. It was unbelievable how sheltered I was. It was a hard adjustment after I graduated."

"Yeah, tell me about it. I think it's hard for everyone."

"I just—if there's one thing I've always wanted to do, Jake —I just want to apologize. . . ."

I looked at Alyssa in disbelief. "What for?"

"For being so judgmental."

I laughed. "I was breaking rules, you know."

"But more than that. There were a lot of things with you— with us. Things I regret."

"You didn't do anything to me, Alyssa. You were one of the few bright spots of Providence."

"I just thought I knew exactly where I wanted to go and what my life should be like. That young naïve girl is gone."

"I remember I really liked that girl," I said.

She nodded and looked down at the table.

You're still that girl, I thought. *You will always be that girl.*

We talked for a few minutes about superficial stuff. A thousand unspoken words and feelings between the two of us, and I found myself talking about the suburb of Summit or the new science building at Providence or listening to Alyssa talk about the house she lived in.

"Or, well, used to live in," she corrected. "Before things basically got flushed down the toilet."

"I'm sorry," I said.

"Yeah. Me too."

She glanced over at me with those soft, haunting eyes I could still remember in my dreams.

"I just never thought I'd have to—that I would be sitting here talking to you about my failed—"

Alyssa couldn't continue. The last few words cracked, and she composed herself.

"I feel like—this is weird, I know—I feel like this huge disappointment."

I reached over and without a thought embraced her hand.

"Hey—I'm the *last* guy who would ever be disappointed in you. Come on. You remember who you're talking to?"

"I really used to believe," Alyssa said.

"Believe in what?"

"Believe in everything. Happily ever afters. The myth. The fairy tale."

"That's funny, 'cause I didn't believe in anything."

"Has that changed?"

"I think you'd be very surprised."

She wanted and expected more, but I wasn't ready. There were many things to tell her. Eleven years is hard to compress into one conversation.

"Let me show you something," I told her.

I opened my wallet and slipped a finger inside one of the pockets. I produced a photo that had been cropped to fit and handed it to her.

She stared at it, her head shaking in disbelief. "I can't believe you still have this," she said, glancing at the photo and back at me.

"It's gone everywhere I've ever gone since college. And let me tell you—that's a lot of places."

She continued to study the picture, her eyes teary.

"I always believed that at some point in my life, somewhere, I'd run into you again," I said. "I didn't know the circumstances and didn't know the how, but I believed I'd see you again. And here we are."

She nodded and handed the picture back to me.

I stared at it. It was taken my senior year at some party. I had my arm around Alyssa, who was laughing and trying to get out of my hug. Her smile told the truth. That there was a chance for the two of us.

Looking at Alyssa now, eleven years later, I wondered if that chance still existed.

January 1994

THE DOOR OPENED, and the pleasant look on Alyssa's face faded when she saw him.

"Jake, look—"

"Don't worry, I'm not stalking you. I gotta meet with her."

"Ms. Peterson?"

"What—I'm not on your little planner?"

"She didn't tell me about it."

"She called this morning. Let's call this unofficial business."

The tall ruler figure of Ms. Peterson came to the doorway and nodded at Jake. "Come on in."

She shut the door behind them.

"All right," Jake said, sitting down in the familiar chair. "What'd I do this time?"

"You're not in trouble, not this time."

"I'm finally getting that student-of-the-year award?"

Ms. Peterson looked like a windup toy that wasn't able to expend its energy. Her face was square, her hair shorter than Jake's. When she looked at him, he thought he could chip ice with the edge of her jaw.

"A few teachers commented on the fact that they smelled liquor on your breath the morning of enrollment."

Jake appeared confused. He tried to remember enrollment. "What are you talking about?"

"Three different people told me that you came through the line inebriated and reeking of alcohol."

"Maybe it's just my minty mouthwash."

"Jake, this isn't funny."

"Bad breath is nothing to laugh about."

Ms. Peterson looked down at her desk, then darted her eyes back to him. "Someone reported seeing you in the parking lot drinking."

"Are you serious?"

"Am I ever not?" she asked.

"What? Me and my flask bottle?"

"Jake, I think it's a sign of a deeper problem."

"Whoa, hold on. Look, I'm not going to deny my breath may have smelled like Milwaukee's finest. But I wasn't in the parking lot swigging gin. Come on."

"How many times have you been in here, sitting across from me?"

"Sometimes you just can't get enough of a good thing."

"Nine times, not including today."

"Did I set a record?"

Ms. Peterson shook her head. "You know, you can flash that smile and try to be cute with the girls, maybe even with some of the female profs, but that doesn't get you anywhere in here."

"So am I in trouble?"

"Not officially."

"But unofficially, I'm what? Grounded?"

"Jake, I'm worried about you."

"'Cause I'm smoking in the boys' room?"

"Because I believe you have a problem."

Jake nodded, suddenly aware where this was heading. "Tell me something," he said. "If you went to the University of Illinois or Wisconsin, what would you find kids my age doing?"

"This isn't one of those universities."

"Why single me out?"

"You signed a pledge before coming to Providence. You agreed to the rules, as much as you've fought to break them."

"Everyone goes to parties and drinks around here," he said. "I'm sorry to burst your bubble."

"Not everyone."

"Most everyone. And okay, maybe I smelled a little funky, but I'm not drinking in the parking lot, and I don't have a problem."

"What happens when you graduate?"

Jake shrugged. The almighty question. He didn't have an answer.

"After a while, actions can become habits."

He nodded. "Look—I've had enough college-imposed counseling because of getting in trouble. I know the symptoms and the signs and all that."

"I'm just asking that you take a hard look at yourself."

"I have. And I'm a college student who isn't hurting anybody and who is just trying to have a fun time."

"And consequences?"

Jake didn't reply. He didn't want this morphing into a theological question about morality and God and sin. Ms. Peterson knew better than to drag them down that path.

"You're not a bad kid, Jake."

"Thank you," he replied cynically. "You're not such a bad dean of students either."

Ms. Peterson sighed. She looked ready to say something else, then tightened her lips. "That will be all," she finally said, her face and body language raising the white flag of surrender.

➤➤ ◄◄

The moving pictures blurred alongside of him. Jake rode like a gliding bobsled unable to stop, the icy world outside lifeless this time of night. He smoked and flicked the ashes on the dirty carpet of Alec's rickety Jeep.

The drive was longer than he'd expected. He knew Alec was drunk, but how drunk was the question. The can of Coors Light in Alec's hand didn't help Jake's curiosity, but he had one of his own, so he couldn't say anything. They had reached Lake Shore Drive after heading up I-55 and now drove between the glowing city of Chicago on their left and the dark waters of Lake Michigan on their right.

"You didn't tell me we were coming in to the city," Jake said.

"Sometimes the 'burbs can be suffocating."

Jake didn't like the way his friend stared at the road ahead, his glassy eyes serious, the usual cocky smile absent. He wondered if maybe Alec was taking him to a strip joint—the only decent ones were downtown—but he didn't think so. Something else was up. Alec just wouldn't say what.

They turned off on an exit and began heading down a side street. It felt crowded for a Thursday midnight. Alec drove for a while and Jake finished his beer, the second one he'd had in the Jeep. Alec started looking for a parking space.

"So what's this all about?" Jake asked again, this time with more frustration.

Alec had showed up at the apartment an hour ago, where Jake had actually been trying to study. That had meant sitting in front of the television drinking some beers and occasionally looking at his business textbook. Alec said he wanted to take him somewhere, no questions asked. His deliberate tone got Jake's attention, so after a few minutes, Jake agreed. His first class didn't start until eleven anyway.

"I said no questions allowed," Alec said.

"Come on. What's the deal?"

"The deal? You want to know the deal?" Alec slowed down the Jeep and stared at him a minute.

"What?" Jake asked, defensive.

"I'm tired of your attitude."

Jake watched the way Alec sucked on his cigarette and tightened the grip around the steering wheel. The violent industrial music blaring through the speakers didn't help his mood.

"And this is going to help it?"

"Well, it's sure going to help mine."

"So why not go alone? Why do you need me and my attitude?"

"Because you're part of the package deal tonight. Without you this wouldn't work."

Alec parked the Jeep in a narrow spot between two cars. They got out, and Jake followed Alec down the sidewalk lined with dirty snow. The windchill was below zero.

It took five minutes to reach the bar on the corner of an intersection. A small sign said *Four-leaf Clover.*

"If we wanted a fake-Irish pub we could've gone to Shaughnessy's," Jake said as they entered the warmth of the bar.

"First, this is the real deal," Alec said. "Plus, we're not going to run into anybody from Providence here."

It took two seconds for Jake to spot the two girls sitting at a nearby table, empty seats beside them.

"Well, nobody except her," Alec said.

"We've been waiting here for an hour," Laila greeted them, standing up and smiling at Jake as if he knew what she was talking about.

Alec grinned at Jake. He gave the dark-haired, shapely stranger a hug and said a few words in her ear, then introduced her.

"Jake, this is Gabrielle, who I told you about."

Jake let out a laugh at Alec's bravado and shook hands with the girl with dark eyes and eyeliner and pouty lips.

"Been awhile," Laila said, slinking up to him and sliding her arms around him.

"Hi," Jake said, his eyes unable to help themselves from gliding over Laila as he followed her to the table.

She wore a black skirt with heels that made her as tall as he was and legs that just kept going. A fuzzy white sweater looked snug around her lean figure. Her crystal eyes followed him as he sat down next to her.

"I'll get us some drinks," Alec said. "Jake—what do you want?"

He gave Alec a look that said *I want an explanation.* Alec returned it with a glance that said *You're going to have fun tonight.*

"Get me a beer. You pick."

Alec asked the girls and then went away, giving Jake a chance to find out what in the world was going on.

"So, Jake, you go to Providence, huh?"

Jake nodded at Gabrielle.

"I just met Alec the other day when I was visiting Laila. We told him you guys should come downtown and hang out for a while."

"You live down here?"

Gabrielle already looked a little loaded. She giggled at Jake's comment and rolled her eyes. "Of course. Else it'd be a long commute to school."

"Where's school again?"

"University of Chicago. I'm a junior."

"I met Gabrielle at a party downtown a year ago," Laila said, detailing how they started hanging out with each other after that night.

Alec came back with something for everyone, including a round of shots.

"Good thing we're not driving back to Summit," Alec said, making a toast with the tequila.

Jake downed his and bit on the lime and then looked at Laila. She gently rubbed her red lips and then licked them, smiling at Jake's glance.

"I love tequila," she said.

And I'm in trouble, Jake thought.

➤➤ ◄◄

"Thanks for telling me about the double date," Jake said as they walked back to the Jeep a couple hours and a dozen drinks later.

"You're welcome," Alec said, almost in his own world. "You can thank me tomorrow."

"Why didn't you just tell me?"

Alec cursed. "You'd say no."

"And why's that?"

"Because of your recent bad attitude toward me," Alec said,

then adding, "and because of your high school crush on the little princess."

Jake cursed back at Alec. "Laila's a head case."

"Yeah, but she's a hot head case. You see her tonight? She really did it up for you, man. She's looking good."

Jake couldn't argue.

"Plus," Alec continued, "I just wanted to get you away from college. Just you and me, like old times."

In the Jeep, the heater on full blast but only blowing out cold air, Jake kept the conversation going, his mind floating now after the continuous rounds of shots.

"Do you really wonder why I've been so annoyed? Just answer this: why'd you disappear?"

"I had my reasons. It was nothing to do with you."

Alec drove down the side streets, looking at the directions Gabrielle had given him to her apartment.

"Then what was it all about?"

"What'd you want? A good-bye note?"

"A heads-up maybe."

Alec shook his head and looked straight ahead.

"It's like—we almost died that night, Alec. And I don't even remember a bit of it. Do you? I never even got to ask you. You were gone the next day."

"I just know we were driving to get a burrito," Alec said, humor on his face.

"That'd be nice on a tombstone. *Jake Rivers. Died from an early morning craving for a burrito.*"

"Yeah, that and six hours of steady drinking."

"I just want to know—"

"What?" Alec hurled back. "What do you want to know?"

"It just would've been nice, you know—just to let us—to let me—know where you went."

"I went to Florida to see my mom. Okay? Enough info for you?"

It wasn't, but Jake figured it was the best he was going to get.

"Here we are," Alec said. "Now we have to find a parking spot."

"My buzz is going down."

"I've got a little something for that."

Jake wondered for a minute what he was talking about, then understood. Everything was happening too fast, and for a minute he felt out of his body, out of control, out of hand.

"It'll be all right, man," Alec said with a smile. "It might be a long night ahead. You need to have some energy."

Alec laughed, and it wasn't the sort of laugh that made Jake want to do the same.

It was the sort of laugh that frightened him.

TEN

June 2005

I SAT ON THE SHAKY propeller plane that was flying over the rolling hills of Napa Valley and heading toward Redding. I had flown in to San Francisco from Chicago's O'Hare, making a half-hour layover before this hour-long trip up north. During my short stint in Illinois, I had used a number Kirby gave me to call Bruce Atkinson. I confirmed that he was still living in Redding and made sure it was okay to come see him. He acted fairly natural, though it had been years since we'd spoken.

I couldn't stop thinking of Alyssa.

We had spent another hour talking in Starbucks, sharing a few memories and shedding more light onto our current lives. Alyssa said nothing else about her marriage, and I didn't ask. By the time she said it was late and she needed to go, I had fallen in love with her again. On my drive back to the hotel, I realized I had never fallen out.

She gave me her phone number and e-mail and told me to call or write sometime. We ended the night with another hug, a lasting and meaningful hug. I didn't get much sleep that night, and prevented myself four times from calling that number. I had to do the same the next morning.

But now, even though I was on my way to visit a buddy I hadn't seen in years, I could not stop thinking of Alyssa. The thought of seeing Bruce and this all-expenses-paid expedition to find a long-lost college buddy suddenly felt insignificant. All I wanted to do was start over again with Alyssa.

But I knew it wouldn't be as easy as that.

➤➤ ◄◄

A 217-foot-tall blade rose high above the bridge and into the fading light of the sky. I had never been to Redding, California, and had never heard of the Sundial Bridge. Obviously Bruce wanted me to take it in, even though he was late to our meeting. I walked across the bridge several times, looking down at the calm flow of the Sacramento River.

Bruce had told me to meet him around five. There was a small restaurant at the edge of the bridge that had outdoor seating. At five-thirty I decided to get us a table. The weather was probably as perfect as it could get, with a light breeze and eighty degrees and a sky full of pockets of clouds resembling cotton balls. I was working on my second Diet Coke when Bruce finally walked up, an hour late.

"Dude, I'm sorry, man," he said as I stood and watched him approach.

He gave me a big bear hug and then let me go. Back in college Bruce was tall and scrawny. If anything, he now looked taller and skinnier. He still had a boyish face with a loopy grin and long, wavy hair that needed cutting about two months ago.

"Been a long time," I said.

"You bet. Sorry I'm late—I had this parakeet and it got out of its cage. The thing is possessed, man, I'm telling you. I got it saying 'Redrum,' can you believe that?" Bruce bellowed out a laugh. "The thing is seriously possessed. It got out and ended up flying away."

If I hadn't known Bruce I would have asked him if he was feeling okay.

"Where'd he go?"

"Up."

We sat, and he looked around to find a waiter.

"You already got something? Watcha got?"

"Diet Coke."

"Oh, all right. Sure. Hey, over here." He waved over a young girl. "What beers do you have on tap?" He ordered a Coors Light, exhaled, and looked up at the sky. "Man, I'm tired."

He didn't act remotely surprised that I was sitting across from him after an absence of eleven years; it was more like we were friends who saw each other every day and were bored with one another.

He glanced at me. "You lose weight since college?"

I nodded. "Probably trimmed twenty pounds or so."

"Exercise?"

"That and a diet that consists of more than burritos and beer."

"Right on," Bruce said in his unique vocabulary that apparently hadn't changed in the past decade. "I'm on that burritos and beer diet myself. But I never gain much weight."

Bruce was a combination surfer dude and stoner. He was the sort of guy who would have a baby face at fifty and couldn't look angry if he tried. The long bangs made it worse, along with his catchphrases of "right on" and "totally."

"So what do you think?" he asked, nodding at the bridge just to our right.

"It's incredible. Sorta Blade-Runneresque."

"Yeah, it was all the talk for the longest time. People around here don't have anything else to do except talk about a bridge. They've gotten used to it."

"How in the world did you end up in Redding?"

He laughed. "How much time do you got? Long story."

"I have plenty of time."

"Yeah, no doubt. I don't know if you remember Pam—this girl I was pretty serious with after college."

"I haven't seen you since college."

"Right on. Really? Seriously?"

"Yeah, I'm pretty sure."

"Well, Pam—we were pretty hard-core, and her family lived out here. I met her, believe it or not, at Shaughnessy's. Like a year or so after college."

"You stayed around?"

"Yeah. Actually got an apartment in the same building we lived in. Sad, right? I know. Totally sad. I mean, I didn't know exactly what to do. I applied to some schools and even started teaching for a while but—whatever. It was nothing. I met Pam, we started dating. She graduated from a local college in the area—I forget which one. Anyway, after graduating she wanted to move back home. And this was home."

"So you followed her?"

"Yeah, sure. We actually moved in with each other. For a few years. I got the whole pressure of marriage and all that, and it was all pretty stupid. Anyway, things took a turn for the worse. Pam actually moved back to Illinois. I still see her parents every now and then. Weird, huh? I mean, I've got no ties to California at all."

"So what are you doing?" I asked, more curious than ever.

"I do sorta everything. I was roofing for a while. Doing construction. You know I bought my own house? Yeah. But after Pam left I sold it. Got an apartment. And that stupid parakeet. I had a dog but it died. Got run over. The apartment isn't much. Hey—do you need to spend the night somewhere?"

"No, that's all right."

"Whatever. Come on. When are you leaving?"

"Probably in a day or so."

Bruce nodded and drained the remainder of his beer. "You smoke?"

"No," I said.

"Man, I want one. Most places around here, you can't smoke. How lame. They probably won't even let me smoke outside. California, you know?" He ordered another beer. "So, like, what are you doing here?"

It had taken him awhile before he thought to ask me.

"I'm actually doing a—what should I call it? Favor? Project? I don't know. I'm helping a guy who is looking for his daughter."

"I didn't do it!" Bruce sounded off with a laugh.

"Yeah, I know. The girl ended up going missing—she didn't show up for her classes at college. Her father thinks she's with Alec."

"With Alec? Really?"

"Yeah. So he asked if I could try to find him."

"You an investigator or something?"

I laughed. "No."

"What do you do?"

I explained to Bruce about my company in Colorado Springs. I didn't go into too many details. Bruce wasn't one of those who necessarily cared about details.

"So like—the guy just said, hey, can you find Alec for me?"

"Yeah, something like that. He said he'd pay me."

"Right on."

"You ever hear from Alec since college?"

Bruce nodded. "You know—I think someone might have contacted me about him. Like a few months ago. I told them I hadn't seen him in a long time."

"Nothing? Not a phone call or anything?"

Bruce thought for a moment. "I don't know. I don't think so. It's hard remembering much. You ever have problems with your memory? Sometimes I wonder if I should get mine checked on. But they'll probably ask me stuff that I don't want to tell them, you know?"

"Still smoke every now and then?" I asked him.

"Well, you know. You know how it is."

I didn't know, to be honest, but I nodded and took this as a yes. The guy who once claimed that he would only wear clothes made out of hemp still probably got stoned on a regular basis.

I had a feeling Bruce was not going to be much help, but I was still glad to be sitting across from him. I told him that David Kirby said hi.

"Kirby? Right on."

→→ →←

Bruce wanted to go out later to one of his haunts, a casino bar. I didn't have much of a choice, so I went along.

"So tell me. How are you doing?" I asked him. "How are you *really* doing?"

"This is it, man. My life." He wasn't done drinking.

61

"Gamble much?"

"Moving to California was a gamble."

"Pay off?"

"No," he said, lighting up a cigarette. "I lost. Big time. Maybe I'll wise up and eventually move on." His eyes looked like slits, like he had a bad sinus infection. He was chalk white and his skin looked stretched over the bones.

Later on, as he started to obviously feel the booze, he was harder to talk with.

"So you came here for what?" he asked. Already he'd forgotten.

"Looking for Alec."

"Yeah? What'd he do?"

"The question is where is he?"

"Not around here."

"You haven't seen him recently?"

"I haven't seen my mom recently."

"Think."

"I get in trouble when I try to do that," Bruce answered.

"He hasn't called or anything?"

"A while ago maybe—I mean, I don't know. I told you— you didn't need to fly across the country for me to tell you that again."

"Maybe I wanted to see you."

"My memory's bad. But it ain't gone. Eleven years is a long time, you know."

"Good memory."

"I was the last to say good-bye. I remember that too."

"What are you drinking?" I asked.

"I've been into Jack and Coke these days. Really sweet. Really need another. What do you want?"

"Beer is fine."

"You've been nursing them all night," he said.

When he came back with the drinks, he picked up where he'd left off. "Remember that hole of an apartment we lived in?"

"Scary," I said.

"It's pathetic. All this time and I'm still living in a two-bedroom apartment. Like life's been playing, but someone hit the pause button for me."

A woman a hundred pounds overweight walked by with pants that looked as tight as Spandex.

"See? See that? That is why this is a beautiful town."

"Maybe we should talk over breakfast," I said.

"This is it right here." He toasted to me and drained his glass. "This is life. You know? Some things never change."

But they do. And I think Bruce knew that too.

→→ ←←

The drive to his apartment was blurry with rain and slow with incomprehension. It was difficult getting anything out of Bruce, who was halfway passed out on the passenger seat beside me, then waking up to drink from a bottle of vodka he had found in his backseat. He kept offering me a sip.

"Just a swig, man."

"I'm driving."

"Man, you've changed."

"When did I pound vodka in college?"

"Your memory's as bad as mine."

"Just tell me where to go."

He slipped in Pearl Jam and cranked it. "You know—I've always wondered something."

"How to get home?" I asked.

"How do you know if it's for good?"

"What?"

"When someone leaves you."

He played the song again. *I know someday you'll have a beautiful life*, Eddie Vedder belted out over the loudspeakers.

"Remember that Pearl Jam concert? With Mike?"

"That was a crazy night," I said.

"Sometimes I wish it could be so easy—you know? No worries. Like it used to be."

"College wasn't easy. That's the myth we believed."

"Huh?"

63

He wouldn't get it anyway. Bruce was still chasing a myth, an imaginary dream.

A few minutes later, when I began to think he had drifted off, he leaned over and whispered to me with half-closed eyes, "Alec is dead. He's a ghost. A spirit. A demon."

Then he passed out until I nudged him awake after we parked outside the apartment complex.

It took a long time just to help him get to his front door. We unlocked it and walked into an apartment that had been turned upside down. At first I thought this was just how he lived, but then I saw the opened drawers and tossed clothes. Papers were strewn all over the floor. Cushions lay on the floor in front of the couch. A television looked tossed aside in the corner. One of the lamps in the main living room area looked cracked in half.

"Bruce—what happened . . . ?"

Bruce stood for a moment, delirious and confused. He knelt over one lamp and then tried to piece it back together, swaying and scratching a white wall with the base of the lamp.

"Bruce, man, why don't you sit?"

He went to the couch and sat on it even though the pillows were tossed aside. I tried to clean up a little, but it was pointless.

"What happened here?"

He kept looking around, surprised and even startled.

"I don't know. But I didn't do this."

"Do you know who did?"

Bruce nodded, then looked at me and tightened his face and lips. "It was Early."

"Who?" I asked.

"Early. My bird. That possessed bird came back with a vengeance."

Then he leaned over and passed out again on his couch.

For a moment I sat in a chair and just looked around, feeling like a stranger invading someone's private life.

Someone had been here recently, looking for something.

Either looking for something or trying to get a message to Bruce.

I wondered for a moment if Bruce had done this himself, but I ruled that out. He might be lost and floundering in his life, and he might be under the spell of booze and pot, but he had never been violent.

Someone else had done this.

And I couldn't help but wonder, and fear, that it had something to do with Alec.

February 1994

IT HAD BEEN THE COLDEST winter Jake could remember. He chose a table close to the fireplace, a spot where nobody else could see them. Not that anyone they knew would be here. Jake doubted she would even stick around to sit down, much less feel the warmth from the flickers that cast shadows over the back room of The Wild Goose. It was a fancy restaurant Franklin had recommended, one the Gotthards went to on a regular basis. The Thursday night crowd were in their forties and up, scattered around the dimly lit rooms.

Jake faced the opposite way so she wouldn't see him. Not at first.

This was a blind date for Alyssa; she had no idea it was Jake on the receiving end. He had spent the last month getting her roommate, Renee, to coordinate it. Renee had been Alyssa's roommate for the last two years; the two were good friends but as opposite as Jake and Carnie. Renee played basketball and softball for Providence, was brash and outgoing and occasionally could be seen at parties having a beer or two. The redhead was one of those tough, just-do-it sort of girls who probably was good for Alyssa.

Jake had concocted this plan months ago, and tonight it was finally happening.

Light music played in the background. Jake made a fist and then breathed in and out, as though he were a soloist about to go on stage. That would truly be a disaster, but this could be even worse.

"Still waiting, sir?"

He nodded at the waiter. *Sir.* Obviously the guy didn't know who he was talking to. Jake sipped his water.

He thought of their first date a year ago, a three-hour series of disasters that ended with Alyssa pushing him off her in the car and leaving without saying good-bye. Jake should have known better, but there *had* been something, and Alyssa for a moment had let herself go. He hadn't draped himself over her and then felt the sting of rejection. It was in the heat of the moment, after an awkward dinner at a dive and then a stint at a party, when Alyssa seemed to let herself go and then get more angry at herself than with him.

He thought about the letter he'd received from her the next day. He remembered every line: *I'm sorry for last night, Jake. Please know it was a nice night and that I shouldn't have ended it without even a thank you or a good night. You and I are two different people. Maybe we should just leave things at that.*

But he didn't want to leave things "at that." And that's why he owed Renee big-time.

"Get me a date with Alec and we're even," she'd said, to which Jake had agreed, even though he knew that task was even more daunting than the one he'd given her.

But he didn't feel bad arranging something like that, especially after the double-date in Chicago that ended up in drunken debauchery.

Don't think about that, he thought. *Not tonight.*

He heard footsteps approaching and straightened up, his dry-cleaned, button-down shirt a little too starchy for his liking. A figure in a black dress drifted by, then stopped by the chair across from him.

She looked exquisite.

"Alyssa!" he said in mock surprise. "What are you doing here?"

For a minute she just stood there, looking around the restaurant. "This isn't happening."

"Is this a joke?" Jake said, unable to keep the smile off his lips.

"Yeah, it is," Alyssa said, starting to walk away.

The host who had brought her over stood off to the side as if watching an act at the circus. Jake got up and quickly ran around Alyssa to block her from walking off.

"Wait, please, hold on."

"No. My ride—I have to get them before they leave."

The plan had been that Alyssa would be dropped off here and that her blind date—that is, Jake—would take her back to the college.

"Alyssa, please."

"Did you get Renee to do this?"

"Yes. I owe her. Sorta like a thirty-year mortgage."

"I'm going to kill her."

"I know. And that's fine. But you don't want to kill her on an empty stomach."

Alyssa shook her head and looked at him with incredulous eyes. "You're really something."

"Just dinner. Nothing else. I swear."

Her eyes rolled over him. "I might not have even recognized you. You actually shaved."

"A guy's gotta try, you know."

She seemed to still be deciding, then she turned around and slid onto her chair.

Jake could feel his heart beating in his throat. He couldn't believe she was actually going to stay.

→> <+

For a while, it had actually felt like a real and legitimate date.

"It's weird to think people come here on a weeknight for dinner," Jake said as he worked on a T-bone.

"It's weird to think we're joining them."

Jake smiled as if to say touché. Alyssa wasn't a steak eater and had opted for a special pasta dish that came out looking like a piece of art. Since she had decided against wine, Jake had done the same, wishing he could have something to ease his apprehension. As hard as he tried not to show it, he knew his nerves showed.

"So, Mr. Rivers. How many ladies have you taken to The Wild Goose?"

"Hundreds," he said. "Then we go down the street to the Hinsdale Marriott."

"I knew it."

"You know I'm kidding. You act like I have some crazy reputation."

"Word gets around."

"What do you mean, *word?* Come on."

"You and Alec—"

"Hold on. Alec is his own man. Don't lump me in with him."

"I've heard stories."

"He's only been back a month."

"Yes, but I've heard stories about you two."

For a moment Jake got a sick feeling in his stomach, and he pictured the night in Chicago again. He wondered what Laila had said about it, especially since he had avoided her around campus ever since.

He buried those thoughts. "Yeah. The movie *Risky Business.* That's our biography."

"You act so innocent," Alyssa said.

"And you act like I'm so guilty."

"Let's see. How many times have I seen you in Ms. Peterson's office?"

"Not for girls."

"One thing leads to another."

"You're wrong."

"And what about Brooke. Diana. *Laila.*"

She knows. She's just waiting to hear me admit it.

"Hold on now. Brooke—we dated, yeah. Nothing there. Diana, I have no idea what you're talking about. And Laila— who *hasn't* gone out with her?"

"It's good to know you're selective," Alyssa said, wiping a corner of her mouth with her napkin.

"You know what I mean."

"Actually, no, I don't."

"This is what drives me insane about you. You make it out like I'm some typical guy, some pig."

"And you're not?"

"No."

"Laila does date quality guys."

Jake didn't want to go there with Alyssa. "I'm not saying you're Laila. You're nothing like that—"

"That what?"

"Laila," Jake finished, being nice.

"See, the thing is, I can see her with a guy like you."

"You have me all wrong."

"Do I?"

"That's why I had to concoct this date, for you to try to get to know the real Jake Rivers."

"And who is that guy? The guy who drove on the soccer field and caused several thousand dollars' worth of damage? The guy who helped take—or should I say steal—every single fork from the cafeteria and decorate the lawn with them?"

"That was Shane's idea, by the way—"

"The guy who seems to like to partake of alcohol quite frequently?" she continued.

"Not tonight."

"Who exactly is that guy then? Tell me that."

"It's a guy who hates fake people and being a hypocrite."

"So stealing forks is being *authentic?*"

Jake couldn't help laughing. "No. But the partying, all that stuff. You know—Ms. Peterson thinks I have a drinking problem."

"Do you?"

"No. Yeah, I know. If you have a problem, of course you deny it. But I don't. I'm just doing what other college kids do. It's just this college we go to."

"Then why are you going here?"

"I went to USC for a while. Flunked out and got into a lot

of trouble. My parents gave me an ultimatum. If they were going to pay for college, I'd go where they told me."

"Must be nice to have a paid vacation."

Jake shifted in his seat and took a sip of water. "Alyssa, tell me one thing."

"What?"

He studied her sweet, reflective face. Sitting across from her was worth it all. Too many nights he'd be sitting in a bar or in his apartment and would close his eyes and picture her there, just as she was now, a picture of innocence and dignity.

"Our date last year. Didn't you feel anything?"

"What do you mean?"

"I mean—I know there was something on the other end of that kiss."

She shook her head, and one hand nervously brushed her hair behind her neck.

"Tell me—don't lie," Jake asked.

"That girl has grown up."

"What does that mean?"

"It means that she isn't looking for a guy she can carry home from a party and tuck into bed."

Jake couldn't help chuckling.

Alyssa went on. "She's looking for someone who shares her beliefs."

"Oh, come on."

"What?"

"Where's that coming from? I believe everything you believe."

"How do you even know what I believe?"

"I know the type of person you are, Alyssa."

"If you did, you'd realize I'm very different from you."

"Don't they say opposites attract?"

"Sometimes. But not this time."

Jake looked at her and nodded. For the next moment, he didn't say anything, just looked at her and tried to find the right words to utter. For once, he couldn't be sarcastic and funny. He suddenly felt very sad, and he wasn't sure why.

They didn't order dessert. When the check came and

Alyssa demanded that she let him accept her money, Jake told her he'd leave it for the waiter.

On the drive home, the heater going full blast and the silence awkward, Alyssa tried to make some sort of amends. "I'm sorry, Jake."

"It's fine, really. This was a bad idea."

"It's not you."

He let out a cynical laugh. "It's entirely me."

When he reached the campus, he drove around to her dorm and stopped the car.

"Sorry this wasn't the dream date you had hoped it would be," Jake said.

"It was better than I expected it to be."

He nodded. Alyssa looked at him, the windows in the car shielding them from the cold and the outside world.

"Jake."

"Yeah?"

"You were right."

"About what?"

"About something being on the other end of that kiss."

He looked into her eyes, then looked away and asked, "What's that mean?"

"It means . . . it means you're not a bad guy. Thank you for dinner."

With that, she opened the door and left. No kiss good night, no small tug on his hand, no mesmerizing glance. Just a polite smile and a departure.

TWELVE

June 2005

SHANE MARCUS AND HIS WIFE, Tracy, were sickeningly perfect but impossible to dislike.

He picked Bruce and me up from the Jacksonville airport
with surprise and elation when he saw there were two of us.
"No way. Where'd you find this guy?"

Shane was shorter than us and trim. He gave us hugs and
patted Bruce on the back. "You've gotten taller and skinnier.
Why can't I do that?"

"Before there was Atkins, there was Atkinson."

"You don't want that diet," I said as we followed Shane outside toward the parking lot.

"So you guys flew out together from San Francisco?"

"I decided to tag along," Bruce said.

He glanced at me, and we both knew the truth. It was
probably good for him to pack a suitcase and get out of town.
Someone was looking for him. Maybe Bruce held some secrets
he still hadn't told me. But he didn't hold any special ties to
California. Not anymore.

"I can't believe both of you guys are here. Good thing you're
packing light."

"How come?" I asked.

We arrived at his car and saw how come. He had a red Mini

Cooper that Bruce was really going to have an interesting time fitting inside.

"They're bigger than they look," Shane said. "Bruce, get in the front."

Coasting down the highway toward his home, blasting the new U2 album, Shane talking a mile a minute, the sun out and the wind whipping in through the sunroof, I realized that sometimes people don't change. And sometimes that's a good thing.

Shane's house sat in the woods in a private development off St. John's Lake. We pulled up to the sweeping driveway and stopped. The three-car garage and two-story house looked impressive even in the fading light of day.

"Here we are."

"This looks just like my place," Bruce said with a grin as we entered their house.

We met Tracy, Shane's cute and friendly blonde wife. They were perfect hosts in an ideal home. Their house was modern with unique framed paintings hanging throughout.

"Like these?" Shane asked, giving me a glass of wine.

"Very cool."

"Tracy painted them."

Of course she did. The wine probably came from grapes they personally trampled from their vineyard in the backyard.

Bruce had already helped himself to a few drinks on the plane, so he welcomed wine. We sat in the large, open living room, light background music piping in.

"You should have come down here a long time ago, though we really only got the place fixed up in the last year."

"So what do you do again?" Bruce asked, needing some explanation for his surroundings.

"Basically sales."

"He lives out of a suitcase," Tracy said from the kitchen.

"I get companies to invest their money with us. We offer 401(k) programs, stuff like that."

"Maybe you could look at my portfolio sometime," Bruce said.

This time Shane got the joke and laughed.

"We never pictured ourselves in Jacksonville, to be honest," he said. "But they have a branch down here, and the opportunity came a couple years ago."

"Yeah—hurricane season is always fun," Tracy said, holding a bottle of Perrier in her hand as she sat beside Shane on the couch.

"You see living here for a while?" I asked.

"Eventually we hope to move. Maybe head back to the Midwest. Buy a place and settle down."

"This isn't settling down?" Bruce asked.

"No way. I mean it's great, but we're going to sell this place sometime and try out new things. I want to go to Colorado and get this guy to take me on a trek around the world."

"It's going to cost you big."

"You're living out your dream, huh? No responsibilities. Your own business."

I nodded, wondering why everybody who heard I owned my own business suddenly thought that I must be wealthy and successful. Anyone can own his own business. That's why so many fail each year.

And that's why you had to take this trip down Memory Lane.

"It's so great to see you guys," Shane said for about the fifth time.

We spent an hour catching up. Bruce spent a lot of that time drinking. He had no shame, and Shane obviously didn't care. He talked about their recent trip to Europe, partially for work and partially for fun, and Tracy's recent exhibit in a local art studio, and the dinner they were planning to make for us. And just when I thought things couldn't get any more picture-perfect for the Marcus family, Shane made an announcement over our second glass of wine—Bruce's fourth.

"Well, Tracy would be toasting, but the doctor has said she can't because she's expecting. In about five months, boom. A little Shane."

"God help us," Bruce said.

"That's incredible. Congratulations."

We toasted and talked about their news. I couldn't tell Tracy was expecting—maybe it was the baggy shirt she had on. She must have a tiny waist to begin with. She was three years younger than Shane, and they'd met when he lived in downtown Chicago working for the same company. Theirs was a love story that really sounded like happily ever after.

As we heard their story, I couldn't help thinking of Alyssa. She'd been on my mind a lot since leaving her a couple days ago.

Shane and I wandered into the kitchen. Shane, always to the point and always the intuitive one, asked me the question he had saved for just the two of us.

"How was going back around school?"

"It was fine."

"Really? That all?"

I looked at him, and he knew I was hiding something.

"Who'd you talk to?"

"Kirby."

"And what'd he say?"

"Nothing. He hasn't seen Alec. Talked about college and the growth of Providence."

Shane nodded. "I get stuff from Kirby all the time."

"I had dinner with his family. He's got three really cute kids."

"And what about you?" Shane asked, leaning against a kitchen counter.

"What about me?"

"No wife? No kids?"

I shook my head. "I've dated on and off. A couple from my church in Colorado Springs tried to get me to do one of those online dating services. That turned out to be a disaster."

"We know a couple who met like that. They've been married a couple years."

I chuckled. "Some people manage to achieve the dream. Some aren't so fortunate."

"Come on now. We both know things always look different on the surface. You peel the layers away and always find something else. Happily-ever-afters take a lot of work."

I looked in their family room and heard Tracy talking with Bruce about video games.

"She's awesome. I'm glad you found someone."

"Yeah, me too. Come on—we should babysit Bruce. There's time to talk later."

⇻ ⇺

Sometimes I think that half of the stunts I pulled back in college were done just so I could sit around a dinner table years later with friends recounting the memories with tears of laughter in my eyes. For an hour Bruce, Shane, and I told an interested audience of Tracy stories from our Providence days. Most of them involved me. Driving on the soccer field. Decorating half of a dorm hallway with shaving cream. Pulling off the mattress stunt. Getting kicked out for drinking. Stealing the stupid college mascot.

I couldn't help but laugh and try to think of something else to top that last story. But Bruce, already good to go from the steady flow of alcohol in his system, managed to top everyone.

"How about the time on spring break when you stole my car and spent the night in it? When all of us thought you were dead or something." He laughed and kept eating.

I couldn't help but glance at Shane, but neither of us said anything.

"What was that?" Tracy asked, humor still filling her pretty face.

"That was just like any other story," Shane quickly said. "You add a bunch of guys, a lot of booze, and the next thing you know you wake up wondering what happened."

"Jake used to have a lot of those stories."

I nodded and only smiled at Tracy.

Bruce looked and acted as if he hadn't said anything. I don't think he knew. I think somehow he had managed to forget all about that spring break. He'd surely forgotten talking with the police and the campus buzz. He'd surely forgotten why that was the last thing any of us would ever bring up. Maybe even why Alec had gone missing in the first place, and why we might be looking for him now.

It was the story we all shared, this specter that hung over all of us, waiting to block out the light and stop the laughter.

→► ◄←

It was around ten o'clock when the power went out. Shane and Tracy didn't seem too bothered.

"This happens all the time," Tracy said.

"Can I smoke?" Bruce asked.

"Yeah," Shane said. "Take it outside."

"Let me get some candles."

Shane got on the phone to report the outage. I followed Bruce outside onto the back deck. We sat in wooden chairs overlooking the large lake.

"I didn't know Jacksonville was by water," Bruce said, lighting up.

"Pretty nice, huh?"

"It's sticky and hot," he answered.

"It's going to get sticky and hot inside if they don't get the power on."

Bruce seemed lost in his thoughts. I decided to bring up his earlier comment. "What do you remember about that spring break?"

"Huh?"

"The last spring break. The camping trip."

Bruce shook his head. I could barely make out his face in the darkness outside.

"We should've gone to Cancun. Or Florida. Maybe down here."

"None of us had the money," I said. "Well, Franklin did. But he was the only one."

"Why'd we go camping?"

I shrugged, not really remembering whose idea it had been. "You don't remember anything?" I asked again.

"Not really. I just remember looking for you that last morning."

I waited, but he said nothing more. Maybe that was all he really did know.

Crickets droned on, but otherwise it was quiet. Woods surrounded us.

"Think we'll find Alec?"

I noticed the way he said *we*. "To be honest? No."

"What're you gonna do if you find him? Handcuff him and take him back?"

"This guy just wants to know if his daughter is okay. That's all."

An hour later, we all sat in the living room lit by flickering candles. Bruce had drifted off due to a lack of interest and a stomach full of red wine. In the middle of telling a story Tracy stopped talking and looked at one of the back windows.

"That's odd," she said.

"What?"

"That looks sorta like a face. Staring at us through the window."

"Huh? Where?"

And then she freaked out, jumping up and dropping her mostly empty glass of Perrier. It hit the wood floor and shattered. Bruce sluggishly shifted up to see what was happening.

"There was somebody there—Shane, I swear there was a face right there, and when I told you it suddenly disappeared—"

We both got up and ran to the back.

"Hey—go out the front," Shane said to me. "I'll go out back."

"Neighbor?"

Shane shook his head. "No. There's an older couple on one side and a family on the other."

I opened the front door and stepped out into the darkness. I walked to the driveway slowly, listening. My heart was racing. I went out toward the trees, walking in the grass.

I heard a slight rustling of bushes on my right and started to turn, but then heard steps. Suddenly something heavy cracked against the back of my skull, and before dropping to my knees I pictured the old apartment and the opened door and the spray of blood spilling on the white wall, and then I was out.

THIRTEEN

March 1993

JAKE PULLED AWAY FROM anxious lips and found himself in
the arms of Laila. She sat behind the wheel of the car, the snow
falling on the windshield, heat blowing out on his legs. Music
pulsated in the two-seater, Sinead O'Connor's voice sounding
off a war cry. He was leaning against Laila, and in the moment,
the picture seemed surreal.

I'm dreaming, Jake thought to himself, but he knew he wasn't.

He kissed her, giving in all over again.

And trying to figure out how he'd gotten here in the first
place.

➤➤ ◄◄

It had started a week ago with Mike Fennimore getting
tickets to Pearl Jam. They had only released two albums but
were already the "it" band (along with Nirvana) for grunge.
Neither Mike nor Jake was a die-hard Seattle sweetheart. Pearl
Jam rocked and Nirvana was raucous and raw, especially after
about eight beers. The other groups that were being anointed
by the movement—Soundgarden, Alice in Chains, even the
pretenders known as Stone Temple Pilots—weren't in the same
league as the bands led by Kurt Cobain and Eddie Vedder. Back

in October, *Time* magazine featured Vedder on the cover, making him their generation's unofficial spokesperson.

Mike just wanted to see them live, so he got three tickets off a scalper for $250 apiece. He said it was an early birthday present for Jake.

"Who else is coming?"

"The biggest fan who will take my bribe."

"Huh?"

"Whoever wants it has to drive."

Jake laughed. "I've taught you well, young Jedi."

A week later, Bruce sat behind the wheel of Mike's white Toyota Celica. It still smelled new—a college gift from his parents. Mike sat in the passenger seat, with Jake in the back.

That was how the trouble started, designating Bruce as the driver.

"No heavy drinking tonight," Mike made him promise after Bruce named every song on the two Pearl Jam albums and even a few on their upcoming release.

Mike forgot, or perhaps just didn't realize, that Bruce's vice wasn't of the liquid sort. By the time they were heading downtown to the venue, Bruce was, as the old saying went, high as a kite.

On the drive to Chicago, listening to rock and barely able to talk over the volume, Jake recalled how he'd first met Mike. It was music. Pure and simple.

After a typical night out, he had come back to his dorm and passed a gauntlet of students hanging out and talking and living a bored life. Mike was among them, wearing a T-shirt that read NIN. Jake paused for a moment and called out to the skinny guy with the spiked black hair.

"You like Nine Inch Nails?"

The kid looked a bit surprised at being singled out. Or maybe he was reacting to the slightly drunk tone and look that Jake gave off. He gave a suspicious nod.

"'Pretty Hate Machine' is awesome," Jake said, then left without waiting to hear the underclassman's opinion.

He ran into Mike again a few days, maybe a couple weeks, later. "You're the guy who likes Nine Inch Nails, right?"

The guy, whose name he still didn't know, nodded. Then said, "You ever heard of Meat Beat Manifesto?"

Jake shook his head, so they talked awhile. Eventually Mike invited him to walk down the hall to his room. He was only a freshman, and Jake could tell, but he didn't care. Good music was good music, and a lot of people around campus liked Poison or Metallica or junk like that. Then there was Carnie, who liked big-haired bands like Firehouse. *Firehouse,* whoever they were. Anybody who liked great music was a kindred spirit.

The first thing he saw on entering Mike's room was a poster of The Smiths.

"You gotta be kidding," Jake said, then noticed the two posters of Depeche Mode.

He saw a CD collection bigger than his own, along with stickers of half a dozen groups adorning the top of a stereo.

That was the start of their friendship. Simple as that. Mike was more mature than most guys his age, but needed to be taught how to have a little fun. And since Jake accepted him, the rest of the guys eventually did the same.

"What's this? Our fifth concert?" Jake asked him now from the backseat of the car.

Mike turned around, a can of beer in his hand, shaking his head. "Sixth. Don't forget Lollapalooza."

"Oh, yeah. How could I?"

"You were hung over all day."

"That was brutal."

"You miss all the fun," Mike said.

"Not tonight," Jake said.

But he was wrong. Again.

→→ ←←

It was easy to become enveloped in darkness. And it happened sometime during the concert.

For the moment, Jake didn't think of anything. He inhaled the music, loud and aggressive and searing. The cup in his hand finally went dry, and he discarded it so his hands could wave around freely. He no longer kept track of the beers he drank, no longer felt the slight buzz those first few gave him. He took some drags from Bruce's hand-rolled and homegrown joints, but he'd never really liked the taste and sensation of pot. It dragged him down and he didn't want to be down, he wanted to ride up this roller coaster.

The music sounded heavy, angry, and visceral, and the singer whom *Time* had dubbed "All the Rage" demonstrated every ounce of it with a mass of hair and a howling voice. Songs familiar and new went by in a haze, and somewhere between the screams of "Even Flow" and "I'm Alive," Jake dipped into that dimension drunks know as blackouts.

But at some point, Jake wasn't sure when, the music slowed and he caught his breath and lit up a cigarette and listened to the slowest song of the night.

What was everything? Vedder sang in the song "Black."

And Jake put an arm around Mike and smiled. He would remember this moment years later. Perhaps the friendship and the times would fade to black, but tonight under the spell of the singer and the song there was something, some connection, and Jake felt it.

➤➤ ◄◄

The cold air outside gave off the impression of sobriety. The walk to the car, the drive back to the suburbs, a soaring high Bruce driving and raving about Eddie Vedder's fall into the crowd and his amazing recovery at the end of the show. Jake dozed off a few times, taking an occasional sip from Bruce's can of beer. Then they reached Summit and faced the almighty question: to go back to the apartment or not. Mike wasn't about to go back to campus; he would crash at their place as he had so many nights before. But they didn't want the night to be over, so they decided to check out the crowd at Shaughnessy's.

It was there that Jake saw Laila. Or she saw him, and walked over to the table where they sat.

"Where'd you come from?" Jake asked. She looked amazing, actually wholesome.

That's why they call it blind drunk.

And now the music throbbed and the lights blinked and Jake kept his eyes on a remarkably long-legged Laila in tight jeans and a mesh shirt that looked see-through unless you studied it as Jake did without a care.

"We've been here since ten," she said. Two of her friends came over and joined them.

Bruce rambled on about the show as Laila pressed up against Jake's leg, looking down at him as he drank a beer and gazed at her from his bar stool. He wondered if his eyes were as revealing with their intentions as Laila's were.

Snapshots of the night downtown with Alec and Laila's friend streaked through his mind. This time Jake didn't bury them. He enjoyed them as the shadows and music and liquor and laughter proved to be too big an equation for his weak heart.

She brushed back her blonde hair and licked her lips. "I was beginning to think you were ignoring me," she said in his ear.

Jake didn't answer her and ignored the voice telling him *Look out—she's a chick and she's got your number and you're a moron not to get up and run away.*

And then, out of the blue, in the haze of the night, he pictured Alyssa's sweet smile, so different from this temptress clinging to him. The image was so out of place in this context, and thinking about her only made him sad. He got up and bought another round of beers.

Sometime later, maybe half an hour and three rounds later, Laila danced in front of Jake. He didn't hide his eyes, the way they moved over her. And she moved closer and his eyes moved lower and then she took his hand.

"Why haven't you seen me since that night?" she asked him.

And he could only smile and pull her close. They had a history and he couldn't let it go, not now and not on a night like this.

"I didn't know you wanted me to," he lied.

She seemed okay with this fib. She moved between Jake's

open legs and leaned down to kiss him. It was a long kiss, and not the first of the night.

"I've missed you," she said.

But instead of replying, he kissed her again.

⤞ ⤝

It was a little later that Jake said something to a bouncer, and the guy took offense to it. But it was true, the guy didn't have a neck and he acted like he had the brains of a bat. Jake probably shouldn't have said it, though, or made jokes about the guy's masculinity and the fact that he needed to lay off the Dunkin' Donuts. It was all that, plus the fact that he was undeniably drunk, that led to Jake getting thrown out of Shaughnessy's.

The guy Jake called Rufus, the bouncer he'd insulted, led him out the door with the help of another guy. Jake tried to go back to tell the gang. The mistake he made was slapping Rufus in the face. It was an innocent slap and not really powerful. But the other bouncer put an arm around him and squeezed, not allowing Jake to breathe until the cold chill of night greeted him outside the door.

They closed the door and Jake tried to open it. He hurled profanities and slammed his fist against the solid oak door several times, the last hurting exceptionally hard, even though he could barely feel much of anything in his body. His legs, his lungs, his breath, his mind. All felt like some endless dub, a high-speed continuous play CD that just kept going, a club song that never stopped.

That's when he took off running, heading toward a destination only his drunken mind could understand. He hit road signs and wavered between the street and the sidewalk and the grass and the parking lots.

Jake didn't remember the car turning into a parking lot of the Denny's and blocking his way. But he saw an eager face behind an open window.

"You left me," Laila said.

"They kicked me out."

"I promise I won't."

Jake didn't realize he had fractured the bone below his pinkie. He got into Laila's car and picked up where they had left off.

✈ ✈

Eventually the high subsides . . . sometimes before a person can make an even bigger mistake.

In the parking lot of Jake's apartment, Laila asked him to come home with her.

Perhaps it was her raw honesty or the fact that it was three in the morning or the fact that something in the music and in her forceful kiss made him reconsider. But as he looked at a snow-covered windshield and took a breath and considered, all he could think about was Alyssa.

Not again. Not now. Not here.

Jake looked at the blonde across from him. In the glow and shadows of the bar, she had looked incredible. But now Laila just looked like a hardened young woman too eager to be with him.

I don't want this, he thought.

He wanted this, yes, sure, and he had once had this, yeah. But not again. Not this head case. If he kept this up she would never back off, and he didn't need anything this heavy and serious the last few months of college.

Yet the biggest reason for stopping was the simple thought of Alyssa.

"I'm done here," he said.

"Jake, come on—let's just go back to my place—nobody has to know—"

But he was already outside and shutting the door and didn't hear her finish her suggestion.

He walked toward his apartment. No good-bye. No nothing. He knew it was better this way.

As he grabbed the door handle to his apartment building with his right hand, he felt an ache that would only worsen by eleven the next morning, when he awoke and looked in the mirror and then glanced at a hand that was half black-and-blue.

This is what you've become.

FOURTEEN

June 2005

"WHAT HAPPENED?"

Shane's voice sounded far off and muffled.

"I'm—I don't know."

I sat on the couch, candlelight making the walls appear to be moving. Shane had grabbed a frozen steak, which I held against the back of my head where a large knot had appeared.

"I'm calling the cops," Tracy said.

"No, it's fine," I said.

"What if someone—"

"They're gone, whoever did this," Shane said.

Tracy began, "Do you think someone—"

"I don't know what to think," he said, interrupting his wife, then quickly apologizing.

"Where's Bruce?" I asked.

"He took off outside."

"What do you mean?"

"He said he was going to hunt down whoever did this to you."

"Great. My heroic, half-sloshed bodyguard."

"You didn't see or hear anything?"

"Just heard someone behind me and then got knocked out cold."

"This is a theme in your life," Shane said.

"What?" Tracy looked puzzled.

"I'll tell you later," he said to Tracy. "Jake—you sure you're okay?"

"I'm fine. Seriously. I just wish that such a great night hadn't ended up like this."

"I don't know what to say," Tracy said.

"It's not your fault," I said. "Better me than you."

"Do you think—you think this has anything to do with Alec?"

I adjusted the mock ice pack and let out a sigh. "I don't know . . . Bruce's apartment got broken into last night."

"Are you serious? What did Bruce say?"

"Not much, except that he needed to get out of town."

"Is he in trouble?" Shane asked.

"I don't know. I don't know anything. I haven't spoken to him—to any of you—for years."

"You need to get some rest," Tracy said.

"You haven't seen or heard from Alec?" I asked Shane.

Shane shook his head. "I told you over the phone—nothing. I didn't even know he was living in Florida for a while. After graduation—I don't know. It all sorta ended with that. With Carnie."

"I know."

"I just thought—we'll all get past this. And still be friends. Still stay in touch. But every time I thought of all you guys, I couldn't help thinking of Carnie."

I nodded. "Me too."

→→ ←←

Ten hours later, after waking up and moving my throbbing head off the pillow and taking four more Advil, I sat next to Shane as he drove his speedboat over the smooth waters of Tampa Bay. The sun was bright, and I'd had to borrow a pair of sunglasses to actually be able to look out. It was just the two of us; Bruce still slept, or was just starting to come out of the stupor that I was beginning to think was a normal part of his life.

Shane talked about buying the speedboat and what he and Tracy wanted to do. Never once did I feel as though he was bragging. He could be sitting in a rowboat talking with the same energy and excitement. Shane was just one of those guys who was always up and high on life.

He paused. "How you feeling?"

"Groggy. Probably a lot like Bruce does. But one of us got socked in the back of his head."

"I'm sorry, man."

"You should be. I mean, I know you deliberately had someone outside ready to assault me."

Shane laughed. "Still—"

"Maybe it was just some random stranger. But I doubt it."

"You think it's to do with Alec?"

"Probably."

"Maybe it *was* Alec," Shane said.

"That'd be ironic, huh?"

"Why wouldn't he want you to find him?"

"I don't know." But I had some ideas. "Can I ask you a question? And ask you to be totally honest with me?"

"Sure."

Shane slowed the boat down so we could hear each other, and eventually brought it to a stop. We floated gently in the middle of the bay, boats occasionally passing by. In the distance was a large and busy bridge that headed toward downtown Jacksonville.

"Do you know what really happened during spring break?" I asked.

Shane shook his head, his eyes hidden behind sunglasses. "I was more wasted than you that night. We were all bombed out of our minds."

"I think we were all nervous."

"Because of what?" Shane asked.

"Because of what we were thinking about doing. Because of what we did."

Shane stood up and leaned against the side of the boat. "I never knew exactly what happened. I always thought . . ."

"What?"

"I thought you knew but didn't want to say."

"The longer time goes by, the less I seem to know. Bruce acts like he doesn't remember anything about it. I don't know. Maybe I knew more back then. I always thought—I assumed Carnie knew everything."

"Alec knew everything too. I think Alec was the one behind everything."

"You think that's why he disappeared?" I asked.

"What I *really* think is that I never really truly knew Alec. But who did? You know? You think you know the guys around you, but college is so different. You have these real intense friendships for a few years, and then they're all gone. Like that. It's weird."

"Things would've been different if—if everything hadn't happened."

"If Brian hadn't come along," Shane added, saying what I couldn't bring myself to say.

"Then Alec disappearing. And Carnie."

"Yeah."

"You know, Alec called me not long ago—actually last New Year's Eve. He told me that Carnie never meant for any of this to happen. That Carnie was the guilty one. That he wanted me to know—but he was never able to tell me."

"That's coming from Alec," Shane said.

"Yeah? So?"

"I never trusted Alec. I loved the guy and had a lot of fun with him, But I never trusted him."

"I thought I did," I said. "Once."

The boat bobbed back and forth. For a moment I just sat in silence, looking at Shane.

"You want to stick around here for a while? Hang out in Jacksonville for a few days?"

"What about my traveling partner?"

"He can sleep in the boat," Shane joked.

"It's tempting. But no—I really need to see the other guys. They'll say the same thing you're saying. I'm sure they don't know anything."

Shane looked at me hesitantly.

"What?"

"Why are you doing this?" he asked.

I could have just said I needed the job and the money. It was true. But it was more than that, and I think he knew it.

"Maybe it's because I never had that final conversation with Alec that I needed to have. We never had our good-bye."

"But what would that accomplish?"

"I don't know. But I think I've waited long enough—maybe too long—to ever try."

"You can't bring Carnie back, man. You can't change anything."

I stared off at the dark blue waters and the bridge in the background.

"Yeah. But I can finally learn why he killed himself."

FIFTEEN

March 1994

CHAPEL WAS EVERY THURSDAY morning, and students were encouraged to go. Jake never did. He had only been in the building three times for large campus gatherings.

The renovation to Vermuclen Chapel was completed a year before he came to Providence. The gothic tower was once the main part of a church built in the early 1900s. A family close to the college had renovated it and added on a building with a modern-day theater inside, with stadium seating in three different sections and a balcony overhead.

This afternoon, he sat alone in a shadowed sea of chairs while play practice took place. Alyssa was a codirector; the play was something an English grad had written that didn't make any sense. It was about waiting for God and featured a bunch of characters sitting around doing nothing but talking and theorizing.

Jake watched the back of Alyssa's head. She'd asked him to meet her here. He was early, but he had nothing else to do.

After the small cast and crew broke, Alyssa found Jake in the auditorium. She walked over and sat down beside him, letting out a tired sigh.

"Sorry we went late."

"That was—interesting?"

Alyssa rolled her eyes, almost in agreement. "I wanted to do a different play. But they had to go with Chuck's."

"What's it about?"

"Providence. Fate, chance, divine intervention. You know, because we *go* to Providence."

"Ah. What's it called? Let me guess. Uh, *Providence*?"

Alyssa laughed and shook her head. "No. Actually, it's called *Waiting For Tomorrow*."

"Interesting."

"How's the hand?"

Jake lifted his right hand, half wrapped in gauze and bandages that covered a splint.

"They had to re-break the bone to straighten it out."

"Does it hurt?" she asked.

"I'm taking lots of medication."

"Really?"

"Yeah. Bud Light. Tequila. Jack Daniels. They're really good, you should try them."

"That's why you broke your hand in the first place."

Jake looked at the earnestness on her face. "I told you—I had a fight."

"With whom?"

"With a big fat door. I think it was solid oak."

"Smart."

"Yeah, well—I lost," Jake said.

"What'd your parents say?"

"I just made up some lame excuse. You know—part of me thinks that the less they know, the less they'll care."

"They're paying your way through college."

"Well—they don't want their only son to be a bum, do they? My sister was the role model, and she stayed out of trouble in college, so they figure I'll turn out like her. I've been making decent grades, and I haven't been expelled yet, so that's all that matters."

Alyssa gave Jake a look that surprised him.

"Hey—don't do that."

"Don't do what?" Alyssa said.

"I hate looks like that."

"Like what?"

"Like you're staring at a kid who's lost his parents in a department store."

"No, I'm not."

"You don't have to pity me just because I broke my hand."

"Pity is a strong word. And if I do—it's not because of your broken hand."

"Then what is it?"

"Jake, I'm worried about you."

"Oh, no. Is this why you brought me in here? To the chapel? To have an intervention?"

"No," Alyssa said, a smile coming on her lips.

"What then?"

"When is it going to stop?"

"What?"

"The partying. The craziness."

Jake found her comments ironic. "Tell me something."

"What?" the beautiful girl next to him asked.

"Why is it that you're so interested in me straightening up, but you're not interested in dating me?"

"The two go together."

"Ah," Jake said, doing his own acting for dramatic effect. "So if I suddenly stopped the partying and all that, you'd go out with me?"

"I don't want you to stop because of me."

"I don't think I would."

"Do you ever think about the big picture?"

"What? Life, the universe, the hereafter? Sure."

"It doesn't seem like you do."

Jake couldn't help thinking how much he wanted to kiss her. "College kids need to have fun. We have the rest of our lives to grow up."

"Do you ever worry about the mistakes you've made?"

"Like breaking my hand?"

"No, like breaking the rules."

"You've been working in that dean's office too long," he said.

"I'm not talking about the college's rules."

He let out a sigh and shook his head. "Alyssa, come on.

95

You're not one of those holier-than-thou people."

"I'm not trying to be," she replied.

"I don't see why God would care in the least about me having some beers with a few friends."

"You make it sound so innocent."

"It is," Jake said, louder than he should have.

"Your right hand is in a cast. Because you *hit a door*. That's not so innocent."

"I hurt myself."

"What happens when you hurt someone else?"

"Oh, man. What? When I get behind the wheel and crash into someone? Come on. I'm not an idiot."

"Yes, you are."

Jake laughed. "Thank you. I needed to hear that. Is that my affirmation of the day?"

"Don't you think about tomorrow?"

"Sure."

Alyssa looked disappointed and moved in her seat as if she was getting ready to leave.

"Look, Alyssa, I don't know what you want."

"It's not about what *I* want."

Jake just looked at her, wanting more.

"What I mean is—there are consequences for your actions, Jake. And I—well—you're heading down a bad path. I don't want you to get hurt."

"I'll be fine."

"Are you sure?"

Jake nodded. "I'm always fine."

He smiled and tried to get a similar look from her, but all he saw was disappointment. He hated that look, especially on Alyssa's face. But there was nothing he could do to change it. He was who he was, and she was right—he shouldn't change just because of her.

Maybe Jake needed to grow up, but Alyssa needed to as well. She wanted to stay out of the world and in the little bubble known as Providence. But eventually she would get out. And she would discover that the world wasn't idealistic or pretty, and that sooner or later everyone failed.

SIXTEEN

June 2005

"MAYBE YOU'RE NOT MEANT to find Alec." Bruce studied his gin and tonic before draining the rest of it. He didn't seem to want a response.

"Maybe you should've stayed in California," I said.

"Ouch. That hurts."

"This isn't some vacation."

We were sitting in an upscale bar not far from O'Hare. We had flown in to Chicago two hours before and were waiting for Franklin. Bruce ordered another drink, and I wondered if he'd been sober since I'd seen him.

"You think Franklin will know any more than Shane?" he asked.

"I'm wondering if he's even coming."

"You want to try his cell again?"

I shook my head. I'd already left him a couple of messages.

"Think he's the same?"

"Probably," I said. "Franklin acted like a forty-year-old back in college."

"How'd we ever end up hanging around with him in the first place?"

"Shane. They were roommates. Remember—they had an apartment off campus that we always went to junior year?"

"Oh yeah."

"He was all right. At least for a while."

"He always patronized me."

I stared at Bruce's disheveled hair and unhealthy paleness. "Don't expect anything different."

"Don't go acting like him now. Why don't you order something?"

I held up the Diet Coke. "This is fine."

"I thought coming with you would be fun."

"Watching you drink twenty-four/seven has been fun too."

Bruce began to get that look in his eyes, the one that said he wasn't all there. Earlier, he had slipped away, and I would have bet my car that he had gone outside to smoke a little weed. He drained his drink and stood up off the bar stool.

"Where are you going?" I asked.

"Just to get some fresh air."

"Sit down."

"Huh?"

"Sit down," I ordered again. "Look—I know we got the okay from Mr. Jelen for you to tag alongside of me. But this isn't some spring break or something."

"You better be lucky it ain't," Bruce said, a darkness in his tone.

"What's that mean?"

"You know what that means."

"You got something to tell me?"

Bruce sat down again and cursed. "Man, nobody told anybody *anything*. Nothing. If I had something to say I'd say it, but I don't. I just have my ideas, you know. Thoughts."

"Like?"

"Like it's better not to think of them. Like it's better to try and get rid of them."

"And getting high is the answer?"

Bruce just laughed. "No. I just like it."

"Don't rub it in my face."

"I recall smoking a few bongs with you."

I nodded. "I never did like pot. You know that." I looked around the mostly empty bar. "Let's give him another hour."

"Then?"

I shrugged. "Then we go get a hotel room."

Bruce ordered another drink and we waited in silence.

"Are you going to call her?" he asked.

"I wasn't planning on it."

Bruce just looked at me.

"What?"

"You want to call Alyssa as bad as I want to go take a smoke break."

"That sounds really romantic."

"Call her," Bruce said. "Ask her out. Make it no pressure. Tell her your pathetic, burnt-out college buddy will be there too."

"Bruce—"

"I'm just joking. Come on."

But this time I knew Bruce was right. I picked up the cell phone sitting on the table in front of me and pressed a number on my speed dial that I had programmed in a few days ago.

The phone rang four times before I got her voice mail. It was amazing. Just the sound of her voice felt refreshing and got me in a different mood.

"Leave a message at the tone, and I'll make sure to get back to you," she said so politely.

"Hi, Alyssa. It's Jake. And Bruce too. We're back in Chicago. We were trying to hook up with Franklin tonight, but it didn't work out, I guess. We're going to be staying close to Summit, and I just thought—well, maybe we could all get together. For coffee or whatever. So give me a call if you'd like."

I gave her my number and then clipped the phone shut.

"'For coffee or whatever.' What was that?"

"What?" I asked Bruce.

"You need to take her out to a nice dinner. *Alone*. I'll be overstuffed baggage."

"You just said—"

"Yeah, I know what I said. Saying my name will make her more at ease. Take off any pressure. But I'm leaving the two of you alone."

"Bruce—"

99

"What?"

"It's not like that."

He nodded, his long hair flopping in his eyes. He brushed it back and laughed. "It's not like what? Dude, you were in love with this girl since the day you met her. I mean obsessed sorta love, you know? You remember how many nights we sat around talking about her? If you don't, well, I sure do, man. And it's cool. You know. Sometimes you're given a second chance."

"That was a long time ago."

Bruce cursed. "Wasn't *that* long ago. I mean, look at us. Does it feel *that* long ago?"

"I don't know."

"So she's divorced. So what?"

"I'm not saying that's the problem. It's just—I'm sure it's the last thing she wants."

"And you'd think I'd be the one with less sense. Dude, she like called you. Out of the blue. Remember? You said she called and it was like this totally magical night."

"All right. Easy there, killer."

"I'm just trying to get some sense in you."

I nodded and watched him stand up.

"I'm going outside for a little smoke. Want to join me?"

I shook my head, knowing Bruce was a hopeless cause. I told him we'd take off in five minutes.

⤜ ⤛

Franklin's being a no-show didn't surprise me. What had surprised me was his assistant saying he would meet us at this bar at 8:00 p.m. I doubted he would be as receptive as Shane and Bruce had been. I could still remember those last few days of our school year. I remembered some of the things Franklin said. Some of the threats. Trying to cover up everything and make sure everyone was on the same page and trying his hardest to get his diploma and then get far away from all of us.

The phone in front of me lit up, and I thought *There she is*. I couldn't help my smile as I reached for the phone and glanced down at it.

But the number was unlisted. Maybe it was Franklin after all, apologizing and saying he was on his way.

"Hello?"

A pause, then a deep voice on the other line spoke. "What do you think you're doing?"

"Excuse me?" I asked. "Who is this?"

The man didn't sound anything like Franklin.

"I know who you are. Think this is some game?"

"Alec?" I asked, knowing it wasn't him but not sure who it could be.

"Yeah, I know about him. And I know about you. And the little games you played in college. I know about everything."

"Look, buddy—"

"No, you look. And pay attention. That knot on the back of your head is just a little sample of what's to come."

"Who is this?" I shouted, angry now.

"Someone who knows everything."

"Is that a threat?"

The low voice cursed at me. "You bet it's a threat. And you better go back home before things get out of hand."

"Why don't you tell me that to my face?"

"You don't want me doing that, Jake Rivers. None of you do."

The line went dead, and I shut off the phone, fury racing through my body. If the caller had wanted to scare me off, he had only managed to incense me. If this was the guy who banged me on the head, I wanted to see him face-to-face. I wanted him to try that stunt again.

What kind of mess am I stepping into?

I thought of the last thing he had said: None of you do.

Who was he referring to?

A sudden fear cut my anger in half. Alyssa. And I knew I desperately wanted to hear from her.

Did he see us meet at the coffee shop?

I didn't know and didn't care. I wasn't sure if this had anything to do with Alec or Mr. Jelen or any of us.

But with the exhilaration and rush of strapping a bungee cord to my legs and jumping off a bridge, I knew I wanted to face this threat head-on. I was done running away from the things that scared me the most. I had spent too many years picking out challenges and conquering them. And this would be another one.

I just hoped nobody got hurt in the process.

SEVENTEEN

March 1994

THREE STORIES TALL doesn't seem that high until you're stand-ing on the roof ready to jump off.

Jake and Shane only had a few minutes, and they knew it. Shane had said he would go first, but he was rethinking it now. It was windy and cooler up there, and the sun was going down. But the crowd below was getting larger, and they needed either to do it now or call it a day.

"Come on, man," Jake said. "If we don't do this we're going to be ridiculed for the rest of the year."

"I know. But—this is insane."

"It was your idea!" he shouted.

Shane just laughed and stood at the edge of the building. The crowd gathering below in a half oval all cheered him on. He looked at Jake.

"Man, I'm telling you—I'm freaking out."

"It's not that high," Jake said.

"Yeah, but that's all we got to land on."

Jake studied the landing point and thought for a moment. Then he raised his arms and heard the crowd cheer.

"I'm doing it."

"Jake!" Shane said as he watched Jake back up.

Jake looked at him and laughed. "If this doesn't work I'm

blaming you." Then he took off and hurled himself over the edge of the building.

It was the most exciting sensation he'd ever felt. Until he landed.

➤➤ ◄◄

Shane had come up with the idea during a studying bout in the library. He posed the question: Could you jump off the top of South Hall and live? South Hall wasn't that tall and had a grassy field behind it that would at least cushion your landing. Jake, Bruce, and Shane debated the question throughout the day and then onward at Four-leaf Clover as they played pool.

"What if you got a hundred mattresses and padded your landing?" Bruce asked.

"How're you gonna get a hundred mattresses?" Jake answered.

But this got them thinking. They began devising a plan to get not a hundred mattresses, but eight anyway. They would make a big square with them, then top them with as many pillows as they could round up.

"How many?" Jake asked Shane, the mastermind.

"Hundreds. We get a bunch of guys to just go around and take pillows."

That was a prank in itself. Jake and Shane needed to get a few RAs in on the joke, not telling them it was in order to jump off the roof. The mattresses could be explained easily enough; they'd say they were replacing them. But pillows—taking people's pillows was like taking their underwear. But they were easy to find.

They enlisted thirty guys to help out on a Saturday afternoon, going through the hallways and into strangers' rooms asking for pillows. Some flat out refused; others gave them their pillows without a shrug. Some watched as they began to put them out in the back lawn close to the edge of the building. As the pile began to grow, students began to show up and watch what they were doing.

The pile looked big, and Shane and Jake tested it out by

jumping in it. Then they proceeded to the roof through a door that Shane got unlocked by bribing someone on maintenance. When they got to the edge and looked down, the interested faces of the students below suddenly electrified by the very notion of the stunt, Jake realized this was going to be harder than it looked.

"What if we miss?" Shane asked.

"It's right below us. There's no way we can miss it."

"What if we break something?"

Jake only smiled. "It was your idea."

"You keep saying that."

"Because it's true."

Jake and Shane stood up alongside the building. For a minute, Jake thought about reconsidering. Then he saw Ms. Peterson walking down amidst the crowd.

He heard the roar of the crowd and a few shrieks from the students gathered below, but what he remembered the most was thinking how quickly he fell. His mind kept thinking *When am I going to land?* And then he did.

His legs were a little stretched out, versus being completely square, but the force of the landing still took his breath away. Something hit his butt hard, and he wondered if a rock or something was in the pile. He was surrounded by a sea of pillows, his breath knocked out of him and his side suddenly aching. Loud applause rang up, and for a moment Jake was terrified.

I can't feel my lower body. I can't feel anything.

But then the moment passed, and he began breathing again. He moved his body up and then felt his rear. It was just from landing on the pillows and the mattress below. Nothing felt broken, but he knew he would have a bruise there for a long time.

Jake stood up, and everyone smothered him as if he were the world champion of a boxing match. He looked up at the roof and gave a thumbs-up to Shane.

His friend couldn't resist. Shane took off and landed more in the middle of the pile. Again the students applauded and cheered and embraced Shane afterwards.

Alec was in the crowd and came up to Jake.

"And you think *I'm* crazy?" he said in amazement.

And for a moment, Jake enjoyed the accolades all around him. Until Ms. Peterson approached and wanted a word with them.

→→ ←←

"How come we almost got suspended?" Shane asked.

"You almost didn't even jump," Jake said.

"You almost didn't stand up."

This was hours later as they were standing around in the living room of Neesa's house. Neesa was a junior that Bruce Atkinson knew. Her parents were gone for a week, so she figured she'd destroy their house one night and then spend the week after trying to repair the damage.

Bruce drove four of them here—Shane, Alec, Jake, and Carnie. Some of the other guys would arrive later. Neesa obviously liked Bruce, because she let them all in for free. Didn't she realize their group alone could account for one keg? Serious lack of judgment. She would learn, however. The night was young, and so was she.

Everybody was talking about the big excitement on campus. At a college so small, something like that went a long way. Alec looked a little irritated that he hadn't been up there with Shane and Jake.

By the time Laila arrived with her group, Jake was already pretty well gone. She had been ignoring him ever since he left her a week ago without a good-bye. It hadn't bothered him. But taking one look at her tonight, wearing another one of her little skirts even though it was ten degrees outside, made him realize who he was dealing with. He was content having her avoid him.

"The big hero," someone said behind him.

Jake turned to see Brian Erwin in all his smugness. He stood several inches taller than everyone there.

"Everybody's bored around campus," Jake said. "Our athletic programs keep letting us down."

Brian chuckled and shook his head. "One day you're going

106

to break your neck because of your stupidity. And I'm going to laugh."

Shane came up behind Brian and tapped him on the back as if they were old buds. "See our act this afternoon?"

The jock continued staring at Jake and nodded. "Don't you think it's getting a little old?"

Shane looked at Brian, wondering what he was talking about. Jake was going to say something, but just then Laila came up and put an arm around Brian's side. She stood on her toes and whispered something in his ear. They both laughed at Jake, then walked off.

"What was that all about?" Shane asked Jake.

"They still think it's high school. They've been watching too much Beverly Hills 90210."

"You sorta remind me of Brandon."

"Get me a beer," Jake said with a chuckle.

➤➤ ◄◄

The music kept getting louder and the crowd kept multiplying. It grew hard to navigate around the house. Jake found himself getting a cup of beer from the keg and pounding half of it in order not to spill any. Near midnight, as he was feeling it bad, he made his way upstairs to use Neesa's parents' bathroom. As he came back out into the master bedroom, he noticed that the door to the hallway was closed. A figure blocked his way across the dimly lit room.

"About time we had some alone time."

Laila. They hadn't spoken all night, but he kept seeing her look at him, eyeing him. She was obvious and knew it too. But she had usually been draped over Brian.

"What're you doing?" Jake asked.

"Getting away from the crowd."

"Great. The room's all yours."

He tried to walk by her, but she moved swiftly and stood right in front of him.

"Where's meathead?" Jake asked.

"He's not here."

107

"Aren't you two a thing or something?"

Laila laughed and slipped her arms around him. "Why do you keep ignoring me?"

"I'm not ignoring you."

"Stay up here with me."

"Come on." He tried to move again, but she continued to stay in front of him, as if dancing with him.

"I know what you want," she said.

"You don't have a clue. Especially since you're plowed."

"Jake—" She gently brushed his side and moved her body close to his.

"Get off me!"

She backed off, and Jake found himself surprised at how loud his voice had been.

"Can't you take a hint?" he asked her.

In the muted light she looked like a lost child. Sad eyes looked at him, and for a moment, Jake felt awful. "Laila—look, come on—"

But then she opened the door and the light blinded him and she walked off. He followed her, walking down the steps and seeing Bruce watching them as they neared the bottom.

Bruce smiled at him as if something had happened. Jake was too tired to tell him otherwise.

➤➤ ◄◄

Moments later, the party still packed and moving like a crowd at a general admission concert, Jake heard a commotion coming from the kitchen. It sounded like Alec. He got up off the couch and squeezed through the crowd.

In the kitchen, a circle had formed around Alec and the much-taller Brian. Alec was cursing at Brian and calling him a bold-faced liar, among other things. Alec's face was red and he snarled like a bulldog, and Jake knew his friend had passed the point of being a happy drunk. With Alec, it was like a switch, and sometimes he became an angry, out-of-control drunk. Surely Brian had provoked this, but he wasn't sure why.

"You're just mad because it's the truth," Brian yelled out.

"Shut your hole," Franklin said, trying to break things up.

"Stay out of this, preppy."

Jake got to the group and pulled Alec's arm. His friend turned around, ready to belt him.

"Whoa," Jake said. "Chill, man. It's me."

"Oh, here we go. The crippled to the rescue."

Jake smiled it off, knowing he was referring to the splint on his hand. "Erwin, man—why don't you realize nobody wants you here."

"Psycho-boy didn't like hearing the truth."

Alec spit out a few more curses.

"Alec, shut up for a minute. Would you guys just relax?"

"I'm relaxed," Brian said.

Behind him stood another jock with blond hair and freckles and arms the size of watermelons.

"Alec, come on," Jake said, figuring this was a bad battle to get into.

"Why don't you ask him why he suddenly bailed on you last year? Huh? What's the story, Alec? Huh?"

"Brian, man," Franklin said, going over to him.

"I said stay out of this. This has nothing to do with you."

Jake still held Alec back.

"I swear I'll kill you, man, I swear—"Alec continued to rant.

"Your mom had a little meltdown, huh? Right? He tell you that, Jake? Doesn't look like it. Your little friend there has bigger problems than just his drinking."

"Shut up!" Franklin yelled.

Alec started to charge at Brian, and all Jake could do was ride along. The big guy didn't move much as Alec landed a shoulder against him. He just slammed Alec's head back to the ground.

"I'll hurt you, man," Brian said, now leaning over Alec, one hand on Alec's face, keeping him down.

It all happened in seconds. Jake looked to his side and saw Carnie smoking a cigarette. He grabbed it with his right hand, still in a splint, the white piece looking like a glove. Then he swooped over and came up behind Brian and put out the cigarette on his generous forehead.

It looked like something out of a movie. The half-full

kitchen exploded in both laughter and gasps. Brian cursed and screamed a big "Owww!" before a quick right arm sent Jake flying back against the refrigerator.

"Oh, I'm sorry," Jake said in a mocking tone. "I must've missed the ashtray. It looked the same."

Brian stared at Jake for a second to register what had just happened. Then the kitchen and the rest of the house broke out in pandemonium.

→► ◄←

Carnie drove Jake home while the rest of the guys tried to clean up the damage. Franklin, Bruce, and a bunch of other guys broke up the fight and got Brian out of the house before things turned uglier. Then they got Jake out in case Brian came back.

"Where's Alec?"

Carnie shook his head, another cigarette in his mouth. "Disappeared. Probably with some girl."

Jake was still out of breath, still angry, still fuzzy in the head. He recalled the series of names he had called Brian.

"Did you hear what he said about Alec?"

Carnie nodded.

"Is it true?"

"Probably," Carnie said.

"I'm so sick of that guy. Walks around campus thinking it should be named after him. They lost in a play-off game. He's not going to play in the NBA. Who's he kidding?"

"You put out a cigarette on his head," Carnie said in a passionless tone, as if to remind Jake.

"A guy thinks because he's some basketball stud with a free pass to do jack around here means he can say and do anything and I'm sorry but he can't."

"Some people won't change."

"Yeah, but some things are off-limits," Jake said. "Hey, give me a smoke."

Carnie looked at him as if he was nervous to give him one.

"Just hand one over, smart aleck."

He handed Jake a cigarette. "You're lucky we got you out of there before Chad could come after you."

"Who's Chad?"

"Brian's friend. The blond-haired guy the size of a tractor."

"I don't care if he has the whole team with him."

"Neesa wasn't too happy," Carnie said, starting to chuckle.

"Who's Neesa?"

"The girl whose house we helped destroy."

"It's her own fault."

They drove for a while, heading toward Burritoville. Nothing topped off a good night of drinking and fighting better than a nice steak burrito with no beans and sour cream. That and a handful of carrots and jalapeños.

It was close to one-thirty in the morning.

After eating the football-sized burritos, a glassy-eyed Jake was finally calmed down.

"Think that's true about Alec's mom?" he asked again.

"Don't know," was all Carnie said. He was lost in burrito love.

"I'm tired of seeing Brian at every party, seeing those white teeth of his."

Carnie nodded.

"He wanted to get in a fight. The guy has had something against me ever since I stole the school mascot and they went on that losing streak."

"I helped."

"I did the time. I take the credit."

Carnie, face full of a thick beard that didn't take him long to grow, nodded again. "Two more notches to add to the belt."

"What belt?" Jake asked.

"The Providence lore. The stories of legend."

"And what notches are those?"

"Jumping off the roof. And putting out a smoke on Brian's forehead."

They both laughed.

"Did you see his look?" Jake asked with a proud look.

"I'll carry it to my grave," Carnie said.

"That guy got busted drinking sophomore year. Just like

me. They didn't do squat to him. Me they send to outpatient counseling."

"You need it."

"Brian had it coming."

"Yeah," Carnie said. He hesitated.

"What?"

"He's not going to forget about this. Not Brian."

Jake only shrugged.

EIGHTEEN

June 2005

ALYSSA STROLLED INTO the restaurant, turning heads and doing serious damage to my already fragile heart. "Breathtaking"
was such a trite phrase to describe the way she looked. She
wore a long, breezy dress with a black, white, and blue floral
pattern and a black top that tied around her neck and revealed
bare shoulders and arms. Her dark hair was pulled back and
tied with a white scarf. And even from where I stood, waiting
at the table for her, I could tell she was more made up, more
polished than the other night.

"Sorry I'm late," she said, a shy smile on her red lips.

"That was worth the wait."

"What?"

"Seeing you walk across the room. I think I need to sit
down."

"Stop it."

We sat, and I couldn't help but say, "You look incredible
tonight."

"Thank you. The thought of going out somewhere fancy—I
probably made more of it than I should have. It's just—it's been
awhile."

"You're telling me. Sorry I don't clean up as well."

I wore khaki pants and a light blue button-down shirt with

sleeves that I had rolled up. I hadn't packed for this trip thinking that I would be going on a date with Alyssa Roberts.

"This is a nice place you picked," I said to her as someone poured her a glass of water.

"I've only heard about it from others."

The name of the restaurant was The Carriage House, and it was about fifteen minutes from Summit in the town of Burr Ridge. Everything about it was dark and fancy—the entrance and the doors opening up to the inside, the heavy oak tables, the shadows and muted light, the corner nooks like the one our table was located in. There was a steady and laid-back dining crowd here for the night.

The waiter came up and announced specials and then asked for our drink orders.

"You like wine?" I asked the stunning woman across the table from me.

"I guess it never hurts to start."

I grinned and looked at the menu, then named off a bottle of Cabernet Sauvignon.

The waiter, a well-groomed man in his late forties, took the wine menu and nodded. "Very good choice, sir."

Alyssa seemed impressed. "So—you're a wine connoisseur?"

"Hardly. It just sounded good. And looked expensive. You've had wine, right?"

Alyssa shook her head.

"What? Never?"

"No. Kyle always tried to get me to have a glass. He said I was such—" Alyssa stopped herself and apologized.

"You didn't say anything," I assured her.

"I didn't mean to start out right away with—" She looked away.

"Alyssa? You can say anything you want tonight. And do whatever you want. Okay?"

"That could be frightening."

"Or it could be really good for you. Just—look. There's no pressure about anything here."

"The Carriage House seems a little more intimidating than Starbucks."

"So does your outfit, but I'm not complaining. You picked this for a reason."

"Oh, I picked it for a reason." She paused for a moment. "The question is whether or not I should tell you why."

"You can tell me anything you want or nothing at all."

"Really?"

"Sure. And if I'm not getting anywhere, then I'll have to get you really loaded with cheap wine."

"I thought it was expensive." She smiled.

"Whatever."

We shared a look that felt like yesterday and like so much more, and it was finally interrupted by the waiter bringing the bottle of wine and pouring me a sample. I went through the motions of swirling and smelling and tasting it.

"Hmm," I said, putting on an act to amuse Alyssa. "Amazing. Taste a hint of blackberry with a slight cedar and even a bit of currant. Smooth and moderately long."

Alyssa looked at me for a moment, and I didn't give anything away.

"You know a lot about wine."

"I just made that all up," I said. "But it sounded good, didn't it?"

Alyssa laughed. The sound felt comforting.

Eleven years and a hard knock on the back of my head almost seemed worth it just for the time spent with Alyssa over dinner. To call it magical makes it sound imaginary. It was the freshest and most intimate conversation I had held in years, and I couldn't help but think that a little wine had something to do with it. At least it calmed down my nerves; surely it did the same for her. We talked about everything. Providence College, of course, and friends and acquaintances from long ago. But each subject morphed into another, and from that came a revelation or an amazing anecdote. I listened, savoring each word like it was fine food.

There were no hidden agendas or awkward pauses. We had a history, and from day one of that history, Alyssa had known where I stood. I liked to think that some time during college, I had begun to understand where Alyssa came from, but I still didn't know for sure. And now, here was a grown-up woman, more beautiful than I could have imagined, living a life I wouldn't have believed until she described it in person.

"Kyle was having an affair," she finally told me, after our dinner plates had been cleared and we continued working on that first bottle of wine.

"I'm sorry."

"It had to be something like that, right? I know you were wondering—if you hadn't already heard."

"I didn't know. I'm really sorry."

"A friend of mine saw him out with this really gorgeous and younger blonde. I mean—he wasn't even trying to hide it."

I didn't say anything. I wanted her to continue to open up.

"You want to know the funny thing? The sad thing, I guess. The reason I'm probably messed up for life?"

"Alyssa, you're not messed up."

"Want to know where she saw Kyle and his bimbo? Here. At The Carriage House. Maybe even sitting somewhere cozy, like we are now."

I hated hearing this, hating knowing that the jerk who had ended up with the biggest hope and dream I'd held back in college had deliberately chucked it away. It wasn't simply that I couldn't imagine cheating on Alyssa. I couldn't fathom breaking her heart.

She continued, her face somber and her thoughts somewhere far off. "I just wanted to see the place."

"When was all this?"

"A couple years ago. It took a year for everything to blow up and then drift away. Kinda like a snowstorm, you know. You get all this heavy snow, and then it eventually gets muddy and ugly, and then it melts away. We tried counseling. He didn't want it. I guess, in a lot of ways, I didn't know the guy I married. I was too busy trying to be the perfect wife, the perfect Christian, trying to lead the perfect life with our perfect little family."

"I might be wrong, but I don't think such a thing exists."

"I know that. Now. But try living around here. Imagine the little families with their perfect little homes and kids and all that. It was hard keeping up."

I smiled. "Why do you think I moved away?"

"You moved because your parents did. Right?"

"Hey, come on. It sounds so noble and adventurous if you leave them out of it."

"I've thought about moving. It's just—my job. That makes it harder. I mean—I already signed a contract to teach next year, but I'm dreading it. I don't want to stay around here."

"Where's Kyle?"

"He's still around. I moved out of the house—it was my choice. I couldn't stomach living there anymore. I'm renting a small place. Divorce is such a wonderful thing, huh?"

"Alyssa—I don't know what to say."

"You can say 'I told you so.'"

"What are you talking about?" I asked her, confused.

"All that babble I used to talk about in college. About finding the right one and about there being a right way and about mistakes and—"

"And you were dead right," I interrupted.

She shook her head, her eyes intense on mine. "I was heading down a dead-end street."

"You couldn't help that you fell in love with a pig."

"Yes, I could. I should have known better. I guess I was just naïve. The world isn't the way I thought it was. Not when I was leading my little sheltered life in college."

"You weren't naïve."

"Sure I was," Alyssa said, finishing her glass of wine. "I was stupid, really. I thought that if you believed in something, that if you really had faith and lived as good a life as possible, things would work out."

"Bad things happen all the time. Things that are out of our control."

"You know the church basically ran me out? They didn't *say* I needed to leave. But my friends, the people I had grown used to being around, suddenly turned their backs on me. They took Kyle's side when I initiated the divorce. They said I wasn't acting in a 'forgiving, Christlike way.' It was just all so—"

"Alyssa—"

"I haven't been to church in over a year, can you believe that? Ms. Little Princess is actually angry at God."

"I don't think God made your ex decide to hook up with some other chick."

"What is it about us?"

"Huh?"

"Now you're on His side?"

I laughed and leaned over to take her hand. "I'm on your side too."

"I thought if anybody could understand, it'd be you."

I nodded. "I understand. I understand that life sucks and that there's this awful, ugly thing called sin that none of us can do anything about. It's not God's fault that things happen. We all make decisions and have to live with them."

"Yeah. But what happens when those decisions are out of your control—when you had *nothing* to do with them? What happens when the mistakes of others end up ruining your life?"

I took a deep breath and thought for a moment. "Sometimes the mistakes of others can bring you closer to where you need to be in life," I said.

"You believe that?"

"That's my life in a sound bite."

"How can you know?"

"I know, Alyssa. I'm not the best at talking about it, but trust me, I know."

The waiter came around to ask if we wanted dessert.

"I'd like to go home," Alyssa said.

I told him to bring the check. As he walked away, Alyssa took my hand again.

"Do you want to come home with me tonight?" she asked in a surprisingly direct tone.

"Yes," I said honestly. "But I can't."

"Why not?"

"Because I don't want to do something I'll regret. Something *you'll* regret."

"Who says we'd regret anything?"

I shook my head, my heart and gut feeling like someone

was using them as a punching bag. "I think the wine agreed with you tonight," I said.

"It's not the wine talking."

"Maybe it is, even just slightly."

Her dark eyes looked at me, confused and almost frustrated. "We're not kids, Jake. There are no rules any more."

"We're not in college. But there are still rules."

She sighed. "I don't get it. Why is it my timing with everything just sucks?"

I chuckled and looked at the beautiful woman across from me. "I think our timing is remarkable, believe it or not."

Alyssa gently rubbed her shoulder, and I couldn't help letting my eyes briefly drift over her. How many nights, how many times had I dreamt of being with her?

What are you doing, Jake?

I was doing the right thing. Saying no had never been my strong suit. But I knew this was the best thing tonight.

"Can I—will you be around for a while?" Alyssa asked. "Do you want to do something again? It doesn't have to be anything formal."

"I'll be around. Next time I'll pick the place, okay?"

She nodded and smiled and looked like the young girl I used to dream about as a student at Providence. I glanced into her gentle eyes and knew that I still loved her, that I had always loved her, and that sometimes, love was an impossible gift to give back.

NINETEEN

March 1994

FOR A SECOND JAKE THOUGHT he heard a tapping noise at the door and looked its way, trying to listen. But there was nothing.

The apartment was empty except for him. He sat on the couch that was ruined beyond recognition from spilled beer and food and cigarette ashes. It was a little after eleven on Saturday night, and Jake sat watching Chris Farley on *Saturday Night Live* and drinking a Bud Light. They were heading out again to meet up with the guys at Franklin's apartment. All of them had been at Shaughnessy's, but it had been packed with the same people and same music and same expensive weekend prices, so they'd left half an hour ago. Carnie dropped Jake off at the apartment to use the bathroom and said he'd go to the liquor store to pick up some stuff.

Jake thought of Shaughnessy's. He couldn't believe he'd seen Laila there. Part of him thought she was stalking him. He knew he shouldn't have mouthed off at her the way he did, telling her to back off and to leave him alone and to stop acting like Sharon Stone in *Basic Instinct*. That last comment had really ticked her off, especially since the other guys had heard it and gotten a good chuckle out of it. At least it had worked—Laila left the bar right after that.

The knocking sounded again, harder, and Jake wondered

why Carnie had brought the liquor up to the apartment with him. And where were his keys? Maybe his hands were full.

Jake passed the "wall of women" they had spent the last eight months putting up, featuring posters of various scantily-clad women in bathing suits and lingerie, all advertising beer. They usually got a free poster every time they went to the liquor store down the street. Jake often joked that he wanted to work in beer marketing. It would be the easiest job in the world.

He opened the door to ask, "Why are you knocking?" when he stopped in mid-sentence. A figure wearing a Chicago Bulls T-shirt and a leering smile stood in the hallway.

It was Brian Erwin.

"What the—"

A second figure behind the first rushed toward him and grabbed him by the shirt.

Jake jerked forward like the start of a roller coaster ride. He was instantly out of breath. Just as he tried to lift up his hand in front of his face, something hard hit his jaw below his right eye. For a moment, he couldn't see and lost all sense of equilibrium. He fell, but before falling he felt another sharp pain in his back, wrenching him sideways so he landed on the floor of the hallway outside his apartment in an awkward sprawl.

He cried out, but something hard, surely a fist, landed on his mouth and cut his lip and muffled his cry. Even before he could realize he had been hit again, another blow landed on his face.

Jake was surprised to hear his own screams, violent and raw. "Stop!" he yelled, but the beating continued.

Something sharp cut into his side; at the same time a block pounded his face. He curled his right fist but felt a shock of pain there, remembering it was in a splint. He waved his left arm toward the blackness.

He heard a vicious curse whispered in his ear before that same ear was pummeled by something.

"God, stop it, please!" he cried.

Then he thought of Carnie and starting screaming for his roommate. "CARNIE!" he howled.

Something as hard as a brick, perhaps an elbow, launched into his gut. Jake exhaled and coughed and tried calling Carnie's name again, but his voice was weaker.

Another fist waled down on his lip and partially against his nose.

"CARNIE!"

The shriek didn't even sound like him.

Where is he?

Then came the worst blow of all. It landed on the back of his head, even as he lay curled up in a ball trying to protect his face with one hand and his broken hand by tucking it underneath his arm. This last blow wasn't a punch but more like a kick from a boot or a cement block.

He tried calling out in between his coughing and moaning and the bitter taste of blood, but he couldn't. His assailant knelt over him and gave him a profanity-laced warning. Jake could feel warm breath against his closed eyes.

Then an opened palm pounded his head back into the floor, and Jake fell into a sea of black.

TWENTY

June 2005

ON MY WAY TO THE MOTEL after dinner with Alyssa, a hundred regrets storming through my mind, I spotted Bruce walking on the side of the road. It was around ten at night.

I pulled into a parking lot and got out of the still-running rental car.

"Bruce!"

He looked at me with squinty eyes, then smiled and walked over. "What are you doing?" he asked.

"What are *you* doing?"

"I got bored watching TV, so I went out."

"Where?"

"This dump about half a mile down the road."

Bruce had a cigarette in one hand. His T-shirt that read "Office Space" was untucked.

"You could've come out with Alyssa and me."

"So—how'd it go? You get a little?"

"Would you shut up? Get in the car."

"I was enjoying my midnight stroll."

"You'll get arrested for public intoxication."

In the car, it took seconds to smell Bruce's combination of liquor and pot breath.

"Bruce—"

"Come on, *Dad.*"

"So is this going to be an everyday thing?"

"Such harassment. I was just minding my own business."

I drove down the street, passing a more developed community.

"You remember driving around here? Completely bombed?" Bruce asked.

"It's lucky none of us killed someone," I said.

"Our guardian angels were working overtime." He laughed.

"Did you get hold of Franklin?"

"That jerk doesn't want to talk to me. Or us. But Mike's available. Tomorrow night."

"Really?" I was surprised Bruce had taken any initiative.

"Yeah. He said to come down. Both of us. He'd love to have us over. Spend the night. Go out on the town."

"You have his—"

"Yes. Anything else?"

"Have a mint."

➤➤ ◄◄

We pulled into the motel and parked close to our room. We were staying on the second floor, the door facing out. We could've gotten a better place, but this was close and fast and it worked for now.

I got out of the car and started walking toward the stairs. I turned around for a moment and saw Bruce, the door half-open, his body leaning toward the steering wheel. For a moment I thought about getting him, then I just sighed and kept walking up the stairs.

I'm not playing dad or guardian.

As I reached the top of the second floor and turned to head down to my room, I clipped the shoulder of a stocky man coming out of nowhere.

"Sorry, man," I called out to the balding figure who said nothing and headed down the stairs.

I walked down the concrete hallway past identical doors and finally found ours. As I reached to get my key card—

It's already open

—I realized that I didn't need it. The door was ajar.

I stared at it for a moment, then poked it forward. A light over the sink in the bathroom was the only light in the room.

Flicking on the switch, I saw everything more clearly.

It was déjà vu of coming home to Bruce's apartment. Except we didn't have that much to pilfer through.

Both of our suitcases were opened, Bruce's tossed over on the floor, with our clothes strewn about everywhere. My leather bag containing most of the info I had—a few pictures of Claire Jelen, names and addresses, nothing really too valuable—had been opened and ripped through.

I took in the scene for a moment, then ran back out to the balcony.

Bruce still remained sitting in the front of our car, his door open. The man who had passed by me in the hall, the only person around besides Bruce and me, was walking across the parking lot to a four-door sedan I hadn't noticed before.

"Excuse me!" I shouted across the still of the night. "Hey, you!"

He finally turned around and stared at me, his face dark from the shadows. He didn't say anything, didn't stop and ask what was wrong. He looked at me for a brief moment, then kept going.

You did this, didn't you?

I began to sprint down the hallway, toward the stairs and into the parking lot.

Lights moved as I tore after the Chevy that was backing up. I reached the tail end of the car and slammed both hands on the back to make sure it didn't keep backing up. The driver shifted into drive and sped away.

For a second I wanted to chase it on foot, but realized that was stupid. I ran back to our rental car and climbed into the car like a NASCAR driver. In a couple of seconds I was shifting the car into reverse and telling Bruce to close his door.

"Huh—what the—?"

"Close the door!"

I neared the turn in the parking lot and could already see

the Chevy turning right onto the main road. I jerked my rental car left toward the front of the hotel, knowing the year-old Mustang rental would overtake the poor Chevy in seconds. I didn't have a plan and didn't know what I was going to do once I overtook him. Maybe just get an idea of who was stalking us, what he looked like—

"Bruce!"

I slammed on the brakes but it was already too late. My unstable friend had been sitting up in his seat and had not taken the turn quite so well. He was sprawled on the pavement behind me.

I cursed without thought and got out of the car again, running back to where Bruce lay. He looked like a corpse, body not moving, head not turning.

For a second he lay still, not saying or breathing or doing anything. But he opened his eyes as I repeated his name.

"Somebody left the car door open," he said with a smile.

"You okay?"

"My head hurts."

"Did you land on it?" I asked him.

"I think I had too many Long Islands."

Helping him up, I realized he was fine. Well, maybe not *fine*. Fine wasn't a word I would use when talking about Bruce. But he wasn't hurt.

Not for now.

↦ ↤

After spending a few minutes picking up our clothes and putting them back in our suitcases, I sat on the edge of my bed, still wired and antsy. Bruce had collapsed onto his bed, but he wasn't officially asleep. His eyes cracked open and looked at me for a moment.

"Alec didn't do this," he said in slurred words.

"That wasn't Alec. But who else would be following us?"

"You believe in ghosts?"

I stared at him and shook my head.

I shouldn't be here.

"No," I said.

"Maybe you should."

"Maybe you should get some sleep."

"You can't fight the undead." Bruce's eyes looked big and he seemed freaked out.

"I think someone's seen a few too many horror flicks."

"They come back to haunt you. I know. I'm telling you, Jake, I know."

His eyes closed again, and a wave of sleep took him, at least for a few moments. Bruce actually looked peaceful, and I envied him for the moment.

For the first time since deciding to try and find Alec, I was worried. I don't know if I'd say I was scared. Maybe it was just bewilderment. And the fact that I was wiping away eleven years in just a matter of days. Bruce, Alyssa, Kirby, Shane—it was all too much in too little time.

Was the intruder who had been through our stuff—was he looking for something in particular? Was he snooping for someone—for Alec, maybe? Or for Mr. Jelen? And was he dangerous? Was I crazy for chasing after him?

Would I get myself hurt?

It wouldn't be the first time.

I thought back to that night. I didn't think about it often, but every now and then I remembered. The fight that started a chain of events in motion.

More like a beating.

I still didn't know where that chain of events would lead. Part of me no longer wanted to know.

But I would finally have to find out.

TWENTY-ONE
March 1994

JAKE COULD STILL FEEL the blows hitting his face, striking his body. But for the few seconds or minutes after crumpling to the hallway floor, moaning and spitting up the blood in his mouth, he saw nothing but darkness.

Then, from far away, a muffled voice at his side.

"okay just wait here I'm going to call just hold on—"

And he thought it was Carnie and he wanted to ask what took him so long but he couldn't work his mouth. He coughed hard and felt his stomach muscles tighten and something soft and gooey came up in his mouth. He spit but didn't know what he was spitting out.

Someone helped him sit up, and a wave of painful blackness covered him like a blanket.

The lights came back on as Jake sat at the table and heard commotion around him.

. . . know who did this to him

. . . out at a bar

. . . keep him up because he's got a concussion

. . . looks awful

In his hand was a warm rag that he just looked at.

"Wipe your face—it's all bloody."

He looked at his side and saw Franklin. Where had he come from?

"Don't talk, Jake. It's okay. We're going to take you to the hospital."

And all he could think was *I don't need a hospital. I'm fine.*

He went to stand up, but somehow the floor and his legs all moved away from him. He heard several voices call to him as he crumpled to the carpet and blacked out again.

➤➤ ◄◄

"You need to stay put."

Jake saw Brian's face for a second and jerked, then realized he was just regaining his sight. The blurriness faded to something concrete, and he noticed a man all in black with a badge on his shirt and a revolver at his side.

"I don't—didn't nothing—it was somebod—"

His mouth was uttering the same gibberish that turned around in his head. He wanted to say he didn't do anything, that he was not guilty. But his tongue rolled out words that made no sense.

His head was killing him.

"It's okay—don't talk now," the cop said. "Have a little more of that."

He sipped something fizzy through a straw. Staring around, he could see quite the party in his apartment. Carnie, Franklin, and Bruce stood by the wall of posters talking to another policeman. They looked as though someone had died. Others moved back and forth—Mike was there, Shane was on the phone.

Where were they half an hour ago?

The door opened, and a figure walked in toward the living room.

Alec roared a curse as he came by Jake's side. "Ah, man, you look awful."

"Thanks," Jake said.

"Who did this to you? Do they know? Do you guys know? Look at him."

"Brian," Jake said, finally remembering, finally getting hold of his tongue.

Alec kept venting his anger. The cop told him to calm down.

"Who did this?" the policeman asked for clarification.

"Brian Erwin," Jake said.

"He's some sports god who goes to our school."

"Providence?"

Alec nodded.

"Someone from Providence did this to him? You sure?"

"I'm positive," Jake said, his voice hoarse.

"Okay," the cop said.

Alec began threatening Brian, vowing to get him.

"Look, just sit over there—" the cop began.

"He got his face pounded in!"

"—and *shut up*. Okay?"

Jake recounted everything that happened. Not that he knew much. He was dragged out of his apartment and beaten to a pulp. By Brian and a friend, someone he didn't know. He thought his name was Chad. Big guy with blond hair.

What'd I do? Jake wondered for the first time.

The cop's partner showed up and talked with some of the other guys. Eventually the one interviewing Jake said he was done for now.

"I'm taking him to the hospital," Franklin said.

"No, man—it's fine."

"You need to get checked out," the cop said. "You got banged around pretty bad. You probably have a concussion."

Franklin helped Jake to his feet and put an arm around his side to guide him. Jake looked at the entryway to the apartment, normally stifling in its off-white drabness. He could see the spattering of blood on the wall and the tiled floor.

That all came from me? he wondered in surprise.

"I'm coming with," Alec said as the rest of the guys stood by the doorway.

The others said they would be there even as Jake said they didn't need to, that it was fine. He looked at Carnie and would almost have sworn that there were tears in the guy's round and usually jovial eyes.

"I'll be okay, man," Jake said. He made a thumbs-up gesture, trying to be funny.

It made everyone laugh. Everyone but Carnie.

TWENTY-TWO

June 2005

"YOU WERE THE REASON I left Providence," a grinning, young-looking Mike Fennimore told me in the bottom of his Chicago condo.

We sat in a room adorned like a tiki bar with bamboo walls and Jamaican artwork, talking about old times and listening to some of Mike's greatest hits. Right now, Morrissey's *Your Arsenal* cranked out of the stereo speakers.

"I mean, what was I supposed to do? All my friends were gone."

"It wasn't my fault I graduated," I said. "I tried my best to stay another couple years."

Mike laughed and took a sip of the martini he had made himself. I had passed on one and drank a beer. Seemed like the civil thing to do. Haley, Mike's attractive wife of three years, had left Mike, Bruce, and me downstairs for the moment. Bruce was drinking a martini, which meant typical trouble.

"I appreciated the invitation to the wedding," I said to Mike.

"Me too," Bruce chimed in.

"Come on. How many years had it been?"

"Did anybody come?"

"Franklin's the only one I've stayed in touch with. And

that's more from business functions. I occasionally do some work with his company."

Mike looked and acted different. He said he had just lost sixty pounds on a diet, but that's why he still resembled the old Mike. It was his tone and attitude that were different. He was no longer the younger kid trying to bond with older students. He was his own person. Married, successful, living a comfortable life in downtown Chicago. No kids, but a little terrier that roamed the condo and occasionally jumped in your lap unannounced.

"So what do you do?" Bruce asked.

"Exciting stuff," Mike said. "I work with stone."

"What—building houses?"

"Yeah. A lot of commercial developments. Or expensive houses."

"You lay the stone?"

Mike laughed at Bruce's question. "I'm more like part owner of the company."

Bruce nodded, looking ridiculous as he sipped his martini from the fancy glass. I could tell Mike didn't particularly want to talk about work.

"Remember seeing this guy in concert?" he asked, referring to Morrissey.

"You rushed the stage."

"I still have part of his shirt."

"That sounds kinda disturbing."

"You got his new album? Came out last year."

"He's still recording? I didn't know."

"That's one of the great things about Chicago. We can go see basically every big group that comes around."

"Still into all the old music?"

"I haven't listened to this album in years," Mike admitted. "I like a lot of stuff. You into Wilco?"

"Haven't heard much of them."

"You gotta get *Yankee Foxtrot Hotel*. Like immediately. They're amazing. Let's see. Poi Dog Pondering."

"Poor dog what?" Bruce asked.

Mike ignored him and rattled off half a dozen other singers

and groups that I needed to check out. I'd been out of it for a while, not keeping up on the latest groups and not reading *Spin* or *Rolling Stone*.

Morrissey's song "We Hate it when Our Friends Become Successful" began playing, and Bruce raised his glass.

"Amen to that."

Mike looked at me for a moment, and I could read his mind.

"You guys can spend the night, you know. I've got a guest bedroom down here, and this couch—"

"Is huge," Bruce said the obvious.

"I don't know. We don't need to." I shrugged.

"How long has it been?" Mike asked me. "Like—way too long. Why didn't you ever call?"

"I always thought it'd be easier that way."

"Yeah. Probably was."

"You ever run into Alec?"

"Alec?" Mike laughed. "Yeah, right."

"No calls or anything?"

"You know—for a while he lived in Chicago. I actually saw him a few times—this was like a couple years after college. I had just graduated. He knew some buddies of mine. Then he disappeared."

"Where to?"

"Nobody knew. No big deal to me."

"Any calls? Anything?"

Mike looked at me with defensive eyes. "You're loaded with questions."

"Yeah. There's a reason why."

Mike opened out his hand to take my beer. "That thing's been empty for ten minutes. Let me get you another."

I looked at his palm and noticed the five-inch scar that ran between his middle finger and the base of his wrist. For a moment I couldn't help staring, then I looked back at him and nodded, giving him my beer.

Something clicked. And I remembered. Sometimes it's just that easy.

﹗﹗

In a different life, another person would have sat in the bar pounding beers and playing pool and listening to music and relishing the moment. It wasn't like I was so against enjoying myself, because I was having a good time in spite of the fact that I've never been particularly good at pool. But playing in the back of the small bar a few blocks down from Mike's place, listening to a steady dose of trip-hop and alternative music, wasn't like it used to be. It wasn't necessarily like I was opposed to drinking more beer—it was just that my stomach felt full. Those times of being able to drink sixteen or twenty beers in a night were long gone. And I didn't miss them one bit.

Bruce and Mike finished playing a game, and Bruce took off to the men's room while Mike came over to the table. I'd just bought him a fresh beer.

"You're a fine man."

"I know," I said with a smile.

"Pool?"

"I'm done. No point embarrassing myself any further."

"This is so weird. I didn't think I'd ever see you guys again."

"I didn't think it'd be in this particular way. And after this long."

An old song from Tricky played in the background and added to the murky red glow of the bar.

"What happened to you last year?" Mike asked.

"What do you mean?"

"I heard some stuff. I don't know—Franklin said some things."

"Like what?"

"Like you became a missionary or something. I don't know. You climbed a mountain and found God."

"I've climbed lots of mountains. But I've never become a missionary."

"Didn't you have an accident or something?"

I nodded, knowing I couldn't escape talking about last summer's expedition. Bruce might not have known about it and Kirby thankfully didn't bring it up. I wasn't sure if Alyssa knew either, but I doubted it.

"My climbing partner died on Everest last June."

"That's intense," Mike said. "You made it out, though."

I nodded. "It was pretty dramatic. Sorta crazy too. You'd think that after everything happened—you know, with Carnie—that that would've gotten my attention. But no. This was the proverbial last straw."

"You quit climbing?"

I quit running, I thought. *I quit trying to do it on my own.*

"No. I just tried—I needed—to get my life in order. I changed some things."

I wanted to tell him more, but I wasn't sure how.

I'm so bad at this.

Bruce came back, his hands holding four beers. Mike looked at me and grinned. "Not everything changes."

"Huh?" Bruce asked. "They were having a clearance sale. Come on. Drink up!"

The beer was at least cold and fresh. I took my time with it. Bruce lit up and seemed in his own world. I thought it was as good of a time as ever to ask the question I'd been wondering about for the last couple hours.

"Mike."

"Huh?" he asked, surprised by my tone.

"Where'd you get that scar?"

"What scar?"

"The one on your hand."

Mike looked at his right palm as if he hadn't seen it before. "I don't know," he said convincingly. "I've had it for a long time."

"You don't know?"

"What? Do you?"

"What do you remember about that spring break?"

He seemed to turn white and looked serious, and for a moment he stared at me, then over at an uninterested Bruce, then back at me. "I remember a lot of drinking."

"Yeah, me too. But how much do you remember? How much do you know?"

"Know? What should I know? What are you talking about?"

"Mike—"

"You saying I got this back then?"

"I know for a fact you got it then. I remember helping you bandage that sucker up—I remember it still bleeding."

"That was a long time—"

"Not that long. Just be honest."

"What about Bruce there? What do you remember?"

"About what?" Bruce asked.

Mike turned back to me. "And what do you remember?"

"Not much," I admitted.

"Really? That's convenient."

"It's the truth."

"And I'm lying?" Mike asked. "Is this why you showed up out of the blue?"

"I told you. I'm looking for Alec."

Mike shook his head. "And I told you. I haven't seen the guy in years. And spring break happened eleven years ago. Sorry I'm sorta foggy about that. Have you seen Franklin?"

"No," I said. "Franklin doesn't particularly want to see us."

"I wonder why."

"We were all there."

"But why now? What's the big deal?" Mike asked.

"Somebody doesn't want the truth coming out. It's like they're suddenly ticked that I'm trying to get in touch with Alec."

"Who would care? That was a lifetime ago. We were all— different. Younger. Stupid, you know?"

I nodded. "This all comes down to Alec. Look—I just need to find him."

"That's all you want? Find Alec, tell this guy, whoever he might be, then what—just forget about everything else?"

"Mike—I thought I understood. . . ."

"Understood what?" He looked irritated.

"After everything that happened with Carnie—I always as-sumed. I assumed—I don't know. I assumed a lot."

Mike finished off his beer and wiped his lips. "I swear to you, Jake, I don't remember getting this scar. You don't have to

137

believe me, but you know me. It's been a long time, but you know me."

I nodded. I still knew Mike. I couldn't call him a liar. He remembered as much as I did. As much as Bruce did. As much as Shane did.

The past can do strange things over time. Sometimes you bury memories, and they're gone.

I stared at a half-full bottle of beer and decided I was finished for the night.

The days of being out of control and feeling fun and alive because of it—it was all a façade. I knew those days were past.

Sometimes you bury memories, and they're gone.

And sometimes you bury a friend and know that the memories he had are gone too.

TWENTY-THREE

March 1994

IN HIS DREAM, THE SUN ROSE and crept into his small hospital room. And so did Alyssa Roberts, with a caring and concerned look that greeted him as he opened his eyes. She was sitting in the chair by his side for some unknown reason. And when he finally focused on the young woman in the red turtleneck sweater, her hair pulled back in a ponytail, no makeup on a still perfect face, Jake knew he wasn't dreaming at all.

"Hey," was all he could muster.

She started to speak, but her face wrinkled and her eyes closed and she began to cry.

"Hey—whoa, Alyssa. It's okay I'm okay—look, I'm fine."

She wiped her eyes and nodded her head and looked at the wall across from them to regain her composure.

"Do I look that bad?"

There were lines under those dark eyes of hers, which made this a first. It had been a night of firsts, in fact. His first official beating. His first filing an official report or complaint. His first time being taken to the hospital. And now, the first time he ever saw a tired and upset Alyssa in tears.

"How long have you been here?" Jake asked.

"Since six," she said.

And why are you here? he wondered.

"What time is it?"

"A little after eight."

"Hey—are the guys—"

"Carnie, Franklin, and Bruce are still out there. The rest of them went home."

Jake went to move his head and felt the jostling of a thousand bricks jarring him. "Ouch."

"You had a pretty nasty concussion," Alyssa said.

"Feels like I still have one."

She just looked at him, sad and almost grieving.

"How'd you hear—?"

"Franklin called me around midnight."

"Sorry," Jake said.

"I am too."

His throat felt dry, but that was probably more from the drinking last night. Jake tried to wrap his mind around what happened.

"The cops picked up Brian Erwin and Chad Hoving this morning for questioning," Alyssa said.

"Chad who?"

"One of Brian's friends. One of the guys who did this to you."

"So they just got questioned? What about arrested?"

"That was all Franklin said. He was the one dealing with the cops. You want me to get him?"

"No, no. That's fine." Jake chuckled. "Franklin the politician."

"Why would they do this to you?"

"I guess Brian's not a big fan of mine."

"Did you do something?"

"Not recently. There was the other night—putting a cigarette out on his forehead. I knew he wasn't happy about it—I guess I underestimated how truly angry he was."

"They're talking about charging them with home invasion."

"Did they invade my apartment?"

Alyssa shook her head and managed a smile for the first time since Jake opened his eyes. "It's a felony."

"Good."

She gave him that grave look again.

"What?" he asked.

"Wait till you see yourself in a mirror."

"It feels like this is pretty bruised," Jake said of his right eye.

"They're both black. That one is black and purple and swollen."

"Nice," Jake said. "I bet this makes me even more attractive."

"You could have died," Alyssa said.

"Don't be so dramatic."

"I'm not trying to be. I'm being honest."

"If I didn't have this hand in a splint, I would've done some major butt-kicking."

"Jake—"

"Okay, maybe not."

Alyssa sat in a chair facing the bed. He never in a million years would have pictured this scene.

"See what a guy has to do to get your attention?"

She didn't smile.

"You don't have to stay here, Alyssa. You look tired."

"I didn't sleep much last night."

"I'm sorry."

"It's not your fault. At least, not all your fault."

"Hey—this time, I had nothing to do with this."

She didn't reply. Jake could actually see anger on her face.

"What?"

"You don't get it, do you?"

"I don't get what?" he asked.

"It's not your fault when you get kicked out of school. It's not your fault when you break your hand."

"That *was* my fault. I take credit for that."

"Don't you see a pattern?"

"Look, Alyssa, if I wanted my parents here, I'd call them."

She shot him an angry and hurt look.

"I'm sorry," he quickly said. "That was mean."

"It's easy to disappoint and then ask forgiveness after."

"Who's asking for forgiveness? Look at me. I didn't do this to myself. I wasn't the one throwing the punches."

"Aren't you tired of all this? I can't believe that you enjoy it."

"I don't like getting beaten up."

"Fine," Alyssa said, picking up her purse.

"Did you wait all this time just so you could start preaching at me?"

"I'm not preaching at you. I've tried hard *not* to preach to you."

"Go ahead. Preach away. I want to hear how you can spin this to somehow make it sound like this is all part of God's grand plan."

"I didn't say that."

"Then how do you sum it up?"

"You reap what you sow," Alyssa said.

Jake cursed. "That is so cliché. You can do better than that."

"It's true."

"How did I *sow* getting my face beat in?"

She shook her head, her dark eyes looking at the floor, then back at him.

"It's a lifestyle. This is the road you're traveling down. This is what happens."

"It's part of college. What am I supposed to be doing on a Saturday night? Studying? I like to have fun. *Fun.* You remember what fun is? And just because I like having fun doesn't mean I deserved this."

"I didn't say you deserved it."

"You just did! Sowing and reaping. Tell me a parable. Of the lost sheep. Of the prodigal son. Go on, tell me."

"You're being a jerk."

"Sorry I don't like someone making me feel guilty after getting assaulted in the middle of the night."

"And you think that's why I'm here?"

He looked at the pure and innocent face of Alyssa and had no answer. "I have no clue why you're here. I used to think that you found my—my rebelliousness—charming. Even if you'd never admit it. But now I feel like your little spiritual project."

Alyssa just stared at him, her lips tightly pressed together.

"And if I am, I want you to try on someone else," Jake continued. "You got that?"

"Yes." She stood up and went to the door.

As it closed behind her, Jake called out her name, regretting his words, regretting that he'd sent her away.

But he was too tired and too woozy for regret this morning. Regret took work, and he wasn't up for the task. Not now. Maybe not ever.

TWENTY-FOUR
June 2005

BRUCE HAD BEEN GONE for over an hour.

One moment he was sitting there, doing what he did best, and then the next thing I knew he was gone. Just like that.

We checked both bathrooms twice as well as the outside sidewalk of the bar, but he was nowhere to be found.

"Did he say anything to you?" Mike asked me.

"Nothing."

"Can you call his cell?"

"I don't even know if he has one."

"Maybe he just wandered off and got lost. Or passed out."

"That's what I'm afraid of."

He laughed. "Some things never change."

"No," I said. "Some things get worse."

Mike drained his beer and thought for a minute. "You want to go check around and see if we find him? You know where my apartment is from here?"

"Two blocks that way?" I said, pointing west.

"Yeah. Let's break up and try to see if he's clumped over in some alleyway."

We left the bar, and I headed right toward Mike's apartment. It was close to one, and my head ached. I wasn't sure if it was from the beer or from the cigarette smoke or from the memories. Or from worrying about Bruce.

Why'd you agree to let him come along?

I wasn't sure about that. So far, it felt like all I'd been doing was baby-sitting him. But I still recalled his look the morning I was heading back to the airport, the morning he asked to come with me.

"I need a break, man," he'd said with sad eyes and an empty stare.

I couldn't tell him no.

⇥ ⇤

The sidewalks were surprisingly busy in the neighborhood of Chicago known as Wicker Park. The night felt warm and close, refusing to let the tiniest of breezes out. Every alley I passed I looked down, occasionally walking down to see where it led. I passed Mike's street and kept walking, figuring I'd do a sweep around his condo.

I reached a shaded street lined with tall trees and rows full of parked cars. How could anybody put up with trying to find parking down here? If you didn't have a garage, it would be a royal pain. The lights on this street either were out or nonexistent—it suddenly got very dark. I passed rows of buildings, finding nothing. A woman walking her dog passed me. Maybe 1:00 a.m. in that neighborhood was like 10:00 p.m. everywhere else.

When I reached the corner I was going to head back to Mike's apartment, but something out of the corner of my eye stopped me. I peered down the street and saw two figures standing and talking. I could only make out an outline, but one of the figures looked like Bruce. Tall with shaggy hair.

"Bruce!" I started walking toward them.

The other figure bolted down the street in a blur. Instead of following, I stopped, wondering if this was Bruce or if maybe I was interrupting something else. A secret tryst on the street or a drug transaction. But I was almost positive that the tall figure was Bruce. I kept walking toward him even as the other figure disappeared.

In the middle of the street, I could see that it was Bruce. He was standing there, not passed out, not even looking drunk, looking as though he had been with me the whole time.

"Who was that?" I asked. "Where'd you disappear to?"

"Sorry, man. I lost track of time."

"We've been looking for you."

"I'm not a missing puppy."

"Where'd you go?"

"I just went out—for a walk, you know. Clear my head. Get some fresh air."

"Smoke a joint?"

"Sure. Clears your head, you know."

I stared down the street. "So who was that?"

Bruce shrugged in an awkward way. "I don't know—some guy who wanted to see if I had any drugs."

"Did you tell him the truth?"

"Nah. We were just talking."

I stared at Bruce for a moment. "You're not a very good liar."

"Who says I'm lying?"

"I've played poker with you a thousand times, Bruce. Come on."

"I'm not lying. Get off my back."

We started walking back to Mike's apartment.

"Bruce—"

I was going to tell him to go back home. To go back to the hole he had come from and stay there and stay far away from me. Baby-sitting was getting old, but this act of making me feel guilty for trying to baby-sit him was getting frustrating.

If you don't want my advice, then back off.

"What?" Bruce said after a few minutes.

I thought of his apartment back in Redding. Of everything he had hoped for when he first moved there and all the disappointments it had brought. I knew nothing I could say would probably change Bruce.

But actions might.

"Nothing," I said. "Just—I'm just trying to look out for you, okay?"

"Yeah, I know. It's just strange."
"How so?"
"Nobody's done that for a long time."

TWENTY-FIVE
March 1994

"WANT COFFEE?"

"Only if you put some Kahlua in it."

That was an attempt at being funny, but Sergeant Cooper's face remained stiff as a corpse. Jake looked across the metal table and watched the sergeant shuffle through some papers. He looked like a military man, with lips that hadn't smiled since he had arrived an hour earlier. They sat in a small, cold, colorless room that might as well have been a holding cell. It was the afternoon after the fight, or what should have more accurately been called the beating. After making notes from Jake's account, the sergeant began asking a few questions.

"So you don't know this Chad Hoving?"

Jake shook his head. "He plays basketball and baseball. That's all I know."

"Isn't Providence a small college?"

"I still don't know everyone."

"You don't play sports?"

"I played soccer my first year. Sat on the bench 99 percent of the time."

"Who threw most of the punches?"

"It's sorta hard to tell. Both of them did their share. And

they weren't just throwing punches. I think they did some kicking too."

"And you didn't provoke Brian at all?"

The sergeant looked as though he didn't like Jake, didn't believe a word he was saying.

"I told you—we've had our share of encounters. The last was at a party. It was nothing."

"What's 'nothing?'"

"Nothing. No blows. I jammed a cigarette in his face."

"And that's it?"

"Yep."

"Were you drunk at the time they came over?"

Jake thought for a moment. "I'd been out drinking. But no, I was fine."

"Drugs?"

"No thanks."

"You weren't on anything?"

"No. But I think they might've been."

This continued for a while, with the sergeant asking him specific questions about when they came over, what exactly transpired.

"Did they ever come into your apartment?"

"I don't know if they ever stepped foot into the apartment. It was more like I was grabbed out of the entryway."

The endless questions hurt his already pounding head, and he wished the police officer would go away.

It was four o'clock in the afternoon. Jake had been driven home around ten and had slept until noon. Alec and Franklin came over with lunch—Brown's chicken, a lot of it. Around two-thirty, he'd gotten a call that the Summit police had picked up Brian Erwin and Chad Hoving at their dorm room on campus. Jake thought of the commotion the scene had surely made. Now he had to come down to the station, make a statement, and identify Brian and Chad.

"And none of your friends saw them?"

Jake shook his head.

"Where was your roommate, the one with you?"

"Our one roommate, David Kirby, went home this weekend.

Probably a good thing too. Bruce was at a friend's apartment. And Carnie—Paul—was out buying more beer. I think he might have been the first one to get to me. I'm not sure. I was out of it."

"Out of it?"

"That's what happens when you get your face pounded in."

"How many times did they hit you?"

"I don't know," Jake said.

"Think."

"Twenty, thirty times each? I'm not sure. Like I said, I know I got kicked too. My back's got a big welt that looks like it came from a boot or something. They rammed my head back into the carpet."

"You're just lucky neither of them had a baseball bat."

"Yeah."

Rehashing this made Jake tired. He just wanted to get it over with.

The sergeant left Jake alone in the bare room for a few minutes, then came back and motioned him to stand.

"Look—this isn't going to be easy. If you had an eyewitness —anybody—that would help us. A neighbor, a friend? Anyone?"

"I already told you—I don't know which neighbors saw or heard anything. I didn't see any opened doors. I was screaming for help."

"They already got a lawyer."

"Who?"

"Brian's family."

"Doesn't surprise me," Jake said. "Maybe the college sent him."

"Why do you say that?"

"He's the school's golden boy."

"They won't like this publicity then."

"Tell me about it."

"Let's go and ID these guys, okay? It'll be quick and easy."

→→ ←←

150

Jake stepped back into the apartment and could smell the fumes from the cleaning supplies that had been used for only the second time that year.

"This place actually looks nice," Jake said.

"Dude, you look like Evander Holyfield after a long fight."

Jake took the beer from Bruce's hand and nodded to his roommate's zany grin. "You look like Kurt Cobain's love child."

"So when are you going to hear anything?"

"They got charged and then bailed out of jail," Jake said. "That's all I know."

"What about the college?"

"I don't know," Jake said. "They should be suspended. Or expelled."

"Just wait," Alec said, sitting on the couch watching television and drinking a beer.

"Wait till what?"

"It's easy to suspend guys like us. But just wait. It'll get a little stickier with them."

"They just got arrested for home invasion," Jake said. "I would hope it'd be a little easier."

"Life doesn't work that way."

"For a Christian college it should."

Alec cursed and downed his beer. His eyes glistened, and Jake knew he'd been drinking since lunch.

"Just you wait and see," Alec said.

Jake looked around and noticed that Carnie was gone.

"He's working," Bruce said. "Regular Sunday night."

"Oh, yeah."

"You going to class tomorrow?" Bruce asked.

"Guess I have to, even looking like this."

"Did you call your parents?"

"Not yet."

"You going to?" Bruce asked.

"I doubt it."

➤➤   ◄◄

151

Jake drifted between sleep and worry. He would close his eyes and find himself thinking or perhaps dreaming about fists punching him in the face over and over. He would wake up and see the glint of the alarm clock reading five minutes later than when he last saw it. A light in the hallway leaked into his room, so he would stare at the crack and try and slow his mind down.

The bed across from him was still empty; Carnie was either working unusually late or at a bar somewhere. Neither explanation made sense. Maybe he just felt bad about what happened to Jake.

At twelve-thirty, almost an hour after he had gone to bed, or tried to go to sleep, the phone woke him up. Someone answered, then Bruce knocked on his door and said it was for him.

Jake picked it up.

"Hey man, it's Alec."

"Yeah."

"I just thought you should know—the guys made it back here on campus. Word is that the charges are being dropped."

Jake sat on his bed and rubbed a hand over his forehead. "How do you know?"

"They were talking to some people tonight. Laughing about it."

"They're being dropped. As in—?"

Alec cursed. "Yeah, as in getting off. As in beating me unconscious and then allowed to go back to the cushy life they have."

"My head hurts."

"This place makes me sick. Those guys shouldn't be allowed within ten miles of Providence."

"Things will get sorted out."

Alec cursed again, this time even louder. "Man, don't you care? Brian saw me tonight and laughed. I swear I wanted to kill that—"

"Easy, man."

"Well, somebody's gotta deal with this."

Jake cleared his voice. "We'll see what happens tomorrow."

"I told you, didn't I?"

"The college hasn't made a decision yet."

"Oh, yeah, they have."

It was too much for Jake to listen to. "Let's get some sleep," he said.

But sleep wouldn't come. Not for a very long time.

TWENTY-SIX

June 2005

I GOT OUT OF THE CAR and stared at the building radiating the afternoon sun.

I'm going to see him whether he likes it or not.

I didn't care if Franklin had a title of Vice President on his business card or an assistant named Brenda who didn't return my calls or even a schedule booked by the minute. This was the same guy I'd bailed out of trouble our junior year when someone took a WWF wrestling jump into his parents' glass dining room table. I'd blamed myself, and it worked. Franklin gave me the money to give to his parents for the table. This was Franklin, and he was one of us and always would be. His passive-aggressive behavior was getting old.

I noted the sign on the front of the building. I wasn't positive what Andersen Investment Corporation did except deal with finances. They probably took people's money and tried to make money with it. Franklin had always had money, so he was used to spending it. I could see his resume. *Background: wealthy kid. Occupation: spoiled brat. Specialty: using ATM machines.*

The five-story building was glass with a black outline. I entered the main door; a registration desk blocked the hall leading beyond the main foyer.

A woman looking at the flat-screen monitor behind her

desk took a few seconds before glancing at me. She took a few more before asking, "May I help you?"

Yeah. How about trying to show a little less attitude?

"I'm here to see Franklin Gotthard."

"Do you have an appointment?"

"Yes."

I did. I made the appointment myself.

Franklin's assistant begged to differ.

"What is your name again?" the receptionist asked me, holding the phone in her hand.

"Kurt. Kurt Cobain."

"Okay," the young woman said into the receiver. "It's a Kurt Cobain."

She waited, oblivious, stupid. Then she got a puzzled look over her face, the first bit of life I'd seen on her chubby cheeks so far.

I decided not to wait.

I dashed away from the desk and past the main open lobby into a narrow hallway. A set of elevators was to my right, but I ignored those, running to get away from the front, then slowing down to a casual pace. At the end of the hallway, another set of elevators greeted me. I got on and selected floor three.

The offices were fancy and corporate, but still basically a bunch of cubicles surrounded by offices on the edges of the building. I walked past a guy who looked like an escapee from a Dockers commercial.

"Excuse me. I was looking for Franklin Gotthard's office. Am I in the right place?"

He looked at me and thought for a minute. "Franklin who? What department does he work in?"

"I'm not exactly sure."

"Head down the hall and ask Lisa. She's sitting at the main desk with a headphone attached to her head."

Lisa, a redhead who saw me coming and continued talking on her headset, didn't keep her eyes off me even as I approached her desk and waited.

Finally she spoke. "Are you lost?"

"I was looking for Franklin Gotthard."

"He's up on the fifth floor. We peons work down here."

"Thanks. Any idea where his office is?"

"Get off the elevator and take a right. You'll walk right into it. Can't miss."

"Nice headset," I told her, thanking her and departing.

So far no armed men had intercepted me. I half wondered if the receptionist had even called anybody. I could be a terrorist carrying a bomb strapped across my chest. What sort of security did a place like this have?

On the fifth floor, I found my way to Franklin's office. A woman in her twenties, who looked like a model for an adult magazine, saw me coming and stood up.

Here's the security. She's going to kick me with one of her stilettos.

"Excuse me, sir, but Franklin is not here," Brenda, Franklin's "assistant," said.

"Where is he?" I'd pictured someone very different.

"What's this about?" she asked.

"It's about not getting a return call."

She looked me over and realized who I was. "You're the guy from his college."

"Where's the meeting?"

"He's down the hall in the boardroom—he won't be getting out for another—sir?"

I was already charging down the hall. This would be fun.

The wooden door was closed, and I wondered how many suits and slicked-back haircuts awaited. I'd never spent a day in a corporate environment and wondered what would have happened to me if I had.

One word: suffocation.

I opened the door and heard a heavyset voice droning on for another second before it stopped.

Twenty faces, at least, turned to look at me. They were sitting, all with papers in front of them, at the largest table I'd ever seen in my life.

There was an awkward millisecond before I broke the silence.

"I need to speak to Franklin."

Franklin stood up. He was wearing a blue suit with a yellow tie. What an aristocrat.

"Sorry about this. Please excuse me."

He didn't look embarrassed. Franklin didn't get embarrassed. The look on his face was annoyance.

He opened the door to the hallway and then gently shut it behind us. He looked at me and shook his head, his face a mixture of shock and disgust. "What do you think you are doing?" he demanded.

"I'm returning that phone call."

"You can't just come and interrupt—"

At this point, a big bald-headed guy wearing all blue came around the corner. Sweat beads dotted his head. In his hand was some black object—at first I thought it might be a gun, then I realized it was a walkie-talkie. This guy didn't *need* a gun. Looking at his arms, and fists the size of my head, I knew he wasn't to be messed with.

"Everything okay here?"

"Yeah, everything's fine, Joe. No need to worry. I know this guy."

"He took off from the main lobby and—"

"It's fine. Sorry about the confusion."

Joe the bouncer looked at me, then wiped his head and turned around. The guy must have been sprinting through the offices. He would've been a funny sight to see, dashing by in his nice little blue jumper.

"Now is not a good time," Franklin said.

His suit fit him perfectly. He was still lean and had a short, conservative haircut, just like it was in college except a little shorter. We were about the same height, and for a moment he glared at me with angry eyes.

"I'm not leaving without seeing you."

"What is the big deal?"

"I wasn't going to leave it with your assistant, if that's what you call that woman back there."

Franklin studied me for a minute, then broke out into a laugh. "You're still out of control, you know that?"

"When's your meeting done?"

"Go back to Brenda and tell her to give you directions to the Grey Lounge. I'll meet you there at—around five-thirty. Okay?"

"Franklin—I'm serious."

"Yeah, I know. I am too. Just ask her and then wait for me there. Get a drink and loosen up. You look like you need one."

"You look like you're applying for *The Apprentice*."

Franklin chuckled. "I'm applying for Donald Trump's job."

"If you're not there, I'm coming over to your house."

Something on Franklin's face changed, and it alarmed me. He was going to say something, probably out of anger, then he stopped himself and bit his lip.

"I'll be there."

I nodded, and was going to let him leave when he said one last thing to me.

"And Jake—I know where Alec is. I know all about Alec. I'll tell you everything so you can stop your little adventure to find the missing college buddy."

He turned around and slipped back into his meeting. I stood there for a moment, just looking at the door and wondering how in the world Franklin knew this and whether or not he was lying.

TWENTY-SEVEN

March 1994

"YOU SHOULD'VE BEEN THERE."

The group hanging out at Four-leaf Clover stopped their conversation and watched, waiting for word. Bruce came in wearing a sweater and smoking a cigarette. Franklin took off his coat and did something surprising; he reached for a cup and poured himself a beer out of the nearest pitcher. Then he sat down at a seat around the two adjoining tables and let out a sigh.

"That's a bad sign," Alec said.

"What?" Franklin asked. His usually perfectly combed hair looked windblown.

"You drinking."

"I'm thirsty," he replied, then added, "and I'm tired of all the fools at this school."

"What happened?" Jake asked, not wanting to hear but knowing he had to.

The meeting that had taken place on campus two hours earlier was all about him. Him and Brian and Chad. The only two from his crowd who ended up going were Franklin and Bruce. Jake didn't want to be at a meeting where they were talking about the fates of Brian and Chad, both suspended until further notice. Alec hadn't gone because he was still furious at everything, and he knew he would probably go off during the meeting. Mike and Shane had joined them at the bar to wait for word.

Bruce cursed in frustration.

"That bad?" Jake asked.

"It was pretty much evenly divided between people who said that Brian and Chad deserve to be expelled and others who said you had it coming," Bruce said.

"Who said that?" Jake asked.

"Quite a few people," Franklin answered. "You'd be surprised how many people were there. Probably 150 or more."

Bruce nodded in agreement.

"Alyssa was there, by the way," Bruce said.

"Did she speak up?"

"No. I think—she left, didn't she?"

"Yeah. They started talking about you and how many times you'd been kicked out and all that stuff, and she ended up walking out."

"So, what?" Jake asked, his brow confused and tight. "People are saying I brought this all on?"

"Some of 'em were at the party where you put out the cigarette on Brian's head," Franklin said.

"You guys were there. It wasn't like I scarred him or anything. It was no big deal."

"Some people were saying it was assault."

"That guy deserves to have a cigarette put out in other places," Shane said.

"They said that the cops didn't have proof, so how could Providence expel students that weren't officially charged."

"I'm not proof enough?" Jake asked.

"And they kept saying 'off-site incident,'" Bruce added. "I swear, if they said that one more time, I was going to explode."

It was interesting to see Bruce incensed. Alec, sure, but Bruce normally just sat back and watched the world pass. Tonight he was different.

Franklin seemed to be the only one there with a level head. "Because this happened off campus, there are certain things they can and can't do."

"They wouldn't want to kick out their star basketball player, would they?" Alec scoffed.

"This has already gotten lots of bad press," Franklin said. "They talked about that. The implications of letting these guys back on campus. And should there be anything done about Jake."

"Anything done about me?" Jake burst out. "Like what?"

"Necessary suspensions. Whatever."

"Am I hearing this right?"

Bruce looked over at him and nodded.

For a moment, they were all silent.

Jake picked up an empty pitcher and waved it at the bartender. He wished Carnie were here. He hadn't spoken much with his big roommate since everything happened. Carnie had said he would meet them at the sports bar, but he never showed up.

"They talked for a while about off-campus parties and what should be done about them," Bruce continued.

Franklin nodded. "Some idiot started talking about my New Year's Eve party, and I was like, 'I don't know what you're talking about.' Everybody laughed, because half of them had been there. Even Ms. Peterson smiled at that."

"She was there?" Jake asked.

"Oh, sure. The president was there, several professors. You missed a big party."

Jake shook his head and grabbed the fresh pitcher.

God bless Budweiser, he thought as he poured himself the only available antidote to this insanity. "So what's the final verdict?" he asked.

"They had to end things because there was no verdict. Some of these self-righteous girls were talking out about drinking and partying and why do people go to Christian schools if they want to do this and on and on."

Alec swore again, and Jake echoed the sentiment. Franklin continued.

"Ms. Peterson eventually had to step in—you know, it was an open forum. But it got a little off track. They said they would evaluate the issues at hand."

"No way those guys should've gotten off," Mike said.

Alec was getting more riled up. "I'm not surprised. Hey, if it was Jake and me pounding Brian's face into the ground, it'd be a *whole* different thing."

"Would it?" Jake asked.

Alec crinkled his face, astonished Jake would even ask. "Come on."

"They didn't have any eyewitnesses. That's what they keep coming back to."

"Are you going to press charges?" Franklin said.

"Then I'd have to involve my parents and lawyers and a whole mess. And if the cops don't think they have a case, what am I supposed to do?"

"You tell your parents yet?" Franklin asked.

Jake shook his head. He didn't know how to begin. Telling his parents would mean getting at the core of the problem in their mind: Jake. His drinking, his friends, his habits, his spending, and blah-blah-blah.

For a while the guys talked about prosecuting. Franklin said his family had a good lawyer that Jake could have, and that made them all laugh. As if Franklin's family lawyer would just step in at no charge.

"The thing the college wants is for everything just to blow over," Franklin eventually said.

"How's it going to 'blow over'?" Alec asked.

"We move on."

"We'll have to see those jerks every day and Jake will be walking around after being knocked unconscious and we're supposed to believe in Christian brotherly love?" Alec cursed God and wasn't bashful about doing so.

"I'm going to put on some music," Mike said, trying to lighten the mood.

"You know—*USA Today* picks up a story on this, they'll be rethinking things," Alec said with anger in his eyes.

"Maybe we should send it to them," Shane suggested.

"Or at least go talk to the president," Jake added.

Alec lit up a cigarette and shook his head. "I don't want to talk to that idiot."

"Ms. Peterson will understand," Franklin said.

"We can get them kicked off campus," Shane said.

"Maybe we can stage a protest," Bruce added.

"Maybe we should all just chill," Jake finally said.

"Meaning?"

He looked at Alec, sitting next to him. "Meaning that really, this is between Brian, Chad, and me. The fact that I don't even *know* Chad is one thing. But I'm partially the reason this happened."

"They want you to think that way," Alec said.

"Yeah, I know. And I'm not saying Providence is being smart about it. If they let those guys back on campus—that's just a reality I have to face. The college isn't in love with me. I'm like a little black stain on their résumé. They just want to get rid of me. Maybe that's all that will matter."

"What?" Mike asked him.

"Finishing up the school year and getting my tail out of here."

"Pretty sad," Bruce said.

"What?"

"That our final semester has to be like this. Or the final semester for some of us."

"Once you guys go, I'm out of here," Alec said. "I hate this place."

"But you came back," Jake said with a smile.

"Well, yeah. Who else was going to take care of you?"

The Depeche Mode song came on, and the loud, thundering drums and the piano filled the entire room. Mike came back just as the lead singer belted out the word *condemnation.*

Jake laughed at Mike's selection. He remembered the concert the two of them had attended last fall. Back when things were normal. When life wasn't so complicated.

Accusations, Dave Gahan continued to sing. *Lies. Hand me my sentence, I'll show no repentance, I'll suffer with pride.*

"Amen to that," Jake said over the music, holding up a full beer and toasting.

The guys laughed, and it felt good to see their smiles. This was his problem, and he was the only one who had to deal with it, not them. Even Alec gave in, and held up his beer to the toast.

"To my friends," Jake said, and they all chorused, "To friends."

Then he noticed the empty chair where Carnie should have been sitting.

TWENTY-EIGHT
June 2005

"IT SOUNDS LIKE you've done well for yourself."

"According to whom?" I asked Franklin, who had just sat down in a plush armchair across from me.

"I hear things. Congratulations."

Dim lights illuminated the aptly named Grey Lounge. Most of the patrons here were like Franklin, except older. Franklin crossed a leg; he seemed comfortable in his tie and suit coat.

"Why the aversion to meeting with me?"

"The gin martini here is great. You should try it."

"Since when did you drink liquor?" I asked him.

"Since when did you refuse it?"

"You didn't answer my first question."

A waitress in a black miniskirt brought Franklin his martini. He stared at her long legs and then focused back on me. He took his time, taking a sip and finally speaking again.

"I didn't come out here to get bombarded with questions. I get that on a daily basis at work."

"You're a regular Joe Businessman."

"It's a check."

"Kirby says it's a hefty check too."

"You saw ole Kirby, huh? This is a regular school reunion week for you."

"Who have you talked to?"

"Another question," he said.

Who was this guy sitting across from me, and what had he done with Franklin? They were the same, yes. But the arrogance factor had grown. I wondered if he still couldn't grow a beard.

"So—you never married?"

"That's a question," I said.

"It's a statement, and it's true."

"I hear you did."

"Sooner or later, it's part of the big plan."

"You gotta meet the right one first. Right?"

"Of course. But some of us aren't romantics at heart like you are."

"How are the kids?"

Franklin laughed in a condescending manner. "You're not here because of my kids."

"A man can be polite, right?"

His cold, hard eyes focused on mine. *We're beyond the polite phase,* they said. *We both know what this is about.*

"Why are you so interested in finding Alec?"

"Someone else is looking for him."

"Who?" Franklin asked.

"Long story."

"Is he in trouble?"

"Might be. That's what I'm trying to find out."

"MIA Alec. Always getting into trouble."

"You said you know where he is."

Franklin nodded. "I spoke to him about a month ago."

"Where was he?"

"First—who is looking for him?"

"A businessman—a suit like you. But older. Alec ran off with his daughter."

He laughed. "She legal?"

"Yeah. Barely."

"Smart move," Franklin said, shaking his head.

"I had no choice but to look for him. He brought up stuff from the past. Says he knows more than he should. Says others might be interested in hearing about it."

"Hearing what?" Franklin asked, putting down his drink and uncrossing his leg.

"I don't know. It sounds like he knows enough. He mentioned Carnie. And Brian."

Franklin looked at me without blinking for a long minute. "What'd you tell him?"

"I told him I'd find Alec. That's why I'm here. That's why I broke up your meeting."

Franklin rubbed the back of his head and then relaxed. "That was a long time ago."

"What happened back then? On spring break."

"Alec never told you?"

"He never told me what?" I asked.

"All this time—your best friend never even . . ." Franklin laughed.

"Never even what?" I asked.

"Why do you think Alec left a week before graduation? Haven't you ever thought that was just a little too obvious?"

"He'd done it before."

"That's what Alec does. He gets into trouble then bolts."

I waited for more, watching Franklin sip his martini.

"Frank—what are you saying?"

"Franklin. It's Franklin."

"Whatever."

"I'm saying that it was Alec's idea, and that when things went wrong, he—"

"How did things go wrong?"

Franklin shook his head. "Uh-uh. No way. If Alec doesn't have the guts to tell you, I'm not going to be the one."

"What did he do?"

"Come on, Jake. What do you think he did? Are you still *that* naive?" Franklin cursed. "Use your head. Your little Alec wasn't as sweet and innocent as you were led to believe."

"Nobody's saying he's sweet and innocent."

"You were so judgmental. So paranoid. Remember?"

"I had reasons to be."

"Then Alec takes off, and your other best friend decides to kill himself."

"I recall he was your friend too."

"Semantics."

"And your point?" I said.

"*My point,*" Franklin said, anger laced in his words, "my point is that you shouldn't be talking to me to get the answers. Your friend Alec has all of them. He knows everything. He took care of everything and then took off. I don't even know everything."

"Where is he?"

"Relax. He's nowhere around here."

"How can you be so laid back about this?"

"Because it was in the past. It was all a long time ago."

"Don't you ever think about those times?" I asked him.

"No. Do you?"

"Sometimes."

"Interesting how you've never come back around here. As if you have something to hide. Like Alec."

I wanted to curse at him, but I held my tongue. I exhaled and balled a fist.

"Where is Alec?" I asked again.

"Last time he called, he was in California."

This surprised me. "Doing what?"

"He was frantic. Sounded like he was in a lot of trouble. Funny—he called out of the blue. A month later, you show up at my door. Seems the two of you need to hook up and sort some things out."

"And you haven't heard from him since?"

He shook his head and took a last sip from his martini. He slipped a twenty in the leather bill holder and stood. "You know—I would love to reminisce about old times and all that, but as you know, I've got a wife and kids I need to go home to."

I stood. This was probably all the information I was going to get out of him. But it had been enough.

"I would say it's been a pleasure," I started to say.

"But you would be lying, and you never lied. Not even back in the days of your debauchery."

"That's a big word for you."

Franklin laughed. "Hope you find your long-lost friend," he said. "Just one more thing."

"What's that?"

"The bum you're carrying around with you—why don't you ask him about Alec's whereabouts?"

"Bruce? What do you mean?"

Franklin raised his eyebrows as if to say *Now you're talking.*

"How do you know—how do you know all this?"

"There's a lot of stuff you never knew, Jake. That we never told you. And there was a reason for that. Maybe—just maybe —it was because you were a wild card. Maybe it was because none of us knew the next thing you'd do. Alec and Bruce weren't the most out of control. Not back then."

I felt like punching him in the face.

"I wasn't responsible for what happened," I said.

"Which one of us got the snot beat out of him? I recall it was you."

Standing there, I breathed out and let my emotions cool down.

"The best thing you can do is find Alec and then leave the rest alone," Franklin said.

"But Bruce—what does he know?"

"Why don't you ask him? I've told you everything I know. That's more than Alec and Bruce have done. Tells you something, huh?"

TWENTY-NINE

March 1994

JAKE FELT LIKE ITEM number nineteen on the president's to-do list as the door finally opened and he entered the office twenty minutes after his scheduled time. Wall-to-wall built-in bookshelves filled with leather-bound and hardcover books surrounded him. He took a seat in a leather armchair facing a rich cherry desk that took up a third of the room.

Dr. Bramson sat down behind his desk, slipped his glasses on, and stared at Jake without any welcome. The fifty-something man was as meticulous as his office. A globe here, a pen and pencil set there, a framed picture. On the wall behind him, next to a window that looked out onto the main courtyard of the campus, a framed Bible verse from Psalms talking about "decreeing statutes to Jacob" and giving the law to Israel. It made as much sense to Jake as speaking in tongues.

"So, Jake, tell me about the off-site incident four days ago." The voice was firm, direct, aloof.

"I'm sure you already know this," Jake said, recounting the familiar story. "After going to a bar, I went back to my apartment. Brian Erwin and Chad Hoving knocked on my door, then dragged me out into the hallway and beat the tar out of me. The police initially pressed charges, but said there wasn't enough evidence to prosecute."

"Had you been drinking that night?" The mostly-bald and narrow head of the president faced him. Dr. Bramson's eyes looked cold and tired behind the large glasses.

Jake nodded.

"Did you provoke the fight?"

"There's been something building between Brian and me for a couple years. But no, I didn't do anything to him that night."

"What about an incident involving a cigarette burn?"

"I smashed a cigarette on his head at a party a week ago. That was all."

"Was it lit?"

"Yeah, but it wasn't like he was being held down and branded. It didn't hurt him. Except maybe his pride."

"There was nothing else? Nothing at all?"

What was the guy getting at?

"No. This Chad guy—I didn't even know who he was until someone told me. I've never talked to him in my life."

Dr. Bramson looked down at sheets of paper on his desk.

"You've been suspended four times since you started in 1991, twice for violating rules on drinking. You stole the school mascot, you tore up the soccer and baseball fields with your car. And most recently, you jumped off the roof of South Hall."

Jake nodded.

"Jake, Providence College prides itself with recruiting exceptional students from all over the country. Students who are interested in learning and growing. We see faith as a key part of the growth of Providence students, and we rely on seniors to be examples for the underclassmen."

The president paused for effect.

"My question for you is this: why come to Providence in the first place? Why not go somewhere else that fits your . . . your personality?"

"Like a party college?" Jake asked, a smile on his face.

"Why did you choose Providence?"

"I went to USC my first year and almost flunked out. My parents were paying for my college, so they gave me a choice.

Go to Providence and they'd continue paying, or I could pay on my own somewhere else."

"You're a business major, correct?"

"Yeah."

"Where do you see yourself after graduation?"

"Good question. I'm not really sure. Got any openings?" Jake said this last line with a smile, trying to get some warmth from the man behind the desk.

Dr. Bramson studied him again. "This is all pretty funny to you, isn't it?"

Jake shook his head. "I was beaten unconscious, *sir*. I've got a black eye that probably won't go away for a month. The police said they can't do anything, and now I hear the school might be letting those guys back on campus. None of that is particularly *funny* to me, but I'm not sure what I can do except laugh."

"Weren't you let back on campus after your mistakes?"

"I'd say they were a little different from this."

"How so?" Dr. Bramson asked.

Jake could feel his head and neck getting warm. "They weren't in the papers, first of all. I never hurt anyone. I've never hurt anyone while I've been here."

"Is that so?"

"Yeah, that's so," Jake said, annoyed at Dr. Bramson's question.

"Tell me about Laila Henson."

What? Jake wrinkled his eyebrows. "What do you mean?"

"Do you know Laila Henson?"

"Yeah, sure."

"And did anything happen the night of the party when you had an altercation with Brian? Anything involving Laila?"

He tried to get a frame of reference for Laila and the night of the party. For a moment, nothing registered at all. All Jake could think of was when she took him home the night he broke his hand.

"Anything meaning what? I didn't have an 'altercation' with Brian."

"When you put out the cigarette on his head."

Jake shook his head. "Laila was at the party. That's all."

"Were you pretty drunk?"

"No," Jake said.

"Are you sure about that?"

"Yes, I'm sure," he said very slowly, annoyed at the direction this was headed.

"I had a talk with Brian Erwin this morning. He had some interesting things to share about that night."

"Really? That's great to hear. I'd love to know what he thought about beating me unconscious."

"He said Laila told him something the night he came to your apartment."

"Okay," Jake said, wanting more.

"He said you tried to rape her at that party."

Jake couldn't breathe. He sat there, trying to comprehend Dr. Bramson's words.

"And you're saying you didn't talk to her at all," Dr. Bramson continued.

Jake couldn't think. This was about the night he got beaten up. Why was Dr. Bramson talking about the party at Neesa's house?

"I don't know if I spoke to her. Maybe. But nothing happened with her. Nothing whatsoever. I didn't *try* to do anything to her. You believe that?"

"I'm just reporting what Brian told me."

Jake cursed. "First off, the guy is a liar. He's had something against me for a while. He's dating Laila."

"You know her, right?"

"Yeah, sure. Half the guys on campus *know* her."

"Laila told him that night about what happened. That's why Brian and Chad came to your apartment."

"Oh, okay. So that makes it all right. If someone told me you'd molested them, I could come to your house and grab you out of bed and leave you for dead. Is that right?"

"There were students who saw you coming out of a bedroom at Neesa's house."

What the—

"But you say nothing happened?"

"Who have you been talking to?" Jake asked in anger.

"That's not your concern."

"Yeah, it is! When you sit here accusing me of something like this!"

"Jake."

He looked at Dr. Bramson and stopped talking for a moment.

"Tell me something."

"What?" Jake asked.

"Do you expect me to believe a word you say?"

The statement not only surprised Jake, it scared him. The detached, callous way the president spoke, the way his eyes didn't waver.

"I guess not."

"You've been nothing but a blemish on this school since you've been here," Dr. Bramson continued. "There is a large percentage of students who come here wanting to learn, wanting to grow up in a safe and healthy environment. Those who love the Lord and want to do good. Do you realize the harm you've done to them, to this college?"

"Harm?"

"By your actions."

"Again, let me remind you, I was the one who got beat up."

"A lot of people say you had it coming."

"Thanks. I appreciate hearing that from the president of my college."

"Brian Erwin has done nothing but good for Providence since he's been here."

"Yeah, I know. Things might be a little different if I could play hoops or hit a baseball. Sorry, I just can't."

"Actions speak louder than words, Jake."

"Wow. I haven't heard that bit of wisdom *ever.*"

Dr. Bramson cleared his throat and rested his thin hands on his desk. "The Bible says the Lord hates the way of the wicked, but he loves those who pursue righteousness."

Jake shook his head, his face flustered and his back sweaty. He wasn't just frustrated; he was furious.

The gall of this man, he thought. *The little weasel sitting behind his big desk trying to intimidate me.*

"So I guess I would fit the part of the wicked, right?" he asked in a biting tone.

"He who ignores discipline despises himself."

Jake couldn't help thinking of Alyssa and their last conversation. "What are you trying to do? Quote the whole book of Proverbs?"

"What is your Christian walk?"

"What is yours?" Jake screamed back. "Is there a reason I'm in here other than to be judged?"

"Sit down," Dr. Bramson said.

Jake told the president what he thought of this meeting.

"I said sit down. Now!"

Jake sat and gritted his teeth. He looked out the window and tried to control his emotions.

"I'm going to tell you something, and I want you to get it into that thick, dense skull of yours," Dr. Bramson said. "I want you to stay far away from Providence for the rest of this semester. You can go to your classes and put in the halfhearted effort you always do and then graduate with the rest of the class. But I don't want you coming on campus for *any* reason except to go to classes."

"So *I'm* being suspended? Brian and Chad get to come back to school, but I get kicked out?"

"You're not a part of this college and never will be, Jake. You've done more harm in your short tenure here than any other student I can think of. I believe Satan has used you in a mighty way."

Jake shook his head. This had gone from bad to unfair to ludicrous.

"If I find you on campus, or if there is any other discipline problem with you this semester—and I mean *any*—you will be expelled without question. Do you understand?"

"Yeah, I get it."

Dr. Bramson glared at Jake and shook his head. "I think we're done here."

"Just one thing," Jake said.

"What's that?"

"I never did anything to Laila, regardless of what she or Brian or anyone says. You don't have to believe me. You can say I break rules and I'm no good for this school, and I can go with that. But don't ever call me a liar. I'm a lot more real than the phonies you have walking around this campus. And that includes your trophy boy, Brian."

Jake stood up and began walking to the door. Then he turned around and faced the man behind the desk.

"Dr. Bramson?"

"Yes?"

"The Bible also says that love is patient, love is kind, love does not envy and does not boast. Love *is not proud.*"

Dr. Bramson sat behind his desk, silent and steady.

"Thank you for being such a godly example. It is truly inspiring."

THIRTY
June 2005

SHE PICKED UP ON the fourth ring.

"I was about to hang up."

"I'm sorry," Alyssa said, out of breath. "I just walked in."

"Busy day?"

"Oh, yes."

"I can call back later—"

"No—I'm just kidding. I was out with my mom. Shopping."

"Buy anything nice?"

Her laugh made the emptiness of my rental car seem endurable.

"I'm sure you want to know all about my visit to Ann Taylor Loft," Alyssa said.

"Ann who?"

"Exactly. Where are you?"

"On the Tri-state. Going about two miles an hour."

"Why are you driving in rush hour?"

"Remember Franklin Gotthard?" I asked her.

"It's impossible to forget someone like Franklin."

"Yeah. We had a nice meeting this afternoon."

"Was it helpful?"

"In a way—yes." I left out the part about wanting to bash his face in.

"Any leads on Alec?"

"Not on finding him. But Franklin did have a few interesting things to say."

She waited for me to say more, then said, "I'm glad you called. I wanted to apologize for the other night. I'm sorry I ruined it."

"Are you kidding? I'll go to the grave remembering that night. Everything about it. And everything that might have been."

"No—I don't know. I guess I just—"

"You were being honest, and for one of the few times in my life, I tried to use some judgment. It comes every decade, so let me have my moment."

"It wasn't my best."

"Alyssa—you've been the best thing about coming back to Providence."

"Then why'd you wait so long?"

I paused for a minute. "Good question."

Traffic crawled down the four lanes of the interstate heading south. If I had to do this every day, I would have to get my head lobotomized. For the next fifteen minutes, we talked about the day and traffic and her shopping excursion. I finally managed to get off on the exit going to Summit.

"Well, since you just got home, what do you think of my coming over?" I asked Alyssa. "I'll pick up something to eat. Something easy. Wine. Or no wine."

"That makes me nervous."

"What—I do?"

"No. It's not you I'm worried about."

I chuckled. "There might be a compliment deep down in that statement. You worry way too much."

"I don't know if I worry enough."

"There's no pressure here—no ulterior motives—it's just—"

"Just what?" she asked quickly.

"Just Jake Rivers. You know where I stand."

"This isn't college, Jake. This isn't a game anymore. Someone fun to flirt with."

"That's what you think I'm doing?"

"I'm just saying—things are different. People change. Lives change."

"That doesn't mean everything about them changes."

"I just don't know."

"What don't you know?" I asked her, finding the street I was looking for and turning down it.

"I'm just—I'm afraid. I'm afraid of—of something—of building something that will eventually disappear."

"I just got here."

"Jake—I don't get you. I mean—why haven't you ever—"

"What? Given up on you?"

"I didn't say that," Alyssa said.

"You fight for something you want. For something that you know is good for you. Even if it is a dream. A fairy tale."

"This isn't a dream."

"I know. But the other night sure felt like one. And you want to know something else? The only thing that could have made it better would have been to have kissed you."

Alyssa was silent for a moment, allowing me to pull the car by the curb and get out.

"I didn't say you couldn't," Alyssa said.

The sun was fading away, and the evening had a warm glow about it.

"If I had a chance to do it again—"

"I don't know," she said.

"What if I were at your doorstep now, looking at you, asking you that same question? What would you do?"

"I don't know. We'll never know." She paused for a minute. "Jake—can you hold on? I'm sorry. Someone's ringing the doorbell."

I could hear the rustle of the phone against her shirt. She opened the door and then stood for a moment, half-surprised, half-amused. She brought the cordless phone back to her ear.

"I'm sorry, Jake. There's some dark and mysterious man at my door who looks like he wants to take advantage of me."

I couldn't help smiling. The orange haze of dusk made her radiant. "Does he look desperate?" I asked into my cell phone.

"Completely. I need to call 911."

I snapped my phone shut and moved closer to her. "I'm not going to disappear anytime soon, okay?"

My arms slipped around her as she looked down for a moment, unsure, shy. Then the dark eyes glanced at me with a look that said *It's okay.* A look, and a welcoming smile.

And I kissed sweet and gentle lips that I had kissed many times in my dreams since college, since 1994, since hearing her final good-bye and never knowing if I'd ever see this woman again.

THIRTY-ONE

March 1994

"NO WAY."

Jake took a bite of the deep-dish pizza and nodded at a disbelieving Bruce. Four of them sat in a booth eating dinner at Gino's Pizza ten minutes from their apartment.

"There's got to be someone we can go to," Bruce said.

"Who? The president? Oh, wait, that's who I just saw."

"Unbelievable."

"Why unbelievable?" Alec said. "What'd you think the president was going to say?"

"Not that," Bruce said.

"Of course that," Alec said, talking through a mouth full of pizza. "Of course the president was going to side with his golden student. Did I not predict pretty much everything?"

"The bit about Laila—you didn't predict that."

"That girl is psycho. I told you that after the first party where you left with her," Bruce said.

"Girls like that are dangerous when they get rejected." Carnie, quiet all night, finally spoke.

They all looked at him, waiting to see if he would say more.

"That's your fault," Jake said to Alec.

"No way. I didn't do anything."

"You sure helped."

Carnie and Bruce looked puzzled; they didn't know about the Chicago excursion a couple months ago. Jake wished he'd never said yes to going downtown with Alec, to staying downtown at Laila's friend's apartment, to giving in to Laila.

The only thing Jake really wanted to do was get drunk. Not just sorta drunk, but really, die-hard drunk. He wanted to escape this insanity, and there was only one way to do it. He drained his cup and filled it up again.

"Only two more months of this hole," he said, pounding beer.

"Thank God," Bruce said.

"No need to thank Him," Alec said. "He allowed this to happen."

No one responded.

"Have another piece," Jake urged Carnie.

"I'm feeling sick," Carnie said. His round, bearded face was downcast and serious.

"Are you guys around spring break?" Alec asked. "'Cause I think we need to do something."

"Something like?" Bruce asked.

"Something big."

"On campus?" Jake asked.

"On Brian."

Jake looked at Alec and saw a sinister grin spread over his friend's face. "What's that mean?"

"I don't know. Wouldn't it be nice to just . . . freak him out a bit?"

"How?" Bruce asked, his voice muffled with pepperoni pizza.

"I don't know. Shane will have some ideas."

"We can't get in any more trouble," Carnie said.

"Oh, come on, Carn. Live a little."

"I don't want to get Jake kicked out."

"He won't even be involved," Alec said.

"Says who?" Jake asked.

"Says me," Alec said. "You took one for the team when we stole the mascot."

"I didn't realize we were a team."

"You bet we are."

"You the captain?" Jake smiled.

"I'm the goalie," Alec said.

"That's a first," Bruce said.

"There's a first for everything. We need to show that to Brian."

Shane and Franklin showed up ten minutes later. Shane dived into the pizza while Franklin ordered a soda and listened to Jake recount his meeting with Bramson.

Carnie cursed and shook his head.

"For once I agree with you there," Franklin said.

Jake drained another beer and was feeling it now. "Whatever."

"No. It's not whatever," Franklin replied, his slicked-back hair stuck together by some unknown force.

"Huh?"

"You pay the same twenty grand to go to Providence that Brian pays," Franklin continued. "The school has no right to treat you any differently."

"President Bramson implied that I was friends with the devil."

"Serious?" Shane asked, laughing.

"Sure. Doing what I can to undermine the school."

"Of course you are," Alec said.

"The president is a weasel," Franklin said.

Alec told Shane and Franklin his idea of doing something to Brian during spring break.

"The baseball team sticks around, don't they? So we know he'll be here."

"What are you going to do?" Carnie asked, his face red and empty.

"What are *we* going to do?"

"Oh, no. I'm not getting involved."

Alec nodded. "Our boy took one on his shoulders for all of us. We need to make things even."

"Things won't be even unless we assault Brian," Carnie said.

"Assault means what?" Alec said, a sneer on his face.

"Come on," Jake said.

"What? They're saying he didn't do anything to you. I'm

looking at you and think differently. We should've found Brian that night and cracked his head with baseball bats. But we didn't."

"Good thing," Jake said.

"No, it's not good. That guy—if he goes off scot-free he'll live his whole entire God-forsaken life knowing he can do whatever he wants and get away with it."

"That's the way life works," Franklin said without any emotion.

"Yeah, but there's also something about getting what you deserve."

"Reaping what you sow," Jake said, remembering Alyssa's words.

Alec cursed in agreement. "That's exactly what it is. If we don't show Brian the way the world really works, he'll never learn."

"So we're like, educating him, huh?" Shane asked.

"Exactly."

Jake chuckled and shook his head. "Look, guys—"

"Come on, Jake. Nothing bad will happen."

"Then what *will* happen?"

"That's what we can decide here and now. Nothing big. No broken bones. No bloody face."

"Then what are you suggesting?" Carnie asked.

They all looked at Alec and his dark eyes that held a hundred secrets. He lit up in a devilish grin and glanced at all of them.

"I just want to scare the life out of Brian Erwin and make him regret the day he ever laid eyes on any of us."

THIRTY-TWO

June 2005

THE NIGHT FELT, simply put, normal. Alyssa had told me to stay if I wasn't busy. *If I wasn't busy.* I wasn't going anywhere. Bruce had gone to see a concert with Mike downtown, and all I had in my grand plan was going back to the hotel room and watching TV—the same thing I was doing in Alyssa's house.

Well, maybe I would have watched something different. We ordered in a pizza and watched an episode of a reality television show.

"So what'd you think?" she asked me as the end credits appeared.

"I can't believe stuff like this is so popular."

"It's a study in human dynamics."

"Those people aren't normal, are they?"

Alyssa laughed. "No. But they're fun to watch."

"I'd use the term 'fun' lightly. Interesting, maybe."

"Kyle used to say I was a reality TV junkie." Alyssa's smile quickly faded, and she looked at the glass in her hand. "Maybe it's just better to watch other people's misery than wallow in your own."

I slid closer to her on the plush couch and offered her a smile. "I was on a reality television show," I admitted.

"What? When?"

"A couple years ago. You ever hear of the *Eco Challenge*?"

She shook her head and I looked at her lips, ones I had kissed several hours ago. I wondered if I would kiss them again before the night was over.

"It's an outdoor race—sorta like *Survivor* meets a triathlon. It's always in a remote place."

"Did you win?"

I laughed. "There are teams of four. Some of my climbing buddies wanted to do it. One of them wasn't in the best shape. He can climb, but this tests endurance. And sanity. We came in twenty-first."

"Out of how many teams?"

"Over a hundred."

"That's not bad."

"My parents taped the shows and everything."

"Wait—you were on TV?"

I couldn't help being amused. "I'm suddenly a different person to you, huh?"

"Shut up."

"They showed it on USA channel. It's more gritty than *Survivor* and *The Apprentice*."

"I would like to see those tapes."

"Sorry. I have the only remaining copy. I burned the rest."

"You've had such an exciting postcollege life."

"Not necessarily," I said.

"Compared to a lot of us. Exhibit A." She pointed at herself.

"This is a strange side of you."

"What side?"

"The woe-is-me side."

Alyssa swatted at my arm. "That's not nice."

"That's not you."

"Sometimes I stand in front of the classroom and feel frightened. Isn't that odd? After all this time, I sometimes question if I have any clue what I'm doing."

"We all do that at times," I said.

"What's the most scared you've ever been?"

I paused for a moment. A quick piercing snapshot blasted through my mind.

*the wet, white body—trying to drag it out—calling out his
name*

"Jake? During your climbing expeditions. Have you ever
been scared to death?"

Another image came to mind. I thought of telling her about
Ray but then realized now wasn't the time. Getting into the details of the climbing partner I had left on the side of a mountain a year ago wouldn't be good for the mood.

"Honestly?" I tried to focus. "It wasn't when I was climbing.
I was rappelling in Georgia."

"Rappelling—like when you lower yourself down a
mountain?"

"Yeah. I was going down the place called the Fantastic Pit
—the deepest free fall in the U.S. It's like a giant train tunnel
pointed at the center of the earth. You just keep dropping."

"Is it all dark?"

"They have lights on it. But you just feel like you're being
swallowed by this huge hole. I was heading down and for a
moment—just a split second—I thought my harness was about
to snap. It just got caught up in a loop and jerked, but it scared
the snot out of me. Funny thing is—I wouldn't have even
dropped that far, all things considered. Still, I would've probably broken my neck or worse."

"What about climbing some of those tall mountains?"

"Sure. But it's a rush too. There's a reason I keep doing it.
The same reason that people like you probably decide to go
back and face a room full of kids every day. Even if deep down
you're slightly freaked out."

We looked at one another, our faces close together.

"Do you want anything—?" Alyssa began.

"Yeah."

"What?" she asked. She looked down, nervous.

I took her hand and held it. "I want you not to be unhappy."

"You're a little late for that."

"I know I am. And I'm sorry."

"It's nothing you did," Alyssa said. "Nothing you could
have done."

"I'm sorry for being gone so long—for not even—I don't know. For not even bothering to try to contact you."

"I'm sorry for making that so easy."

The sitcom on television was a little too loud, so I grabbed the remote and turned the television off.

"We should stop apologizing so much to each other," I said.

"I know. It's probably not very healthy."

"It's not very fun either."

My cell phone rang, and I looked at the caller ID. "It's a Chicago number."

"It might be Mike," Alyssa said. She was right.

→→ ←←

"Jake—man, you gotta come downtown."

He sounded out of breath and frazzled. More than frazzled, in fact. He sounded frightened.

"What's wrong?"

"Bruce got shot."

"What?" I shouted out.

"Bruce got shot tonight."

"Where? How—"

"We saw Blue Merle at the Riviera—and we were coming out and walking to our car and someone came out of nowhere—like seriously out of the dark. They hit him over the head and then fired a shot in his gut while he was lying on the ground."

"Is he—"

"He's in intensive care. Cops are here and I was questioned and—" Mike cursed. "It's major, man."

"Where are you?"

"We're at Loyola Hospital downtown. Know where that is?"

"I'll find out."

"I don't even know how to go about contacting his parents."

"You might not want to," I said.

"The hospital is trying to get hold of them."

"Did you see the guy?"

"Not really. It happened so fast. We were talking about cars or something stupid and laughing and I walked ahead and then heard a muffled sound and looked back and Bruce was on the ground."

I stood up. "Look—I'll come on down now. Just—just let me know if you get any news, okay? Call me."

"Jake. There's something else."

"What?"

"The guy. The one who shot Bruce. He said to tell you to back off. To go back home."

"What?"

"Yeah. He said, 'Tell your buddy Jake to back off and go home or things will get worse.' What'd he mean? What's this all about? Are you in trouble?"

"No—look, just stay there, Mike. I'll head out soon. We can talk when I get there."

I looked at Alyssa, who had been standing, listening to my side of the conversation, ready to take action.

"When we get there," she said.

THiRTY THREE

March 1994

THE COLD AND GRAY of the last week had evaporated into a beautiful blue spring day with temperatures in the high 60s. Unfortunately, good weather couldn't compensate for an intense hangover. Jake had gotten bored with beer so he had tried wine, which seemed fine last night. But there was something different about wine. You didn't want to overdo on the vino. Jake knew that now.

After an easy hour of business marketing discussion with other seniors, Jake carried his backpack over his shoulder as he walked across campus. He felt as he always had while walking around school—like an imposter. While the president's words had been harsh and cruel, they also were half true. Why *was* he here? Simply because his parents were paying his way? What a lame reason. But there was still no excuse for the president putting him in his place, making him feel guilty for doing nothing.

As Jake walked toward the parking lot where his car waited, he saw a figure emerging from the dorm. A dark-haired girl in jeans and a yellow top. Even from far away, Jake could tell it was Alyssa. He quickened his pace. The jerking of his body made his head hurt, but that was okay. She was headed toward the cafeteria building, which was crowded now that it was lunchtime. Jake managed to get on the same sidewalk and walked up to her.

"Hey," he said to her in a casual greeting.

"You're not supposed to be here," Alyssa told him.

"News spreads fast."

"You forget where I work."

"You gonna turn me in?"

"Only if I have to," she said in a distant tone.

"Going to lunch?"

"It's lunchtime."

"Any chance you'd want to go somewhere off campus?"

"I pay to eat lunch *on* campus."

"Alyssa?"

She looked at him and waited.

"Can I talk with you?"

"About what?"

"About everything," he said.

"I don't have much to say that I haven't already said." Her eyes refused to look into his, her lips tightened.

"Did I do something?"

"Did you?"

"Look, we need to talk," he said.

"*Now* we need to talk?"

"Yes."

"Are you forcing me to?"

Jake thought of the president's question about Laila. "Alyssa, please. I just—just this one time. That's all I ask. Just one more time. Then I'll leave you alone. Okay?"

"You could start now."

"Why are you so angry at me?" Jake asked.

"I think you know."

Alyssa seemed bothered by the students passing by, watching them talk.

"I think we need to talk somewhere away from here."

"Jake, look, I don't want—"

"Please, Alyssa. I need you to hear me out."

⤛ ⤜

They sat in a booth at McDonald's. Even though he'd tried to pay, Alyssa had bought her own chicken sandwich and Diet Coke.

"What'd you hear?"

"I've heard a lot," Alyssa said.

"About?"

"You. And Laila."

Jake shook his head. "The president believes I tried to rape her. I haven't had anything to do with her. Not this year."

"Really?"

Jake nodded. "Yeah, really. Well, I mean, there was one night."

"One night?"

"Yeah, something stupid. I was drunk and—"

"That's surprising."

"Alec set me up on a double date. He just wanted to get with her friend. It was a mistake."

"But you haven't had anything to do with her."

"I hadn't. Not until then."

"People saw you in a bar making out."

Jake nodded, closing his eyes for a minute. "I was drunk."

"Maybe you did more," Alyssa said.

"I know for a fact I didn't. She wanted me to go home with her, and I didn't. Period."

"And the night of the party?"

Jake shook his head. "Look—I can't make you believe me. But I thought you might."

"Why is that?"

"Because you know I'm not interested in Laila."

"How do I know that?"

Jake shook his head. "Because for the past few years all I've ever tried to do is get you to go out with me. You know how I feel about you."

"That hasn't prevented you from dating other girls."

"I know."

"Or making out with other girls."

Jake scratched his head.

"You'll never get it, will you?" she asked.

They kept eating in silence.

Jake breathed in. "Would you have given me a chance if we had met in a different way? Would you have been interested in me if I was someone different?"

"Maybe. I don't know."

"It used to be fun," Jake said, looking out the window at the playground full of young kids running around.

"What?"

"All of it. The parties. The guys. Now I'm just really—tired, I guess. I just want to graduate and move on."

"Move on to what?"

"Something different. A change of pace."

"Some of your habits will be hard to break," Alyssa said.

He returned her straightforward glance. "I know."

"You have a long night last night?"

Jake nodded. "It's hard work partying. You torture your body. It's not for the weak of heart."

"Is that supposed to be a joke?"

"Yeah. No good, huh?"

She shook her head and finished her sandwich while Jake watched her.

"What?" she asked.

"You're beautiful, you know that?"

"Stop."

"The only reason I've ever thought about changing—about quitting all of the craziness—the only reason has been because of you."

"That's not a good reason."

Jake nodded. "Maybe not."

"You shouldn't change for someone else, Jake. You should change for yourself."

"And how should I change? Stop the drinking? Stop the cursing? Go to church?"

"Stop the lying," she said in a soft voice.

"Who am I lying to?"

"To yourself. To your parents. To everyone else."

"I didn't do anything to Laila. The only thing I did to her at that party was push her away."

193

Alyssa didn't say anything.

"Alyssa, look at me. Please. Look at me. Look in my eyes. I swear to you and to God and to anyone else I can that I *didn't try to rape Laila*. I don't know how and why that rumor got started—I don't know what that has to do with anything. I've made mistakes, and I've made mistakes in the past with Laila, but I didn't hurt her or do anything like that. I've never done anything that she didn't want to do. Got that?"

"Okay."

"No, I want to know that you at least believe that."

"Okay."

Jake didn't finish his hamburger. "I'm sorry," he said to Alyssa.

"For what?"

"For ever thinking—for ever trying . . ."

"Jake —" Alyssa began, her eyes tearing up.

"No. Look. I've tried harder with you than I've tried for anything in my life. It's like chasing after a rainbow or something. I've always thought that somewhere deep inside there was a part of you that liked me—a part of you that might be open to me. Mistakes and all. But I think that's how I've been lying to myself. I've convinced myself there was a chance and really, there never was. Was there? Tell me I'm wrong?"

Alyssa wiped her eyes and said nothing.

"It's one thing to get the life punched and kicked out of me. Or to be told by the president that I'm going to hell. But you gotta know, Alyssa. I'd gladly take that over having you sitting there, giving me that look. Saying nothing."

"I'm sorry."

"Yeah, I am too."

He drove her back to Providence, a quick five-minute ride, and pulled up to the dorm. They hadn't spoken during the drive.

She looked over at him and, for a brief second, Jake believed she was going to say something else.

Then she turned and got out and closed the door behind her.

Whatever tiny thing they had ever had between them was over and gone.

THIRTY - FOUR

June 2005

"THAT FAT NURSE IS getting on my nerves." Mike glanced at me with bloodshot eyes as he dropped down into the chair across from me.

"Did you tell the cops—"

"No," he answered.

This was the first time we'd been able to talk, to really talk, as Alyssa had excused herself to go to the restroom.

"What'd you tell them?"

"I said the guy wanted Bruce's money and he had none. No lie there."

"What'd he look like?"

"Forties maybe. Nondescript. Seriously nondescript. Little hair. Pudgy. I don't know. He could be twenty-four and blond as far as I remember."

It was closing in on 1 a.m. and I was on a second cup of coffee. Mike had been pacing back and forth since we had gotten there.

"This is about more than just finding Alec, right? What's really going on?"

I looked at Mike and shook my head. "I don't know."

"What's Bruce doing here anyway?"

"He wanted to tag along. He has nothing back there in California."

"No job?"

"No nothing. I think he'd been looking for an excuse to leave."

"And he ends up getting shot in Chicago. Nice." Mike swore.

"He'll be fine."

"How do you know? Nurse Betty over there won't give out any information except that he's in intensive care and to wait and sit down."

I stared at Mike's shiny black shoes. "You call your wife?"

He nodded. "You think Alec has something to do with this?"

"I don't know. All of this—this didn't just happen. Someone doesn't want me finding Alec. Who else would it be besides Alec himself?"

"He wouldn't get someone to shoot Bruce."

"People change. Franklin wasn't too happy to see me either."

Mike shook his head, looking a bit too pale in the harsh glow of the hospital light.

"This is karma, man. Our karma. We've had this coming for a long time."

"I don't buy it."

"That's the truth," Mike answered.

Alyssa walked up holding a can of soda. "Everything okay?"

I looked at Mike, and he stood up and said he was going to get an answer.

"We were just talking about karma. You believe people reap what they sow?"

She nodded. "I used to."

"Maybe Bruce—maybe all of us—maybe we had this coming."

"What? Getting shot?"

I looked at her. "There's a lot I haven't told you, Alyssa."

"About Carnie?"

"Yeah. About all of them. There are a lot of things about our last spring break that I tried to just put out of my mind."

She sat down beside me, and for the moment ignored her soda.

"There's stuff I should've gotten to the bottom of," I continued. "That I should have told someone about."

"What stuff?"

"That's the thing—I don't know. Mike doesn't know. Bruce doesn't know. Here are all these grown men who have no idea what happened ten, eleven years ago." I inhaled and shook my head. "This is—intense. I feel like it's my fault. I should never have let Bruce come with me."

"He can make his own decisions, you know."

"No, I don't think he can," I said. "He has the same maturity level he had back in college."

Mike came back, his wrinkled black shirt hanging out and his face dotted with stubble. "Well—it doesn't look like he's going to die."

"Way to put it delicately," I said.

"What do you want me to say? That's all I could get out of them."

I stood up and threw away the Styrofoam cup I'd been cutting with my fingernails.

"Mike," I said, for the moment ignoring Alyssa's presence. "Did the guy say anything else? Anything to do with me. With Alec?"

"I told you his exact words, give or take."

I nodded. "I think maybe I'm going to follow them."

"Sounds smart to me," Mike said.

"Jake—" Alyssa had come alongside me, curiosity in her eyes.

"Mike—I want to take her home."

"I'm fine," she protested.

"No—it's okay," Mike said. "It's cool. I can stay here for a while. They said he's stable. Stable. How can someone be stable if he just got a thumb-sized hole in his gut?"

"Can you keep me posted?"

"Yeah."

"I'm sorry, man."

I couldn't help but give Mike a hug. He received it awkwardly.

"Be careful, okay?" I asked him.

"Yeah, always. You taking off then? Leaving?"

Alyssa's eyes widened momentarily. It was too late for being discreet.

"I don't know," was all I could say.

On the drive back to the suburbs, the interstate's lanes open and inviting speeding, I looked over at her. She was still wide-awake.

"Sorry about everything," I said again.

"What are you apologizing about?"

"Coming into your life out of the blue and putting this in your lap."

"I called you," she said.

"I asked you out."

"I accepted."

"I kissed you."

"And again, I—"

"Okay, I got it," I said, the banter helping ease my mood. "This just—I don't think I should be here."

"Who doesn't want you here?"

"Alec?"

"Why? Why wouldn't Alec want you around?"

"I don't know."

I kept the car at a steady seventy-five miles per hour. We were maybe fifteen minutes from Alyssa's house.

"Jake?"

"Yeah?"

"What happened on spring break?"

"It was just going to be a prank. That was all. And even then, it wasn't my idea. It was out of my control."

She didn't answer, and after a moment I continued. "You know—I used to think it was fun waking up not remembering the night before. That was college. I thought—I just assumed it was normal behavior."

"For some, it is."

"Yeah, maybe," I said. "But I can't get those times back. Whatever happened, those memories are black and done. When Carnie died, he took those memories with him."

"And Alec?"

"Alec kept tons of things from me. I don't know if I ever fully trusted the guy."

"Alec? Your best friend?"

"Best friend. Yeah. Even after—after everything happened—it just all started out of—just all of us being stupid."

And I tried to tell her what I recalled but it seemed to come out wrong. I hadn't talked about any of this in years.

I had just started my jumbled story when we arrived in her driveway.

"Jake?" Alyssa put a hand on mine. "Can you—look, I don't want to be alone tonight. I'm not asking for—I'm just a little freaked out."

"Yeah, sure. Don't say anything more—I understand."

I turned off the lights and locked the car, then followed her into the house.

THIRTY-FIVE

April 1994

THE DOOR TO HIS APARTMENT swung open without a knock.

"I wanna hear it," Alec said as he approached the kitchen counter where the answering machine stood.

Then he took a look at Jake.

"You're looking nice today."

Jake hadn't shaved in a week and hadn't showered for a couple of days. Red eyes, a nice little beer gut, disheveled hair. He didn't care. All he cared about was the message he'd gotten this afternoon.

He played it for Alec. The others were at school, doing what college students did: Sitting in class. Learning. Studying. Talking. Socializing. Eating. Laughing. Living. But not Jake. He was getting threats while he slept off a long night.

He pressed the machine. The voice started by greeting Jake with a juicy four-lettered curse.

"You think this is over, don't you? You think it's done, but it's not. And you better watch out because we're gonna finish what we started. I told you once, and I'll tell you again. Nobody screws with me. Nobody."

It clicked off.

Alec stood there, eyes wide open, unblinking.

"What should we do?" Jake asked, tired and without energy.

"Nothing."

"What? We shouldn't let the cops know about this?"

"Oh, no," Alec said, going to the fridge to get a beer. "No, this is between you and him. Between Brian and all of us. Spring break is almost here."

"Yeah," Jake said, too drained to care.

"That guy has a lot of nerve. But we'll see just how much nerve he's really got. Just you wait."

Jake nodded. Alec handed him a beer. It was two-thirty in the afternoon, and Jake could still feel the aftertaste of a case of beer the night before. He hadn't eaten anything all day.

"I don't know, man," he said to Alec, looking at the beer in his hand.

Alec opened it for him.

"Drink up. Spring break starts now."

➻ ➺

Blink.

The setting sun is gone and you're listening to loud music and you're laughing.

Blink.

You're on the road in the passenger seat watching the yellow lines roll by.

Blink.

You're on a sidewalk smoking a cigarette following the footsteps in front of you.

Blink.

You're entering a dark hallway with suffocating beats and soulless stares.

"Hey, wake up," someone says on the couch next to you.

Everything races, glittering and pecking and blinding. You swear Kurt Cobain is screaming in your ear and he's really angry.

"Huh?" you say.

"Don't fade on me now," the voice of Alec says from somewhere above or below.

"I won't."

"Need something to keep you up?"

"Sure."

And it's that easy.

Before Alec, you'd managed to stay drug-free, not counting pot, twenty years of your life, but that's just a phrase, a notion by a government, a slogan for a television network.

This is not some crossroad you're at. It's simple and easy and your best friend laughs and makes it seem as easy as passing a bottle of salt and in a way it is.

Blink.

The day and night mesh and overlap.

Blink again.

You're on the road, sitting in the backseat next to a stranger with long dark hair, laughing uncontrollably.

Control is for the weak.

Reality is for the foolish.

All you do tonight right now is feel and you're invincible and the stars are out and you never want this feeling to end ever never and for a fleeting moment you believe it never will.

⇥ ⇤

"Trent Reznor is a god," Mike said, turning up the volume on the Nine Inch Nails album he had purchased a few weeks before.

"Or maybe he's the devil," Jake replied, throwing a dart into the board on the wall.

"Sounds more like it," Carnie said.

"Come on, you love it."

"Sounds like he's on heroin and got locked in the room with a synthesizer and a monkey."

They all laughed at Carnie's joke, always a rarity but always worth it when the time came.

"Monkey?" Mike asked.

"Listen to that. It's sounds like he's torturing the poor thing."

"We need to go out," Alec said, coming back from the bathroom.

"I managed to go through a hundred bucks last night," Jake said. "The bad thing is I don't even remember most of it."

"You brought home someone named Jen or Jade," Carnie said. Jake looked at him. "Shut up."

"Seriously."

"What?" Jake stared at Alec.

"He's kidding. I mean, we were hanging out with a couple of girls. Sorta freaky too. Goth chicks into The Cure. We should've had this CD last night."

"You should've invited me," Mike said.

"No thanks," Carnie said. "I spent $7.89 on beer and a burrito."

"We were celebrating," Alec said, hitting a bull's-eye and making the board sound off.

"Celebrating what?"

"Freedom."

"This guy really hates himself, doesn't he?" Carnie said about the album.

"He's taking grunge and industrial and combining them," Mike said, hitting the wall next to the dartboard.

"Stick to music, my young friend," Carnie said, hitting a triple twenty and hearing the board celebrate his shot.

Alec began discussing where they needed to go. It was seven in the evening but it felt much earlier—like they had just gone out and just woken up.

"What day is it?" Jake asked, suddenly and completely forgetting.

"Saturday," Carnie said.

"Does it matter?" Alec said.

And as Jake delicately sipped his first beer of the day, his mouth still raw from the previous night, he listened to angry, fierce vocals of the music as they wailed, *I do not want this.*

➤➤ ◄◄

"Tell me about your parents," Bruce said to Jake as they sat in the forest preserve on the sunny day, the mercury pushing seventy.

"What do you want to know?"

"I don't know. You just never talk about them."

"What's there to talk about?"

Bruce shrugged.

"My older brother is the hero and my older sister is the brains and I'm the youngest they don't know what to do with."

"They made you go to Providence?"

"Sure. They wanted someone else to try and save my soul. They've sorta given up."

"Do you like them?"

Jake took a sip from his beer. "It's not like I don't. It's just— I don't know. They don't get it, and I feel like they're so old, you know."

"My dad is nonexistent and my mom overprotective," Bruce said.

"They're divorced, right?"

"Yep. That does wonders for a family."

"You know—we go to college when the divorce rate is higher than ever and AIDS is rampant and the world might be coming to an end, and they wonder why we listen to this music and do the things we do."

"Gen X, man."

"I wonder if it's going to keep getting worse," Jake said. "Like if the next generation of kids are going to be even more jaded. And imagine the music—how angry that's going to be."

"It's all circular. They were enraged in the sixties, right? And the seventies too. But look at the eighties."

"Sometimes I wonder what I'm going to do once I graduate. I don't even want to graduate . . . but I don't want to stay around here."

"If you could do one thing in your life, only one thing for sure, what would that be?"

For a second, Jake thought of Alyssa. It was a fleeting, foolish thought, but she came to his mind.

"Climb Mount Everest," he said.

That's actually attainable.

"Really?"

"Sometimes I've stood on the edge of a mountain and

thought, it can't get any better than this. The view, the height, the intensity of the moment. You know?"

"Yeah," Bruce said, taking a drag from his cigarette.

"What about you?"

His longhaired friend thought for a moment and pushed the hair out of his eyes. "I'd get my father to admit he loves me. Or that he even knows I'm alive."

"That's cool," Jake said.

"It's pathetic, but it's a goal."

"I wonder," Jake said. "If and when I get older . . . if I'll do any better. If I'll be a better man. A better person."

"I will," Bruce promised. "I swear to God I'll do better."

→> <←

It was Tuesday, April 5, a little after lunch. Jake lay out on a blanket watching the clouds and waiting for Alec. This would be the third day in a row they had come to the forest preserve. The weather was unusually warm for this time of year, and they were making good use of it. In a way Jake felt like he could put the winter's woes behind him, even for the moment.

The door to his CRX was open, playing Pearl Jam. This early in the day, and in the year, they wouldn't be bothered by cops or strangers.

Alec arrived and came out of his car holding a case of Bush Light Draft.

"I don't think you have enough beer," Jake said.

"I've got another case in the car."

"Nice."

"We're going through both of them today."

"A case apiece?" Jake asked, laughing, his stomach turning.

"You bet."

"I think at this rate I'm going to be dead by Friday."

"We can arrange that." Alec laughed.

"Don't you get tired of drinking?"

Alec cracked open a beer and handed it to Jake. "My man, when will you ever learn? Life is only manageable when you're out of hand." He opened his own beer and raised it.

"What are we toasting?"

"The grand scheme. The master plan."

"We're not still going through with it," Jake said.

"You bet we are. I've got it all planned out."

"Alec. The stuff with Brian is over."

"Oh, it's not over. It's *far* from over."

"Alec."

"What, *Dad*?"

Jake swore.

"That's the spirit," Alec answered. "You don't worry about anything. Just drink up."

"I thought we were going camping this weekend."

"Oh, really?" Alec laughed. "That's all part of the plan. Part of the alibi."

"And Brian?"

"He doesn't have a clue."

"About what?"

"About what's going to hit him."

Alec grinned one of his uncontrollable, unbridled grins. Suddenly, drinking sounded like a really good idea to Jake.

June 2005

I SAT UP ON THE COUCH in Alyssa's living room, unable to sleep anymore. It was around seven, and the morning looked overcast and gloomy. Seemed appropriate. I felt wired and restless, and my dreams had been like paddling a canoe in an ocean storm.

Alyssa had apologized for not having a spare bedroom, since it was being used for storage. Now I stood and looked around the bare house. Nobody could have guessed that Alyssa had been living in this town for the last decade. It still felt like she had just moved in.

I knew what it was like to live on your own. You got used to it, sure. But you also got lonely. And even with a family in the area, those nights of coming back to silence were sometimes hard to take. No amount of volume on the television or surfing the Internet or talking on the phone could erase the fact that you were alone. And for Alyssa, who had tried to make a go with having a family and sharing another's life, this loneliness probably felt extra painful.

I thought of this last night when I hugged Alyssa before going to bed. There had been no thought of something happening between us, not with the mood both of us were in. I've always thought it was crazy in movies when characters are being chased and almost killed and then they suddenly stop everything to get together for a good ole romp in bed. It's Hollywood, sure, but it's also ridiculous.

I looked around the living room, the only halfway-decorated room in the house, at a shelf on the wall with photos of Alyssa and her parents, her sister, other relatives. She looked so beautiful, so innocent and pure. There was a shot of her on her graduation day from Providence; I held it for a moment, examining it carefully.

You never put on a robe, a voice whispered to me. *You never got a chance to walk to get your diploma.*

I decided to head out and find some breakfast.

→→ ←←

The phone rang, and a woman picked up.

"Yeah, I'd like to talk with Mr. Jelen."

"May I ask who's calling?"

"This is Jake Rivers. This is about his daughter, and it's urgent."

The woman put me on hold, but seconds later a no-nonsense voice picked up and got right to the point. "What is it?"

"I'm done. I've had enough. You can find someone else to track down your daughter."

"What are you talking about? What happened?"

I was standing in the parking lot of Dunkin' Donuts, a hot cup of coffee on the hood of my rental car, talking on my cell as I watched morning work traffic pass on the street in front of me.

"Someone doesn't want Alec found," I said. "Maybe it's Alec, I don't know. Last night one of my friends got shot."

There was silence on the other end.

"Yeah, that's what I think," I continued. "Look—whatever is going on with Alec—I'm not a part of it. My friends aren't a part of it. And whatever happened years ago rests with Alec. He's the responsible one."

"Jake, you agreed to—"

"I know what I agreed to. Your threats helped."

"Do you know anything?"

"I know that he had a lot more to do with our college exploits than I realized. And maybe—maybe he doesn't want me finding him. Maybe he doesn't want you intruding in his life."

"It's not his life I'm concerned about," Mr. Jelen said.

"Your daughter is an adult. She can make her own decisions. Right or wrong, you can't do much about it."

"I could at least make a plea—if I knew where she was."

"You gotta get someone else. None of my friends know anything. And the longer I keep looking, the worse it gets. And there are people—people I'm worried about getting hurt."

"Like your young lady friend?"

I paused for a moment. "You spying on me?" I asked angrily.

"Let's say I'm keeping track of you, Mr. Rivers."

"My father is Mr. Rivers, so don't call me that again. And secondly, I don't need to be kept track of."

"She might be interested in knowing what happened back in your wild college days."

I gripped the cell phone, wishing it were Mr. Jelen's neck.

"You got something to say, say it. Tell her. Tell me while you're doing it. Everything I knew I told the authorities. There was nothing else I could say. About any of it."

There was only silence on the other line.

"You're quiet because, you know what? You don't know jack either. I thought maybe you did, maybe you had learned something I didn't know. But that's impossible. So go ahead. You tell anybody anything you want. The answers lie in the man you're looking for. You find him, you let me know. I gotta few questions I want to ask him myself."

"Jake—please, hold on."

"What?" I yelled into the phone.

"You don't have a daughter—a family. You can't understand."

I thought of the woman I'd left back at her house, probably still sleeping comfortably in her king-sized bed.

"I understand well enough."

"I just want her back." Mr. Jelen sounded desperate and weak, two adjectives that probably weren't usually associated with him.

"Sometimes there's nothing you can do about it. Claire's not your little girl anymore. She's going to make decisions, even if they're bad ones. You just got to hope and pray that she'll wise up."

Again there was a silence, as if Mr. Jelen had been surprised and didn't know what to say.

"I have to go."

"Jake? If there's anything—anything else that comes up—please, can you at least let me know?"

"Yeah."

"You can still use the credit card I gave you for any additional expenses on your way home."

. . . *your way home.*

The thought felt odd. For the moment I didn't want to think about it.

"I'll be fine, thanks."

But there was nothing fine about any of this. The only fine thing was back in a house five minutes from here. Maybe I would prepare breakfast in bed for her.

→→ ←←

Any such romantic notions were shot the moment I returned.

Alyssa was carrying a cup of tea across the living room when I opened the front door. She let out a high-pitched shriek and jerked the cup, letting the liquid swoop in an arc over the carpet.

"It's just me," I blurted out, too late.

Alyssa held her hand on her chest. I put the box of donuts down on a table and told her I'd help clean up.

She exhaled. "I thought you'd left."

"I'm sorry—I was hoping I'd get back before you woke up."

"I woke up when I heard your car start."

"I didn't want to freak you out and wake you up," I said. Then I looked at her colorless face. "I guess that plan didn't work."

"I look awful—I didn't think you were coming back."

"What? I'm going to just leave without saying good-bye?"

She didn't say anything.

I took the cup from her hand and laughed. "This just proves what I've thought all along."

"What?"

"That you truly are beautiful."

Alyssa held up a hand to her face, embarrassed. She wore white pajamas that looked comfortable and appeared almost too nice to sleep in.

I went to the kitchen and grabbed a wet rag and towel and spent the next few minutes trying to clean up the stains. We eventually ended up on her couch, eating donuts.

"I didn't know what kind you liked," I said as she looked through the box.

"So you got a dozen?"

"Actually, just eight. One for you and seven for me."

"Chocolate glazed are my favorite."

"Strange. I guessed that."

"Did you hear anything from Mike?"

I shook my head, taking a bite of a maple donut. "I'm going to call later."

"That's nice, to see what you're eating."

I swallowed before saying, "Excuse me."

I wanted to try and figure out a way to tell Alyssa that I had called Mr. Jelen and given up my quest. Or whatever this was called. It was as if I had been called for some magnificent journey but had never really gotten started. I knew as much about the whereabouts of Alec now as I knew several weeks ago.

April 1994

OH GOD NO PLEASE GOD NO

Jake looked up at the heavens and then back at his bloody shirt.

This is a bad joke it's gotta be

His watch said eleven, but he didn't trust that. Then he looked at his right fist and saw the cuts and the bloody knuckles and the purple color and he wondered if he had broken the hand again.

How'd I do this?

He didn't know the day. Friday? Saturday? His head hurt to think about it. All he knew was that he was alone.

Trying the ignition didn't work. Someone must have run out of gas the night before. Probably Bruce. But then where did he go? To find gas?

And what's that gun doing in the backseat?

It looked like Carnie's handgun, the one he had bought not long ago. New Year's Eve. Remember that?

Jake shoved the gun under the front car seat in case someone came by and looked inside. Then he locked up the car and began walking, in which direction he wasn't sure. Maybe his friends were playing a prank on him. A really bad prank. Was he horrified? Oh, yeah.

Jake kept walking for what might have been a mile, his head foggy and eyes squinting at the sun. Then he turned and went another direction, trying to find a main road. Trying to find anything.

He searched his thoughts and tried to come up with something from the night before. Anything at all.

Three of them drove out here with him: Alec, Bruce, and Carnie. They'd arrived on Thursday night and had brought enough booze for half the state of Illinois.

Jake could remember sitting by a fire with the guys, their tents behind them. Laughing and eating and drinking. And that was it. It was late, how late he didn't know. He tried to remember if anyone else was there.

Where am I?

And more importantly, *what happened?*

Finally the dirt road ended at an intersection with a two-lane road. Jake stepped onto it and looked in both directions.

Nothing. No campground, no farm, nothing around. No oncoming traffic or noise.

He felt the back of his pants. He still had his wallet. He looked inside. No money. At least he had an ID on him.

The sun was warm, so he took off the bloody shirt and crumpled it up. He began to stuff it into his pocket when he noticed the bulge. Jake reached inside and found a folded pocketknife. The blade was bloody and the blood still felt wet.

No no no no no

The blade itself when opened was about six or eight inches long.

This is not happening

Jake once again examined the blood covering his pants and his Doc Martens.

What the—

He looked around. What if a car came?

Yeah, they'll pick me up looking like this.

Without hesitating he headed into a cornfield and ran for several minutes until he was deep inside. Then he kneeled and began to dig like a madman. When he'd made a hole several feet deep, he dropped the knife down and covered it over.

God please help me please God

But something told him he was alone on this. He'd been alone and wasn't getting any help from anybody. Except maybe his friends, wherever they were.

➤➤ ◄◄

Jake had walked for an hour along the side of the road and seen only two cars. One was a truck that flew past and the other a station wagon that he didn't look at. Then the sound of an oncoming car made him slow down. It began to honk when it got within sight of him.

Jake recognized Alec's Jeep. He stopped and just watched as the Jeep skidded to a stop and the passenger door was flung open. Alec rained curses down on him.

"Where have you been?" he yelled. "I've been trying to find you for the last three hours!"

"I don't know," Jake said, his voice hoarse and weak.

"Get in the car!"

"Where've you been?"

"Where've *I* been? What about— What's all over your pants and shoes? And what's with your hands? Have you been digging?"

Jake climbed into the Jeep. "What happened last night?"

Alec shook his head and cursed.

"Is everybody okay?"

"Everybody's fine. Where've you been?"

"I woke up in Bruce's car."

"Where is it?"

"It needs gas."

"We gotta clean you up. You look awful." Alec was speeding down the road, looking ahead. "What do you remember?"

"Nothing," Jake said.

"Nothing as in . . . ?"

"Nothing as in nothing. Blackness. Nothing. The last thing I remember is sitting around the fire."

Alec swore. "And you say I got a problem."

"What happened?"

"Just chill for now, okay? The guys are waiting for us at the camp."

"Who?"

"Bruce, Shane, and Mike. Shane's like you—he got plowed last night. Passed out in a field."

"Where are Carnie and Franklin?"

"They left already."

They came to a stop sign, and Alec turned right.

"You know where you're going?"

"I got acquainted with these roads this morning."

"Alec, just tell me—"

"Just shut up and relax. Look in that bag in the backseat. I've got some clothes. Grab a shirt. And get rid of those jeans."

"Where'd this blood come from?"

"Things went bad," Alec said. "That's all I know. For a while, we even thought—we were wondering if you were dead. Look, we gotta meet up with the rest of the guys before anything else happens."

"This isn't a joke, is it?" Jake said, putting on the T-shirt.

Alec looked at him with wild bloodshot eyes and the gaze of a sniper. "I swear to God this isn't a joke."

"Then how'd this happen?"

"I don't know. It was just—it was a long night. It got totally out of hand."

"Did anybody get hurt?"

Alec arrived at a gas station and parked at the side of the small building,

"You need to get cleaned up, okay? And you need to relax. I'm going to get some gas."

Jake wiped his eye with a muddy finger. Everything was intense and extreme and he felt like it wouldn't turn down, like the volume and the rage in his head would not silence.

"Tell me one thing," he said, afraid even to ask but having to.

"No. I said go clean up."

Jake broke down and started to cry. "I'm scared," he said.

"Yeah, I know," Alec said, putting his hand on Jake's shoulder. "Look, man. You're still half drunk. It's going to be fine."

"No, it's not. No way it's ever going to be."

Alec looked intense but didn't appear worried.

"Jake, come on. Just do what I tell you, and things will be fine."

He was going to tell Alec about the knife, but he couldn't.

"Does this—does this have anything to do—"

Alec knew where he was going and nodded. "Don't say his name. Don't. Clean up and let's get out of here."

Jake prayed that Brian Erwin was still alive.

➤➤ ◂◂

They gassed up Bruce's car and drove it back to the campground. Jake took Carnie's .45 and put it in Alec's bag. Alec didn't seem surprised.

Back at the campsite, the three guys were waiting in silence, knowing something was very wrong. Bruce came up to him. "You took off with my car, man. I had no idea where you went."

"Sorry."

"I'm just glad you're okay."

"Let's go!" Alec said. "Jake, come with me. You guys ride with Bruce."

In the Jeep, Jake asked why Carnie and Franklin had gone home earlier.

"They left me to clean up the mess. You know Franklin. He doesn't want to be around if things get too messy."

"How messy are they?"

Alec looked over at him. "Like I said, just do what I say from here on out." He grabbed a beer from behind his seat. "Want one?"

"I'm giving it up," Jake said.

His friend only laughed and popped open the can.

They rode back along the interstate through the Midwestern flatland, the radio blaring to prevent any words spoken between them. Nirvana's "All Apologies" played.

The song ended, and the DJ announced that Kurt Cobain, lead singer of Nirvana and the spokesperson of their generation, had been found dead in his Seattle home that morning.

"I guess this is a good morning to die," Alec said, almost to himself, gazing ahead at the street and lost in his own world.

THIRTY-EIGHT

June 2005

I ENTERED MY MOTEL room and went straight toward the bathroom. The large cup of coffee had worked its way through my system. I came out and headed toward my bed when I got a jolt similar to the one I had given Alyssa.

"That bed doesn't look slept in," a familiar voice said out of nowhere.

I jerked my head toward the unlit corner of the room where a chair stood, now occupied.

"Now you might say you made it before going out this morning, but I highly doubt it."

My heart was pounding, and I froze, looking at the outline of the figure. I flicked on a light.

"Long time," Alec said, a devilish smile on his face.

"What are you doing here?" I asked him, still standing ten feet away from him.

"The real question is, what are *you* doing *here?* I mean, come on. A guy gives you an all-expenses-paid trip down Memory Lane, and you check into this crummy motel? Man, I'd be at the Ritz downtown."

"Tell me one thing and one thing only," I said, trying to be as controlled with my emotions as possible. "Tell me you had nothing to do with Bruce last night."

Alec looked the same after eleven years. His hair was cut very short and he looked tanned, his white teeth standing out on a dark complexion. His face looked thinner, healthier than I remembered. But the same smirk and reckless abandon lingered in his dark brown eyes.

"I could say I didn't, but would you believe me?" He cursed. "All this time, and you still don't trust me."

"I don't even know you."

Alec's smile disappeared for a moment, and he looked genuinely hurt. "The answer is no. Of course not. I didn't have anything to do with Bruce getting shot."

"Then why are you here?" I asked him. "And how'd you know he got shot?"

"Why are *you* here? That's the pertinent question."

"Looking for your sorry tail."

"Didn't have much luck, did you?"

"Alec, this is not a joke."

Alec nodded. "Bruce, by the way, is doing better."

"How do you know that?"

"Because I just came from the hospital."

"Where've you been?"

"Around. You know, all this nonsense about trying to find me. It really wasn't that difficult, you know."

"Where's Claire?"

Alec stood up and laughed. "She's not around, that's all I've got to say about that."

We faced each other for a moment. I felt unsure what he was going to do. A part of me wondered if he was carrying a gun, if I needed to be worried.

"Look at you, man," Alec said, shaking his head.

"What?"

"You look scared. Scared of me."

"Should I be?"

"Man, I'm disappointed in you. Seriously disappointed."

"Coming from you, that means absolutely nothing."

"Well, at least you're honest." Alec crossed the room and opened the door.

"Where are you going?"

"Giving you some space. Don't worry—I'm not going any-where."

"Uh-uh—no way," I said, starting to follow him out.

Alec looked me over. "Take a shower—you look like you need one. I'll be in my rental car."

"What? Just waiting?"

"I'm the one who found you, Jake. Just—just stop being all jumpy." Alec cursed. "Man, I thought you'd be a little more ex-cited to see me."

"I just don't want you to disappear."

"Don't worry, I won't."

"And why is that?"

"'Cause there's stuff you need to know. It's time to tell you everything."

THIRTY-NINE
April 1994

JAKE STILL FELT GUILTY, but he wasn't sure why.

It was Tuesday when he drove back to the apartment after going to see his parents for a few days. He told them he needed laundry done and a good home-cooked meal and a quiet place to study, but the truth was that he simply wanted to get away from everything. From the guys, from the school, from the memory of waking up in the back of Bruce's car covered in blood and carrying a stained knife. As if getting away might cover everything, like burying the knife deep in a hole.

Ever since arriving at his parents' late Saturday night, Jake kept wondering if somebody was going to call. If the police were going to pound on the door. If something was going to come out. He still didn't know what had happened, but he knew it had something to do with Brian. And his imagination had been running rampant.

Now he would find out the truth. Whatever it was.

Arriving at his apartment on this rainy morning, Jake just wanted to wake up and find that this all was a bad dream, or a mistake that he would have to get suspended for and then move on.

What exactly happened?

That was what bothered him the most. He had ideas—he

could conjure up a hundred different scenarios. But none of them were good.

➤➤ ◄◄

No one was at the apartment, so Jake grabbed his backpack full of books and headed off to his eleven o'clock class. Franklin and Carnie would be there. He had not seen either since drinking with them at the campfire.

He got to class and sat next to Carnie.

"Where've you been?" his roommate asked.

"I went home."

"You should tell people."

"Yeah, sorry."

"Franklin disappeared too."

"What do you mean?"

"He took off and nobody's seen him."

"We gotta talk," Jake said. "Let's go to Four-leaf Clover tonight."

"I'm partied out," Carnie said.

"Yeah, me too. Just to go somewhere we can talk."

Jake didn't hear a word the professor said. He doodled in his notebook and thought about the camping trip and looked over at Carnie. His friend's face said it all. Worry, fear, anger.

After class, Jake walked with him to his next class. "Carnie, man, tell me what happened."

"I know as much as you do."

"I'm worried," Jake said.

"You need to talk to Alec."

"Does this have to do with the—with the practical joke?"

"Is that what it was?"

Carnie kept walking, and Jake grabbed his arm. His big friend stopped and looked angry enough to launch a punch at him.

"I'm going to class."

"Carnie, man, I'm afraid. I mean did something happen— do we need to —"

"Tonight, okay? Not here. Act normal. That's what Alec said. Got it?"

"I'm just freaking—I mean, what if —"

Carnie put up a hand. "It'll be fine. I'll see you tonight."

>> <<

The apartment was still empty when Jake returned. He knew Carnie and Kirby were at the college. He wasn't sure about Bruce.

He turned on the stereo for background noise and the television to give him something to stare at. But he still felt empty and alone.

What'd I do?

The more he replayed events from that day and that night, the more hazy they became. It wasn't like some memory from childhood, buried beneath two decades of more vivid recollections. This section of tape was just not there. It had never been recorded, had never been edited, was unable to delete.

He wanted to just get up and go. Climb into his car and drive. But it wouldn't help anything, and he didn't know where he would go.

A phone call got him off the couch.

"Where've you been?" It was Bruce.

"I went to my parents.'"

"You had everybody worried."

"Sorry."

"I just wanted to see if you were back."

"Can you make it to Four-leaf Clover tonight? I want all the guys to get together."

"I don't think that's such a good idea. We need to lie low for a while."

"Bruce—you gotta tell me what happened out there."

"I can't."

"Why—why can't you?"

"Look, I don't know anything either. I just—you guys disappeared, and the next day everybody acted funky."

"What's the last thing you remember?"

"I can't talk about this now. Later. I'll be there, okay?"

The silence punished Jake. He felt like the rest of the world

222

was going on as normal outside, and he was bearing the weight of some horrible awful sin.

I believe Satan has used you in a mighty way. President Bramson's words were now ridiculing him. He was probably right.

He's just waiting to see me get in trouble. Just like Alyssa. And my parents. And everybody else.

➤➤ ◀◀

On a night when he'd decided he really wouldn't drink, Jake had already polished off three beers by the time Alec showed up.

"Big gang," Alec said with a smile, looking around at the empty seats.

"Where've you been?"

"Where have *you* been?"

"My parents' house."

Alec ordered a beer. "So how you doing? I see you're off the wagon." Alec's fiendish grin looked particularly scary tonight.

"Alec, I'm dying here."

"Yeah, I bet."

"What am I supposed to think?"

"About?"

Jake pounded the beer on the table and cursed.

Alec seemed unfazed. "You went camping with the guys," he said. "You tied one on. And I mean *really* tied one on. Major bender. Ended up running around in the cornfields at night. Took off in Bruce's car and spent the night in it. You woke up the next day and you came home. End of story."

"What about —"

"End of story," Alec repeated.

Jake finished his beer and ordered another. "It's really not, is it?"

"For you, for now, yes, it is."

The door to the mostly empty bar opened and Carnie ambled in, smoking a cigarette. His forehead and shoulders were wet. "It's been raining all day," he said, taking off his coat. "No pitcher?"

"You can get one."

Carnie obliged and sat down, exhaling. "Where is everybody?"

"I think we're it," Alec said.

Carnie nodded. "Doesn't surprise me."

"I'm doing a little one-on-one counseling over here."

Jake cursed. "You guys are screwing with my head."

"No, *you're* screwing with your head. You gotta relax."

Jake wanted to grab Alec's head and shake it, to just force him to tell the truth. But nobody could get the truth out of Alec if he didn't want to go there.

"Where's Franklin?"

"I haven't seen him since the trip," Alec said.

"Parents', I think." Carnie poured himself a cup of beer.

"You guys worried?"

"About what?" Alec asked.

Jake shook his head and filled a cup with beer. He was actually beginning to feel a little better now that the alcohol was kicking in.

"You better get the story straight and stick to it," Alec said.

As usual, Carnie just sat back and smoked.

"What if I don't exactly know what that story is?" Jake asked.

"I just told you. You went camping. You had a bunch of beers. You woke up the next day and you came home. That's the story. Any additional information is unnecessary. Even where you woke up. Wandering around in the country. What you were wearing."

"And all of you guys?"

Alec shrugged. "Shane passed out cold. He's worse than you in terms of memory. We shouldn't have bought that tequila. José Quervo did a number on us, didn't he?"

Carnie didn't smile.

The door opened again, and Mike came rushing in. He sat down at the table without taking off his wet coat. "Did you guys hear?"

"Why don't you be a little more loud?" Alec said.

"Sorry. I just—you want to know the buzz?"

"I can only guess," Alec replied.

"What?" Jake said, his stomach suddenly feeling queasy.

"Brian Erwin. He's missing."

FORTY

June 2005

THE BAR AND GRILL was named Tommy's, and I entered to find Alec in a booth. He'd agreed to meet me here after I showered.

"I'm still here," he said, waving up his hands as if I were the police. "What'll you have?"

I saw the bottle of beer on the table. "It's not even noon."

"I had to bribe this out of them. Don't let my efforts go to waste."

"I'm not thirsty."

"I sure am."

I sat in the booth across from him. The bar looked and smelled like a hangover. It was a Friday morning, and the Thursday night crowd must have been obnoxious.

"Remember Shaughnessy's?"

I nodded.

"Well?" he asked.

"Well, what?"

"This is where it used to be."

"What? Here?"

"They tore the building down and put this up. Sorta smells the same, if you ask me." A grin filled his face.

"The area looks different."

"A lot of things change with time," he said. Alec's gaze didn't waver as he took a sip of beer.

"Where'd you take Claire?"

"Why this fascination with someone you don't even know?"

"I have my reasons."

"Yeah, I know. Mr. Father-knows-best Jelen paying you to find me. Yeah, that's right. I knew from the beginning."

"So why didn't you just save everybody the time and the headache and say where you were?"

"Nah. I wanted to see where it would go."

"Bruce is in a hospital thanks to you."

"Don't blame me," Alec said.

"I don't trust a word you're saying."

"Did you ever?"

"Yeah, once I did."

Alec cursed at me. "You know that's crazy. You didn't trust a word I said at the end of college."

"Disappearing didn't really endear you to anybody, you know. It's hard to trust somebody whose best trait is running."

"Nobody ran."

"Oh, you ran. You got your tail outta there when the going got rough. By the way—I'm not sure if you got the memo, but Carnie died."

"Cute." He gave me a venomous glare.

"No, it wasn't cute. You want me to describe to you in all the grisly detail how I found him?"

Alec bit his lip and looked away. I'd finally gotten his attention.

"Were you around at all?" I continued. "I don't know when you found out, but did you ever bother to call? I mean—I don't care, it was a long time ago. But at the time, it hurt. One of the few people who was in my shoes was missing. Because that's what you do best—go missing."

He shook his head. "Carnie was not my fault."

"'Bruce isn't my fault. Carnie wasn't my fault. Claire isn't my fault.' Do you see a pattern here? You've got a problem, pal."

"You're the one with the problem."

"Not anymore. I was just on the phone with your—with your whatever—your future father-in-law. And I said enough. I said I was done."

"No, you're not."

"Oh, yes, I am. All of this—it's over. You can keep running and keep trying to tell yourself it's okay."

"You have all the answers, don't you?" Alec asked, glaring at me.

"Who's saying that?"

"It's easy to judge now, isn't it?"

"Why don't you tell me what happened, Alec? Tell me everything. Let's have the conversation we should have had years ago."

He drained his beer and waved to the waiter to bring him another.

"That's not going to help," I said.

"This—this—" he said, holding up his empty bottle and waving it in my face, "is the only way I'll be able to tell you anything."

"That weak, huh?"

"Yeah, okay, maybe so. But look at Bruce. Look at Franklin —or Mike. Look at you. All of us have lost ourselves in our own little worlds. We all have ways of coping."

"Coping?"

"Yeah. What? Going off to the Himalayas and finding God on the top of a mountain—what, that's not coping?"

"You read about that in the Providence magazine?"

"I know more about you than you think."

"Everybody knows more than I know. And I'm getting really sick of it."

"Just—just give me a little time."

I stared at him. "What's a little more time?"

"You've waited eleven years. What's another few hours going to be?"

I stared at this guy, this stranger across from me, not knowing what to think. I didn't believe a word he said, yet I still wanted to hear those words. Maybe he'd make me believe him again.

Maybe.

➤➤ ◄◄

The sun had set on a tiring day, and I sat in a lounge in Chicago with Alec drinking beers. We had spent a couple hours at Tommy's, playing some pool and eventually having lunch. Then we decided to drive downtown and go to a couple of places before seeing Bruce. Alec was well on his way to being gone, and there was no stopping it. I figured I'd at least have a couple beers to get my nerves at ease.

It was interesting seeing Alec, watching him pound beers with complete abandon. Interesting because I wondered if that's what I used to be like, how I used to act. The coherent and smug guy from the morning slowly became cynical and annoyed.

Finally, in the evening, after I'd actually bummed a cigarette from Alec, perhaps out of boredom, perhaps out of desperation, my frustration boiled over.

"Is this fun for you?" I asked.

"What?"

"This. All of this. Me having to ask you fifty times to tell me what's going on."

"What do you think is going on?"

"I think that someone wants to find you and that someone else doesn't want you found."

"That's logical. You're a logical sort of guy, you know."

"You're becoming worthless."

"And you're becoming a nag," Alec said.

"Did you have anything to do with Bruce getting shot?"

A shadow fell over Alec's face. "Do you think I did?"

"I have no idea."

"Yeah, you do."

"Did you kill Brian Erwin?"

"Wow."

The name and the question shocked even a drunk Alec.

228

"That's all I want to know."

"You didn't have to wait eleven years for the answer to that."

An attractive woman walked by but Alec just glared at me, his eyes cold and narrow.

"What happened to him?"

"Whose story are you going to believe?"

"Franklin said you were the one behind it."

"Really? There's a shocker."

"Yeah. Who do you think I should believe?"

"Why do you think I left?"

"Because you were scared."

"Wrong."

"You were the hero then?"

"Carnie was falling apart, and you were too much of a mess to even notice. And don't look like that. Come on, Jake. Get off your high horse. You're pathetic. You're a hypocrite the same way those phonies were at Providence, the ones we used to mock."

"Not all of them were hypocrites."

"Listen to you. Listen. Can you hear it? The manure spewing out of your mouth."

"At least I'm not slurring my words."

"At least I can remember spring break. Yeah, that's right. If you hadn't been so deep in your own personal blackout, you'd remember. You'd know. And maybe, just maybe, Brian would be alive."

"Shut your face," I said.

"Oh, now you don't want to hear about anything? Tell me something. Who picked you up on the side of the road? When you came out of your binge? Who cleaned you up?"

"It's interesting that out of everyone there, you're the one who knew what was going on."

"And that's supposed to mean what?" Alec said, his voice loud enough for a few women sitting at a table nearby to glance our way.

"Brian went missing, and nobody heard about him ever again. Not even after the cops interrogated us. I told them everything I could. I didn't have anything to do with his disappearance."

"Oh, so then I must be the one? Right? You're pathetic. I don't know why I'm sitting here."

"I had a right to know—"

"We were protecting you! How stupid can you be? Don't you get that?"

"Protecting me how? What would I have done?"

"Told the cops. Or little Miss Princess. Or God knows who. You were weak then and you're still weak now."

"You've turned into a mean drunk," I told him. "You never used to be this way."

"And you've turned into a crushing bore."

I finished the beer I was drinking. "Tell me about Claire."

"Tell me about Alyssa."

"Been spying on me?"

"Ask Bruce," Alec said.

"About what?"

"Ask Bruce about me. See what he says."

"What's that mean?"

"That means that your little friend who's been tagging along with you—who you're asking if I helped *gun down*—he's been actually keeping tabs on you."

"For *you*? Why would Bruce be spying for you?"

"Why would my best friend get paid to come hunting for me?"

"Why are you hiding from Jelen?"

"Questions, questions, questions." He cursed again. "Did you see him? Did you? You think a guy like him wants me to have anything to do with his daughter?"

"I don't much blame him."

Alec smirked. "That's friendship."

"Where is she?"

"Would you relax with the questions? I'm getting tired of hearing my own voice, much less yours. This whole day has tired me out."

"Then why are you here?"

Alec shook his head. "Because of my friend. Because of Bruce. I was worried about him."

"Just like you were worried about Carnie, right?"

"No. I learned my lesson that time. That's never going to happen again."

"Bruce might die," I said. "There's nothing you can do about it."

"I can be there if he does."

But I wasn't ready to go back home. Not yet. Not until I knew whether Bruce would be okay.

FORTY-ONE

April 1994

YOU SEE THE GUY with his arms tied behind him wrapped in layers of construction tape. A single silver piece is over his mouth. His eyes are wide open and he breathes in through enlarged nostrils hungry for air. He's in the backseat and you grab his shoulder and he stumbles out on the ground.

"Get over here," you tell him.

He gets to his feet and looks at you and mouths something underneath the tape and you tell him to shut up. This only makes him scream louder.

And for a second, you look behind you. Then you look back, and he's taken off, sprinting toward the cornfield. You go off after him, shouting for him to stop.

And then you're in rows of corn, much higher than you remember them being. You're following the trail and the noise.

You look down in your hand and see that you're carrying a knife.

And that's the image Jake always has when he wakes up, out of breath, gasping for air.

That's what keeps him from sleeping again.

→→ ←←

"Okay, I just need a little information from you," the deputy said to Jake in a casual, routine manner.

Jake didn't remember this guy from his prior visit to the police station. This deputy, a guy named Jim Doogan, was maybe in his thirties, lean with a friendly smile. Nothing about his body language or his attitude said that he suspected Jake of causing Brian's disappearance.

"This is just a formality, as I told you on the phone. We've already spoken to a few of your friends."

Jake nodded and breathed in. He could feel his heart pumping.

First, Jim Doogan asked him a bunch of questions he had already answered several times before, about the home invasion and the beating. Jake recounted them without emotion.

"So where were you the first week in April?"

"That's spring break," Jake said. "I was around our apartment for the most part. We decided to go camping Thursday and Friday nights."

"Much of a camper?"

Jake feigned a smile and a chuckle. "Not at all. Hardly ever do it."

"And what'd you guys do while you were camping?"

"For the most part? Drink."

"Several campers in the area said you guys were pretty intoxicated."

Jake nodded.

"Did you have any interaction with Brian Erwin that week?"

Jake shook his head.

"When was the last time you saw him?"

"On campus sometime."

"Did you talk with him?"

"I avoided him."

"He never came up to you—said anything to you? Or any of his friends?"

Again, Jake shook his head.

Calm. Steady. Tell them everything you know. Just as easy as that.

"What's your general feeling about Brian Erwin?"

I like him a lot. He's swell.

Jake knew now wasn't the time for sarcasm.

"Can't say I really liked the guy. Since he nearly killed me and basically got away with it."

The policeman nodded, almost as if in agreement.

"But you have had no interaction with him since then?"

Jake thought of the voice mail and almost told the cop about it. But that muddied up the already filthy waters. No point in bringing that up.

Especially since Brian Erwin had been missing for two weeks.

They talked for another ten minutes, then Doogan thanked Jake for coming. "What is the best place to reach you at if we need to ask you anything else?"

Jake said his apartment and then left, relieved and hopeful that this was all he needed to do.

→→ ←←

The phone was ringing when he opened his apartment door.

"Yeah?"

"What'd you tell them?"

It was Franklin. No greeting, no explanation, nothing except the urgent question.

"How'd you know—?"

"Carnie told me."

"I told them what I know."

"And what is that?"

"Where're you calling from?"

"Just tell me."

Jake cursed. "You've disappeared off the face of the planet."

"No, I haven't. I just want to know what you said."

Jake recounted his explanation. "That good enough for you?" Then he asked, "Where'd you go? That morning?"

Franklin's voice sounded remote. "I had to be back home to study."

Jake laughed in disbelief. "Franklin—"

"Alec says you're breaking down on us."

"What's that mean?"

"It means exactly what it's supposed to mean."

"I just want someone to be honest with me."

"I'm being honest."

"I want one of my friends, one of my *friends,* to simply tell me the truth."

"You don't get it, even after everything Alec's told you."

"Don't get what?"

There was silence in the phone, and Jake shouted his question again.

"We're looking out for you, Jake. You might not see that, but we are."

Jake wasn't sure what to say.

"Just hang in there, okay? Everything's going to be fine."

➤➤ ◄◄

Music has this way of making you drown out life's worries and warts. Music and booze.

This was what Jake was thinking about as he submerged himself in both.

"I wish I could've gone to the memorial service."

"Huh?" Jake asked Mike.

"For Kurt Cobain."

"Oh, yeah."

"Can you believe it?"

"No," Jake said as an afterthought. "There's a lot I can't believe these days."

The music at Shaughnessy's was louder than usual as their playlist honored Cobain's memory. It had been two weeks since spring break and the camping trip and since Brian Erwin had officially gone missing. The local Chicago news stations had picked up the story and gave daily updates on the progress of the search for Brian.

"That's my favorite song, I think," Mike said, as the jukebox started playing "Come As You Are."

235

"Mike," Jake said above the music. "Just here. Just one time. Tell me what happened that night?"

"Come on, man." Mike shook his head. "It's no good."

"You know I tell you everything."

"Sure. I do too. It's just . . ."

The place was crowded. Jake and Mike were in no fear of someone overhearing their conversation; they could barely hear each other.

"You guys took him, didn't you? That night?"

"Jake . . ."

"Didn't you?" Jake shouted. "Just tell me."

"Of course we did."

"Who?"

"Franklin, Carnie, me."

"How—did anybody see you?"

Mike shook his head. "No. It was late. You guys were back at camp. We deliberately got you loaded so you wouldn't suspect anything. Alec stayed back with you."

"But how?"

"He was going to his car. Parked in the distant lot on campus."

"How'd you get him to go with you?"

"He was heading to work. Late shift on the garbage truck. Franklin knew about it."

"So what'd you do?"

"Nothing. I mean, we tied him up with duct tape and brought him out."

"Then what happened?"

"Jake, come on. I swore."

"To who?"

"To Franklin."

"I'm glad to see where your loyalty is."

"This has nothing to do with loyalty!" Mike shouted and drank his beer. "I'm telling you. Franklin warned us not to say anything. He said that—he said it would protect you."

Jake's stomach felt sick. "Come on, Mike. What happened then?"

"I don't know. I just—he got away. And I . . ."

"What? What do you mean he got away?"

"It's really blurry," Mike said.

"Don't lie to me."

"I'm not. I swear. It was insane. I mean, I don't think things were ever as out of hand as that night. You were—you were pretty gone. And Alec—he had the grand plan, you know. And Carnie—everybody was just so messed up."

"I know."

"I mean, *really* gone. I was pretty freaked out by everything. You ended up disappearing. Alec went missing. Franklin. Carnie. Bruce."

"That's great."

"I'm telling you what I know."

Jake looked at Mike and knew he was telling the truth. "Just tell me one thing," he said.

"What?"

"How'd you get that cut on your hand?"

Mike shook his head. "I don't know."

"Come on."

"I swear, man, I don't know."

Jake stared off at the bar. His thoughts were random and heavy and he couldn't sort them out.

"Jake?"

"Yeah?"

"That guy had it coming."

"Nobody deserves to . . ."

Mike looked at him and nodded. "Maybe he, maybe he just went missing."

"And what?" Jake asked. "He's going to come back around?"

"Franklin would kill me if he knew I told you this."

"I don't know anything more than I already knew."

"Jake—this is serious."

"Think I don't know that?"

"It's serious for you."

"No. It's serious for all of us."

Mike took a drink and watched Jake, waited for his response.

"We all have to live with what happened. All of us. This isn't going to go away."

"I know."

237

They listened to the fierce music and kept drinking.

Jake remembered opening the door to his apartment and seeing Brian Erwin and Chad Hoving standing there, waiting for him.

Grabbing him and punching him and kicking him.

He didn't deserve this, Jake thought. *No matter what happened to me, he didn't deserve this.*

"Hey," Mike said.

"What?"

"Can I get you another beer?"

"Get some shots. I need to get rid of this."

"Get rid of what?"

"This guilt."

FORTY-TWO

June 2005

I STOOD AT THE END of Bruce's hospital bed while Alec sat in a chair on the other side. Bruce was conscious, but he didn't react when we walked into the room. His hair was slicked back, and he looked tired and pale. Tubes were attached to his arm, and he breathed slowly.

"Doing okay, buddy?" Alec asked him.

Bruce looked at him in slow motion, his eyes reminding me of a hundred nights spent with him completely stoned.

"Who did this?" Bruce said in barely more than a whisper.

"Who did you see?" I couldn't help asking him, wanting to speak before Alec could.

"I don't know. No one I knew."

"You're going to be okay," Alec said.

"They didn't know how to contact your parents," I said.

Alec shot an angry glare at me. "His mother passed away a few years ago."

"Alec . . ." Bruce murmured, still wanting an answer.

"I don't know."

"Why?" Bruce asked him.

"I think you know why."

"Do you know why?" I asked Alec.

"You *still* think I had something to do with this?" Alec cursed in frustration. "Bruce, tell him. Go on, tell him."

"What?" Bruce asked, his voice weak and quiet.

"Get him off my tail."

"Jake—get off his tail."

Alec looked at me and couldn't help laughing. "No—tell him the truth."

"About?"

"Did I trash your place? Or knock Jake out? Or do this to you?"

"Maybe you should've just let me find you," I said to Alec, "and none of this would have happened."

Bruce said he was thirsty, and Alec gave him a cup of water from the table next to the bed.

"It's nobody's business what I do with my life," Alec said. "Not yours, not Jelen's, not Claire's, nobody's."

"I'm not going back home," Bruce whispered.

I wondered if he was referring to Redding.

Alec stood beside Bruce and gently brushed back his hair, the way a father might do with his child. He glanced at me, and for the first time that day, I trusted him. Something about that act and that look said that he genuinely cared about Bruce, that he wouldn't have done something like this, that it wasn't his fault.

The phone in my pocket vibrated. I picked it up.

"You're there—Jake, where are you?"

It was Alyssa. She sounded terrified.

"What's wrong?"

"A man came by tonight. To my house. I didn't mean to open the door, but I thought it was you surprising me, so stupid me I opened the door—"

"Are you okay?" I barked out, already heading toward the hospital exit.

"I think—I don't know. I called the police."

"Is he gone? Did he hurt you?"

"He just threatened me. He came inside my house—and told me to call you."

I was running, keeping the cell phone to my ear as I made my way down a hallway.

"You called the cops?"

"Yes."

"Okay. Just—what'd he say?"

There was a pause.

"Alyssa?"

"He told me that if you didn't leave—he would come back. And that he wouldn't—" She was crying now.

"Alyssa, are you all right?"

"He said that he wouldn't leave me untouched."

I was outside now and heading to the parking garage. "I'm going to be there in a few minutes. Just hang tight."

"Jake? What's going on?"

"I don't exactly know. But I think I finally understand who's behind this."

"I'm scared."

"Just—don't say anything to the police."

"About what?" she asked.

"About me. Just say—say a guy came over and threatened you."

"Are you in danger?"

"I think so. But I won't be for long. I promise you that."

I was pulling out of the parking garage when a figure darted in front of the car. I jammed on the brakes and saw Alec waving me down.

"Where are you dashing off to?" he asked after I rolled my window down.

"Someone threatened Alyssa."

I saw the look change on his face. It grew more grim. I still didn't know what he was thinking, but he appeared surprised.

"I swear—if something happens to her—"

"What do you want me to do?" Alec asked.

"You've done enough."

"How can I prove I didn't have anything to do with this? With Bruce. Or Alyssa."

"Show me."

"And if I do—then what?"

241

"I don't know," I said. "I just—I gotta go."

"Give me your cell number."

I listed off the numbers as Alec saved them in his phone.

"I'll call you in a little while," he said.

"What for?"

"For proof. For answers."

FORTY-THREE

May 1994

EVERYTHING WAS DIFFERENT. Everyone and everything.

Except maybe Bruce. He seemed like the only one who *hadn't* changed after a month of lies, secrets, and silence.

"You gotta stop smokin' that stuff," Jake said, coming out of the bathroom.

"Huh?" Bruce said.

"There's a bong in our tub."

"Oh, sorry 'bout that."

Bruce lay on the couch smoking a cigarette, his eyes droopy and barely able to stay open. Jake wondered what the guy's lungs looked like.

"That's making your mind go to mush."

"Yeah, I know," Bruce said.

"You seen Carnie?" Jake asked.

"Nah."

"He's never around anymore."

"Nobody is."

"I'm worried about him."

Bruce looked at him with the same absent expression.

I'm trying to have a deep conversation with a guy who's been stoned out of his mind for the last two weeks.

"Never mind," Jake said.

"Sure thing," Bruce said.

Maybe it would be better that way, Jake thought. *Maybe that's what I need to get through these last few weeks of school.*

Bruce didn't seem to notice when Jake said good-bye.

⇥ ⇤

He was walking from class when he saw her.

So the rumors were true.

Alyssa walked alongside a tall guy he had only seen but didn't know. He was a jock. Probably had been friends with Brian Erwin. He was good-looking with short hair and a smile he flashed as he spoke to Alyssa.

They held hands as they walked.

Wonderful, Jake thought.

He tried to find a way to go the other direction without Alyssa seeing him. But her dark eyes spotted him. By the time the couple reached him, they had stopped holding hands. Jake passed them and simply nodded. Alyssa looked as if she wanted to say something, but the guy she was with continued talking.

Jake kept walking for a few moments until he heard Alyssa's voice call out his name.

He stopped and turned around. She was standing there alone. Her boyfriend or friend or guy or whatever was still walking toward the classroom building.

"Hey," she said. "I haven't seen you for a while."

"I've been trying to be a diligent student to finish out my Providence career."

She looked at him as if to study his face. "Things going okay?"

"Never been better," Jake said, trying to make a joke. It came out sounding hollow.

God, what it would be to tell someone—to tell her—the truth.

"Jake—the last time we talked—"

"Don't worry about it," Jake said, giving his best smile as if he had moved on.

"I'm sorry."

"No need to apologize. It's fine. No big deal."

244

Alyssa didn't believe it, and Jake knew she didn't. The truth was out there, and it was awkward and it hurt. He liked someone who didn't like him. That was reality.

It used to matter. Now things like that seemed trivial.

"Still acing those classes?" Jake asked.

"Sure, I guess," she said, not wanting to change the subject.

"I better go. You know. Big brother is watching."

Alyssa looked as though there was more she wanted to say, but she just nodded. She forced a smile and told him to take care.

Take care, he thought. *Yeah. Sure.*

⤐ ⤙

"Get in the car."

Jake looked at the Jeep that had pulled up on the grass next to the sidewalk and saw Alec behind the wheel. He looked like a wreck. Dark stubble covered his face and his hair looked more spiked than usual. There were huge rings beneath his eyes.

Jake kept walking. "I got class."

"Get in the car now!"

A freshman girl passing by looked at Jake. He opened the door and climbed in.

"You moron," he said to Alec.

"Why don't you shut your hole and just listen, okay?" Alec tore out of the college driveway and headed away from the campus.

"Going anywhere in particular?"

"No," Alec said.

"Then why'd you pick me up?"

"You weren't doing anything."

"I was going to class."

Alec cursed.

"Yeah, well, I've got a sinking GPA, and I need to try and do something to resuscitate it."

"It doesn't matter anyway."

"Have you been drinking?" Jake asked, smelling Alec's breath.

245

"Surprised?"

"It doesn't smell like beer."

"Gin usually doesn't."

Jake decided to put on his seat belt, and this amused Alec.

"A little uptight?"

"Alec, come on. What's the deal?"

"What's the deal? What's *my* deal? You're the one who won't hang out, who leaves when I come over, who doesn't want to go out."

"Why should I?"

"That's what friends do."

"Friends are honest with each other," Jake said as Alec swerved into the turnoff lane to get onto the expressway.

"And what are you implying?"

"I'm not implying anything. I'm telling you point-blank."

"You think I've been lying to you this whole time?"

"Yep. You and Franklin and Carnie."

Alec scoffed and sped up. It was around ten, and traffic was light. "Don't compare me to Franklin. I'm nothing like Franklin."

"You're more alike than you know."

Alec's leg jammed down on the accelerator.

"Slow down," Jake said, gripping the armrest.

"All I've done is try to help you."

"That's what Franklin says." Jake looked at the speedometer. They were going over a hundred miles an hour. "I said slow down!"

"You don't believe me, do you?" Alec shouted. "You think I had something to do with Brian's death, don't you?"

"Who said he's dead?" Jake said.

Alec cursed at him again and kept his foot on the gas. "Who's lying now?"

"I don't know what I'd be lying about!" Jake watched the lanes in front of him.

"I picked you up and you were drenched in blood. Am I making that up?"

"Slow down!"

"Didn't I tell you to just shut up and get in the car?"

"But you didn't tell me anything about that night."

Alec turned the wheel and crossed four lanes and ran up along a four-wheeler and then in front of him. They were going 120 miles an hour. The car was shaking, as if it was giving all it could.

"Alec, come on."

Traffic was getting more dense ahead.

"I don't care about any of this. Not a bit, you get that?" Alec shouted.

"Yeah, I get it."

"No, you don't. I don't want you thinking I'm a liar. I don't care—"

"Alec!"

The Jeep swerved and almost careened out of control.

"Remember that time you were driving and almost killed the two of us?" Alec asked.

"Get me out of this car."

"You owe me for that night."

"Yeah, fine, okay."

"Tell me you trust me," Alec said.

The car continued to shake, and Alec veered violently and clipped the back of a Ford.

Jake tried to grab his leg.

"You do that again and I'll let go."

"You're insane."

"Yeah, but I'm not a liar."

"Fine."

"Say that you trust me."

"Fine. I trust you."

"I want you to mean it!"

Alec's intensity terrified Jake.

"I mean it."

Jake jerked the wheel to avoid ramming a car that was going half the speed they were.

"I swear to God, Jake, I don't care—"

"Fine! I believe you!"

"You swear?"

"Slow down!"

Alec looked at him and then jammed on the brakes, making

the Jeep jerk and go sideways for a second. He released the brake, and they continued to drive with the regular traffic.

Jake realized he had been holding the arm of the door for dear life.

"I may be a lot of things, but I'm not a liar," Alec said. "And all I've done is try to help you."

"You're trying to kill us."

"And so what? Would it be any worse than things are now? Would it?"

Jake didn't answer.

"Yeah, that's what I thought," Alec spit out.

It was the last conversation, if it could be called a conversation, that Alec and Jake would have for another ten years. A week later, Alec went missing, just like Brian Erwin. No goodbye, no hint of where he was going, no nothing.

FORTY·FOUR

June 2005

IN THE SANCTUARY of the car, I prayed. The only sounds were the high pitch of the engine pushed to its maximum as I headed south down the interstate.

God please don't let this end bad please God be with Alyssa please protect her

I realized how little I'd prayed recently and how much of a fraud I felt, suddenly tossing up one of those self-serving trench prayers. But there was nothing else I could do between the hospital and Alyssa's house. Even after calling the police myself, making sure they were on their way, I wanted to make sure she was safe. I wanted to make sure

she doesn't end up like Carnie

she was protected and not worried.

I let out a curse in the middle of my prayer and apologized. I was so bad at this, so new. I didn't know what I was doing, and I knew God probably listened to me and thought *What a mess.* But I knew He was watching and listening.

I wished they had a manual for dummies on this whole faith thing. Because I didn't know the right words to say, the right actions to follow. I just knew what I felt and what I believed and the truth of that.

no judgment against anyone who believes

I thought of what Alec had told me about his innocence and wondered how he could prove it to me. Would I ever believe anything he said? I didn't know. All I knew was that I wanted Alyssa to be safe. All I knew was that her danger had been my fault.

Help me to do the right thing, whatever that is. And help her to be okay. Please God. I'll do anything you ask of me. Just keep her safe.

➤➤ ◄◄

When I pulled up to the house, there were two squad cars outside and several cops inside. Alyssa ran toward me and embraced me. She didn't let go for a few minutes, crying into my shoulder.

"Are you okay?" I asked her.

"Now I am."

And I couldn't help thinking this was all my fault. All of it.

I sat with the police for half an hour, not saying anything but listening to them continue to ask Alyssa questions. Eventually they asked her if she had somewhere else to stay for the night.

I thought of my hotel room, but then remembered the stranger pilfering through our stuff and decided against it.

"What about your parents' home?" I asked.

"What am I going to say?"

"Just tell them the truth. Tell them a strange man came to your door acting weird. Tell them you want to stay over."

We left the house with a squad car still outside on the corner. As I followed Alyssa's directions, she asked me what was going on.

"I saw Alec," I told her.

"What? When?"

"Today."

"Does this have anything to do—"

"I think so," I said to her, grabbing her hand and squeezing it tight. "I think it has to do with Bruce, with Alec, with everything."

250

"I didn't know what to say back there—with the police—"

"You told the truth."

"I didn't tell them about you."

"I know."

"Jake—I'm scared."

"You'll be at your parents' in a few minutes."

"No, it's not that."

I looked over at her and saw her haunting gaze.

"What?" I asked.

"I'm scared for you."

"I'm going to be fine. Everything's going to be fine."

The clock on the dashboard read 11:35.

"Don't worry about anything. I promise you—everything's going to be fine. Okay?"

"Why? How do you know?"

"There's stuff I need to tell the cops. About Alec. About—about a lot of things. I need to do it and I need to do it now.

"Will it help?"

I took Alyssa's hand in mine. "I don't know. I just know it's the right thing to do."

FORTY-FIVE
May 1994

JAKE HAD MANAGED TO GET Carnie to come out to the forest preserve with him. This was the same place they had once gotten a pony keg and invited thirty of their fellow underage sophomores to celebrate the warmth of springtime. The same place where an inebriated Alec and Jake had swum across the lake, getting to the middle and feeling their legs cramp up and laughing and wondering if they were going to die in the Summit forest preserve. The same place they had often come for beer and conversation and to pass away the time.

Now Alec was gone. Franklin ignored them. Bruce was high most of the time. Shane was studying like crazy, ready for graduation. Mike was talking about changing schools at the end of the year.

And then there was Carnie. Jake was worried about Carnie. He didn't usually say much, but something was different with him since spring break. Something was different with all of them, sure, but not like Carnie. He carried the look of death on his face. If he caught Jake looking at him, he would just look away, silent and secretive.

Even after a few beers, Carnie wouldn't talk about spring break. But Jake kept hoping that they could get past it. Past Brian's disappearance and the rumors and the secrets and the lies.

It felt like summertime had arrived, and Jake had a nice buzz going and felt the memories of three years here in the woods of this remote location.

"Where do you think you'll be in ten years?" Carnie asked out of the blue.

Jake shrugged, staring up at the sky. "I don't know where I'll be in ten minutes."

"Take a guess."

"My guess is, uh, jail." Jake let out a chuckle, then realized the bad taste of what he had said.

I used to laugh a lot more. Joke a lot more. But there hasn't been much to joke about lately.

"I'm serious," Carnie said.

"I don't know. Doing something outdoors. With people. Having fun. I think I'd die having a nine-to-five job."

"Yeah."

"What about you? What do you see?"

"I don't know what I see anymore."

Jake looked up at Carnie, surprised at his tone. "What do you mean?"

"I just want to get away. But I don't know where to go."

"Come to Europe with us," Jake said.

"That wouldn't help."

"Then what would?"

Carnie was silent for a minute, then he said, "All the stuff they say in class and chapel. The stuff about God and heaven and hell. You believe all that?"

"I don't know. Some of it. I believe in God."

"What if it's really true?"

"About God?"

"About everything. Eternity and hell and damnation and all that."

"That's the stuff I wonder about," Jake said.

"Yeah. Like—how can God really do such a thing, you know? How can He send people to hell? That's what I always wonder, what I can't get my mind through."

"Yeah."

"I was listening to Metallica the other day—"

"Ah, such good taste."

"Their song 'Nothing Else Matters.' And I wondered—does anything matter? Does it really matter if we're drinking beers or having sex with someone we barely know or if someone disappears and nobody knows the story behind it? Does any of it matter in the first place?"

"Are you trying to tell me something?"

"I told you a hundred times, Jake. I don't know what happened."

"You've acted different ever since spring break."

"I know," Carnie said.

Jake watched his friend, took a sip of his beer, and then waved a hand. "I don't know what happened, and frankly, I don't care anymore."

"You believe in that notion of joining your friends in hell?" Carnie asked.

Jake laughed out loud. "You're drunk."

"Maybe. But do you?"

"Do I what?"

"Do you believe it will be better to have a fun time in hell with your friends than spend eternity with a bunch of holier-than-thou people in heaven?"

"This past semester has been a journey into hell," Jake said, trying to make light of the conversation.

"Do you really think there is a hell? Honestly?"

Jake looked at Carnie. He felt like a teenager having a talk with his father about sex.

He didn't want to tell Carnie what he really believed.

In the first place, he didn't know exactly what he believed. But it scared him, just like a lot of things deep down scared him. But he could put a Band-Aid and a case of beer over them and the fears would subside. The fear of tomorrow, the fear of the unknown, the fear of ever after. The fear of what really happened to Brian Erwin.

He had grown adept at ignoring those fears.

"Carnie . . . a week from now, we'll be walking down getting our diplomas, and all this madness will be over and we'll be free."

"Free to do what?"

"Free to be adults. To do whatever we want."

"Haven't we been doing that the last couple of years?"

"You know what I mean," Jake said.

But Carnie seemed distant, lost in his own ocean of doubts and insecurities.

"It'll all work out, man," Jake said.

And he believed it too. That he really, truly believed.

FORTY-SIX

June 2005

"JAKE." ALEC'S VOICE SOUNDED harried on my cell.

"What is it?"

"Where are you?"

"Heading to the cops."

"Jake—"

"It's over. I'm through. With everything."

Alec cursed. "You said you wanted proof."

"Proof of what?"

"I've got it."

I had left Alyssa ten minutes ago. I wasn't exactly sure where I was driving and what I was doing, but I wanted this to be over. Tonight.

"I'm supposed to actually believe you?"

"This one time," Alec said. "One last time."

"I'm tired—"

"Come to the campus."

"To *Providence*?"

"Just meet me there in an hour. And I promise you, you'll understand."

Something in me still believed him. I didn't know why.

Another part of me was scared that Alec's lie would be his last.

I could remember driving these same streets, a different person. It wasn't that long ago. The past decade didn't feel that long. Thirty-three years old didn't feel that old. But I wouldn't have recognized that kid driving that car. I wouldn't have known what to say to him.

Had I been given this chance only to discover the truth about myself? The truth I had suspected all along? That I was guilty, that I was more guilty than I realized? That they had been covering up for my sins. That they had taken the blame for me.

There's only one person who can do that, who's ever done that.

I saw the shimmer of the street lamp. A nearby church I'd never visited still remained on the corner. A restaurant. A health club.

I spent three years existing around here but never really living. Never really opening my eyes to the world around me.

I turned onto the street where the sign said Providence College.

If I could go back, I would. If I could simply go back and try again, I would try harder. I would change and do something good. I would stop ridiculing the so-called phonies I labeled and judged without knowing them. I would finally acknowledge that I couldn't do it alone and that I needed help and that God was the only person who could help me.

Help me now. Help me tonight.

I'd spent so much time running and I'd tried running far away but God had caught up with me

I don't understand why, God. Why me?

It wasn't fair and it wasn't right but that's why it was called grace. I was learning about such things. I'd heard about it but hadn't really understood it until a year ago.

The college parking lot was empty except for a lone car with its headlights on.

Let this be the end, I thought. *Let this be over and done with, regardless of what happens.*

I opened my car door and breathed in the cool summer night.

"This better be good."

The voice I heard belonged to Mike. He turned off his car and opened the door, leaving the parking lot suddenly coated in darkness.

"Alec called you too?" I asked.

"He said I needed to get down to the college. That it was urgent. I figured—after everything with Bruce—is that what this is about?"

"It'd better be."

It was closing in on one o'clock. I watched Mike light up a cigarette.

"This is crazy," he said. "I thought we'd go the rest of our lives without bringing all of this up."

I wanted to reply, but for the moment I leaned against his car looking up at the stars. It was a brief moment of relaxation.

Then I heard the engine approaching and knew Alec was near.

FORTY-SEVEN

May 1994

THE STILLNESS WOKE HIM. A hollow quiet that nudged him and made his subconscious perk up with alarm. His body was slower to follow. The familiar remnants of the past night, of the past four years, covered him like a blanket. The dry mouth, the smoky clothes, the crusted eyes, the pressed skull. Jake looked at the wall and wondered where he was, if he'd slept in his own bed and how he'd managed to get there from the party the night before.

He tried to replay the last memory but it didn't come. He'd gone through this too many times, and now he just didn't care. Sometime between Shelli's graduation party and now, he had lapsed into that too-familiar state. The long tail of a falling night when darkness and silence eclipsed everything.

Jake sat up and tried to get his bearings. He thought of the party, which made him think of toasting graduation, which made him think of the cap and gown, which made him think of

10:30 sharp

The clock said 10:45 a.m.

The class of '94 would be walking in fifteen minutes.

He could make it to school in seven minutes, still have time to adjust his cap onto the gnarly-looking mass of hair sticking over his head, and could smile as he walked and heard his name.

Why didn't his roommates wake him up?

Last night was a blur. This morning was a blur. Everything in the past week had been a blur.

Jake walked to the bathroom. He looked in the mirror and saw a large bruise on his forehead. It looked like he had run into something, or someone, last night. A pipe or a cabinet or who knows what. He shook his head and rubbed his eyes.

He only had a few minutes. He turned on the faucet and took a cup to run water over his face. He quickly brushed his teeth.

Then something caught his eye.

What . . .

He looked to his right and stared into the tub.

The stained plastic shower curtain was half torn off its rings. Something was weighing it down. Maybe someone had been sick and had left a morning surprise in the shower. Maybe that someone had been him.

With one hand still brushing his teeth, Jake casually tried to open the curtain. It wouldn't budge, so he jerked it off its rings.

And saw the wet, white head of Carnie looking at him with blank, open eyes.

Every ounce of strength and life in Jake poured out of him in a gasp as he grabbed Carnie by his wet shirt and tried to pull him up and out of the tub.

His bulky friend weighed too much, and all Jake did was stretch the shirt.

"Carn, come on, man, hey, wake up."

But his words sounded hollow. Carnie's face was dead white and ghostly, and Jake thought the worst. Why not? Why, after everything, wouldn't he think the worst, because the worst had already stopped by their front door and delivered a whole case of hurt and sorrow and misery. Maybe it had stopped again last night and delivered its final present for the year.

The voice, his voice, now surprisingly loud, surprisingly

scary, rose as it called Carnie's name. "Carnie! Come on, man! Come on! Paul, for God's sake, wake up! Paul, wake up!"

And he called out and cursed God and screamed for help and nothing did any remote good. He tried to find a pulse but didn't know where to look and all he knew was that Carnie didn't feel warm, he didn't feel real, he didn't feel *alive*.

And as Jake dialed the phone, he knew his twitchy fingers and his sweaty back and his hoarse voice and his frantic words all meant that this was real, that in the almighty words he and Carnie used to sing together he was alive, truly alive, and that this was a living nightmare that he couldn't wake up from or forget.

He would remember this moment every day for the rest of his life.

FORTY-EIGHT
June 2005

I HEARD A CURSE SHOUTED in the semidarkness and knew it wasn't Alec's voice.

"This your idea, Jake?"

I could see Franklin walking around the car to face Mike and me. Alec turned off the engine and the lights.

"So he got you to come too?" I asked the figure approaching me. "What'd he have to—"

Franklin's fist came out of nowhere and landed awkwardly against my ear. I fell back and gasped out loud.

"Don't try that again," Alec said, now out of the car.

"Or what? You gonna use that?"

Holding my ear in my hand, I looked at Alec and noticed his arm pointed at Franklin.

"Alec—"

"He's got a gun," Mike said to me.

"Everybody just calm down. Jake, you okay?" Alec asked.

"I'd feel better if you told me what you are doing."

"You wanted proof. Here's proof."

I could make out the shadows of their faces under the glow of the moon.

"You're holding a gun," I said. "What sorta proof is that?"

"Tell him," Alec said, still aiming his handgun at Franklin.

"Tell him what?"

"The truth."

"The truth died when Carnie decided to swallow a whole bottle of pills one morning."

"Shut your face," I said to Franklin.

"It was your idea from day one," Alec said. "Go ahead, tell 'em."

"Tell them what?" Franklin asked.

"We were at Shaughnessy's and I said we should do something to get back at Brian, and that's when you devised the plan. It was all you, Frankie."

"I don't recall you objecting," Franklin said.

"I wanted to do it. I thought it was going to be hilarious. I thought it would be a good prank."

"You guys never told me the exact plan," I said.

"You knew," Franklin barked out.

Alec shook his head. "No, he didn't. He was barely functional when I told him. And he was out of it the entire time we were out there."

"And that makes it all okay, right?" Franklin asked.

"You, Mike, and Carnie got him," Alec said.

Franklin didn't say anything.

"Come on. Lay it out. Right now."

"What?" Franklin said. "You gonna beat it out of me?"

"I won't have to," Alec replied.

"And why's that?"

"Because it's over," Alec said. "All of it. It's over."

"What are you talking about? What's over?"

Alec wiped his forehead and looked up at the sky. "I just want to set the record straight. Right here and right now. And then I'm gone, and you'll never hear or see me again."

"Haven't you said that once before?" Franklin asked.

"All of us were responsible in one way or another. It's just time to get the truth out and settle it and go our merry ways."

"Carnie can't speak for himself."

"Carnie doesn't have to. It was the three of you guys who got Brian off campus. What's that? Kidnapping? That's something, and it's probably not a misdemeanor."

"And what do you call coming into my house and pointing a gun in my face? Huh?"

"Put the gun down," Mike said.

"What do you guys want from me?"

"Resolution," I interrupted.

"And you're getting it," Alec said. "Just tell us here what happened, and then it's done."

Franklin stared at us. "Don't you guys get it?" he asked. "I've only been trying to help."

"Trying to help? What's that mean?" I asked.

"What that means is I'm trying to keep you from stumbling into any more trouble. You think I didn't know what was going on with Jelen? I was the one he came to first to try and find Alec. He didn't know how I left things with you—with all of you. He didn't need to know. But he freaked me out when he pulled out this blackmail threat. I didn't bite. But I knew that someone would. And that someone was our Mr. Jake Rivers. Resident hero. The prodigal son."

"What was I supposed to say?" I asked.

"Why didn't you come to me?" Franklin asked.

"Oh, yeah, Papa Frankie," Alec said in disgust. "I'm sure you would have been a comfort."

"Jelen got involved because of you. This is all your fault."

"So what'd you do?" I asked.

"I just—I just wanted you to lay off. To not stir up anything."

"Frankie, you see, has this nice little comfortable life set up for himself, and he doesn't want anyone interrupting it, right?" Alec rested his arm against his side.

Franklin looked as though he wanted to lunge at Alec, but he was wise not to.

"But wait—that wasn't you in Chicago with Bruce and me—" Mike began.

"I don't wave guns around like an idiot."

"You—you just get people to do it for you."

I looked at Franklin's unchanging face and couldn't believe it.

"What's that mean?" I demanded.

"I was just trying to keep you from doing something stupid," Franklin said. "I asked an associate to take care of things."

"An associate," Alec interrupted, mockingly.

"I asked him to get someone to scare you off. That was it."

"Who was it then?" I asked. "The same guy who conked me on the head in Jacksonville? The guy who threatened Alyssa?"

"Threatened who?" Franklin for once sounded believable.

"That's right," Alec said. "Now he's threatening women. Who's next? Jake's parents?"

"That was all just for show."

"And the bullet in Bruce's gut?" Alec demanded. "The one that almost killed a former friend of yours? Was that all for show?"

"Things got a little out of hand."

"Yeah, they always do with you," Alec said. "They got a little out of hand years ago, and they did now."

"What were you thinking?" I asked as Alec propped himself on the hood of his car.

"I was the only one thinking. Period. You take off trying to figure out the past and asking questions—"

"I was looking for Alec."

"You think this Jelen is going to let things just stay the way they were? You think he's going to back off?"

"He will now," Alec told Franklin.

We looked at him, not knowing what that meant.

"Alec—"

"No, this is about Franklin," he said to me. "What happened that night? After you picked up Brian? Did our little ride here bring back any memories?"

"Why don't you ask Mikey here? He knows."

"No, I don't," Mike said. "I swear I don't."

"You were the one who opened up the trunk. You don't remember?"

"No."

Franklin shook his head. "We taped him up, Carnie and I. But I guess we must not have done a very good job. I don't know. A lot about that night is foggy to me too. I was pretty loaded. We opened up the trunk, and Brian bolted out and went after the first person he saw. That was Mike. Man, don't you remember—you were bleeding like a pig all night long? He cut you pretty bad with a knife—a knife that came out of nowhere."

"Then what happened?" Alec asked.

"It was crazy. I don't know. Brian took off after me with that knife and then Carnie was there and things got out of hand—"

"You're lying," Alec said.

"No, I'm not."

"Carnie went to find me," Alec continued. "When you guys got here, you parked on the side of the road. You were supposed to let Brian off in the middle of nowhere to fend for himself. Carnie found me by the campsite, and by the time we got there you were standing over his body."

Mike and I both looked at Franklin. He didn't say anything at first, just looked tired and angry.

"The guy had just tried to kill Mike and he hurt him pretty bad and—"

"And what?" Mike suddenly shouted out at Franklin.

"And I just—yeah—I was doing it out of protection."

"Carnie told me Brian was shot in the back," Alec said.

"You *shot* him?" I asked.

Mike cursed and walked to the side of the car saying "No" over and over again.

"It was self-defense."

"It wasn't Carnie," Alec said, looking at me. "And it wasn't me."

"It got out of control—we're talking about Brian. You know—the guy who almost beat the life out of you? You remember that? That guy had it coming. It wasn't supposed to turn out that way, but he was out of control."

For a moment we were all silent. Distant car engines resonated in the background. Crickets in the surrounding forest droned on. I wondered what a gunshot would sound like out here in the middle of nowhere.

"It was never supposed to happen," Franklin said.

"A lot of things weren't supposed to happen," I said.

Alec watched us carefully, his hand and the gun resting against his side.

"So you just—you just let me—let all of us believe it was Carnie?" I asked Franklin. "How gutless was that?"

"I couldn't control Carnie's demons. We all have them, I couldn't help it. You think I was happy to hear about that?"

"You sure weren't sad."

"At least I didn't bolt," Franklin said, staring at Alec.

"Tell me something," I said. "Something I've always wondered. How—how did I get all bloody? I woke up in the back of Bruce's car with blood all over me."

"I think that was mine," Mike said out of the darkness.

"What?"

Alec answered. "I told you he was bleeding—almost bled to death. We couldn't get it to stop. But we didn't want him going to the hospital."

"How'd I get it all over me?"

"I think you were helping him put pressure against it," Alec said. "But I don't think you were much of a help. You didn't know how to say your last name."

"Jake the hero," Franklin said.

"What's that supposed to mean?"

"Kinda ironic, huh? The big famous adventurer used to be a messy drunk we'd all babysit."

I walked over to Franklin. "You're going to tell me who you hired and where he lives."

"And why's that?"

"What if he threatened your wife? Huh? Your kids?"

"So, what? You married to Alyssa?"

I was about to punch him in the face when Alec came and held me back. "Jake, hold on. I just need to know one thing."

"What's that?"

"Where'd the body go?"

Franklin tightened his lips and looked down. "I got rid of it."

"How?" Mike asked.

"Carnie and I did. That morning when you guys were searching for Jakester here."

"Carnie said you got rid of it in the Cal Sag," Alec said.

I thought of the murky channel nearby where a body could easily decompose without moving or being found.

Franklin didn't say anything. But his silence confirmed it.

"All this time—all these years—I've thought . . ." I couldn't believe this.

Alec nodded. "You should trust somebody once in a while."

"Who? You?" Franklin asked. "Where're you going to run off to this time? Huh?"

"Actually, I think I'm going to have a chat with the Summit police. I think they might be interested in all of this."

Franklin laughed and cursed. "You're as full of it as Jake."

"Nobody's going to hang anything over my head anymore," Alec said. "Nobody's blackmailing me anymore."

"So you're doing this out of love?" Franklin asked.

"No. I'm doing what I should have done if I'd stayed around. I'm doing it for Carnie."

FORTY-NINE

May 1994

WHAT ELSE DO YOU HAVE IN MIND?

Jake no longer tried to sound civil. No longer tried to appear agreeable. All he wanted and needed was to be rid of everything and everyone.

The last five days had been like a smear across a freshly painted picture. What should have been the warm and beautiful start of summer and beginning of his adult life had been smudged with Carnie's wake and funeral in Tennessee. Meeting family and friends, crying and being cried on, walking in silent numbness, all the while just wanting to get out of there. Jake and Bruce had just gotten back from the twelve-hour drive. And Jake wanted to get real drunk real fast.

He had graduated, yet had not received any diploma. Nobody said his name out loud last Saturday morning except for the shouting, shrieking voice of Carnie's father when Jake spoke to him on the phone and delivered the news.

"It shouldn't work out like this," Bruce's voice said across from him.

But Jake didn't care. He didn't give a rip. He could try to be cute or coy but those days were gone. Long gone.

You're not the man you used to be.

Amen to that.

You and I weren't meant to be together.
Hallelujah.
I might be a lot of things, but I'm not a liar.
Yeah, sure, but you're a deserter.
Do you really think there is a hell?
And I don't know, I don't know anymore, because if there is, I'm really afraid now, I'm terrified, because what then what then WHAT THEN, CARNIE?
You're going to get what you deserve.
Jake drank. Of all the things he could do or should have done, he sat in Shaughnessy's drinking. Sitting across from Bruce, having a beer, a smoke, trying to comprehend the carnage that had taken place this past semester.

"You still gonna go to Europe?" Bruce asked.

"I have to get outta this place. This country."

"You going with Franklin and Shane?"

"No. I've said four words to Franklin this past month. The guy never said a word to me about Carnie. Not a word."

Jake felt anger but knew he couldn't put it anywhere. All he could try to do was swallow it, drink it up, and let the drinking numb his pain.

He had found Carnie's body five days ago. His roommate had taken an entire bottle of prescription medication and given nobody a reason why. There was no note, nothing.

And in the black and blue and blurry days since, all Jake could conclude was that Carnie felt guilt from Brian's disappearance. That maybe he was the cause.

What about your own guilt?

Carnie had done something about his. Now Jake just sat back and did what he had always done. What his whole life had led to. This grand, climactic moment. Lots of people had adventures and went on quests and sought out their hopes and their dreams and their loves and their lives, but he sat in a bar across from a half-baked stoner doing nothing and saying nothing and giving nothing back.

Nothing. Everything turned out to be nothing. Hemingway said it and Kurt Cobain said it and his entire angry generation said it.

Nothing

He had lived twenty-two years for nothing. Carnie was the brave one because he had checked himself out permanently.

Liar

Bruce tried to talk a little more, but Jake was done. Bruce didn't understand what was going on. Perhaps his stoned mind just couldn't comprehend the guilt and the madness overflowing in Jake.

Sinner

All Jake could do was drink. And even after Bruce left, calling a cab because he knew he was too drunk and telling Jake to do the same, Jake kept it up. He didn't care anymore.

Though it all looks different now, I know it's still the same.

At some point, he played darts with a seventy-year-old man who laughed at him. The guy told him not to drive back home, but Jake lived ten minutes away and, come on, who cared anyway.

On the drive home, the night lights bright and shiny and rapidly passing by, he blared Nine Inch Nails. It was angry and agitated and fit his mood.

Thank you, Trent, thanks a lot for adding to my pain.

He thought of his last drive with Alec.

Where are you, Alec?

The farewell to Mike in the parking lot. The tears and the hug from Shane. The rest of them.

The rest of who?

You know who I'm talking about, don't you? You did this to me and I know you did. You take every good thing away from me and I never deserved any of this.

The drive seemed longer. The roads felt stranger.

I didn't do this on purpose and I never meant for it to work out this way.

He cranked up the stereo.

Hear me?

He passed a slow-moving car.

Hear me up there out there mystical magical man?

He opened his sunroof and felt the gush of air blow down on him.

Are you there and I don't think you are I bet you aren't I bet my life you aren't.

"*Grey would be the color if I had a heart . . .*" the singer sang.

Is there a hell

He could see Carnie's face after he asked, a haunting, needing, desperate face looking toward him for something he couldn't give him.

Is there a hell because if there is maybe I'll find out maybe I'll be seeing maybe I'll be checking in soon maybe I'll be seeing you Carnie see you Carnie see you Alec I'm coming

Flying, speeding, racing, cursing, gripping, bracing, Jake in his Honda CRX jumped the curb and tore through the ten-foot shrubbery lining the street and then clipped a tree and rolled.

I'm down to just one thing, the voice on the stereo still screamed out, *and I'm starting to scare myself.*

FIFTY

June 2005

THE SUN SHONE on the courtyard outside the library on Providence campus. I sat on the edge of a cement bench, watching Alec come up the walk.

"You can pull off miracles, you know that?" Alec said.

In another life, this might have been our farewell. Me graduating, saying good-bye to Bruce and Mike and Shane and Kirby and Franklin *and Carnie*. And finally wishing Alec a happy-ever-after.

It was another thought, another life.

"Why's that?" I asked.

"You got me to come back. I never thought I'd set foot on this campus again."

Alec sat on a cement bench facing mine and lit up a cigarette. His eyes squinted from the sun. "So why'd you want to come back here?"

"I wanted you to see it in daylight."

Alec only laughed.

"Honestly? Because I've been to more bars and pubs and clubs in the last month than I have in the last ten years."

Alec laughed. "I feel like I should be having a beer for this conversation."

"We've had very few without being inebriated."

"Yeah."

The campus was still today, with students out for the summer and most of the faculty either on vacation or in their offices working. I never could remember just sitting on campus and looking around, enjoying the tranquility. I never pictured my college days in sunny serenity. I remembered the shadows.

"How'd it go with the cops?"

Alec shrugged. "I told them everything. I know you did too."

"And Franklin?"

"He was released on bail. Should be interesting. They're going to want me—want all of us—to testify."

"I know."

"Guess I can't disappear then, huh?"

"Probably not."

Alec smiled and took a drag from his smoke. "I gotta go back home," he said.

"And where's that?"

"Well—going back to see my mom. She's still living in Florida."

"And Claire?"

"She broke things off a few weeks ago. Things were, in her words, 'a bit too intense.'"

"What's that mean?" I asked.

"It means we're over. And Mr. Jelen doesn't have to worry about me being his son-in-law."

I nodded. For a while we sat in silence, each waiting for the other to speak. Alec broke the quiet.

"I never did get a chance to explain my New Year's Eve voice mail."

"I'm still waiting," I said.

"Carnie told me what happened near the end, before I left. Back then—I don't know. It didn't seem like a big deal . . . in light of everything. But I got it wrong. I should have said something. But I was—messed up."

"We all were," I said.

"It wasn't just the drinking. It was something worse."

"What's that?'

"Selfishness. Arrogance. All those things I've been guilty of all my life. It just—the stuff he said didn't mean anything to me because it didn't affect me."

I waited.

"You remember the night you got beat up?"

"Sorta hard to forget."

"Before the end—before I took off—remember how Carnie just suddenly stopped being around? We all assumed it was because of what happened on spring break. And that was part of it. But there was more."

"How so?"

"Carnie got liquored up one night and told me how he was outside of the apartment the night you got the snot beat out of you. He was in his car and saw Brian and his buddy storm inside."

I looked at Alec and tried to think for a minute. "Did he know what they were going to do?"

Alec nodded. "It was pretty obvious."

"But . . . I don't get it."

"I didn't either. Carnie told me this, and he was bawling, man. I mean, he was a wreck. It was weird to see this big guy crying like a baby. I was like, 'Why didn't you do something?' and all he could say was that he was scared."

"Carnie? Scared?"

Alec nodded. "Yeah, that's what I said. That's what we all thought. Big guy who could crack anybody's skull. But he was—well, Brian freaked him out."

"There's no way."

"That's what he told me. He felt responsible for what happened to you that night. That was why—that was why he was bothered so much by everything that happened afterward."

"I don't get it. Why couldn't he have just—just come into the building—"

"He did. He heard you yelling out and screaming."

I looked out across the campus. I could picture Carnie and me ambling our way to a class, sharing a smoke, trying to walk off a hangover, planning what we'd do that night. With Carnie by my side, I always felt somewhat invincible. I couldn't believe Alec's words.

"So you see why—you see why he—"

"Yeah," I interrupted. I wiped my eyes and sighed. My heart felt heavy. "Everything that happened—all of this—it was my fault."

"No, it wasn't."

"In a sense it was. I provoked stuff with Brian so that it escalated. Everything that happened afterwards—"

"Was *not* all your doing. Franklin's going to jail, and you're not."

"I thought it would be easier," I said.

"What?"

"Finding out the truth."

"I never wanted to get back into all of that."

"Me neither. But God has a way of putting things in your life you don't want."

Alec laughed.

"What?"

"Jake—come on. You really buy all of that stuff?"

"I have to believe it. It's not a choice."

"Why?" Alec asked.

"Because if I don't—if it's nothing—then I gotta cope with blood on my hands. Don't you get it? It's selfish, I guess. But if these mistakes and sins can't be taken away—then I'm stuck with them. I'll live my whole life with these things on my soul."

"Yeah. But what if you don't have a soul?"

"Then I go to my grave guilty."

"You're not guilty," Alec said.

"We're all guilty."

"I don't think so. They did it to themselves."

"That makes you no different than Carnie."

"How so?"

"You'll die without hope."

"I won't *kill* myself."

"Maybe not. But twenty—forty—sixty years from now—you'll die. And then what? Then what?"

"Blackness."

"I don't want to go my whole life without hope, Alec. I did it for almost thirty years. I didn't want to keep going. Not believing in something. Without believing that the pain I held—those awful memories—those failures that haunted me—that they couldn't go away."

"Have they?"

"Yes."

"Sounds like a fairy tale. Or a good shrink."

"You remember the last thing—the last conversation we had? When you almost killed us in the car?"

Alec thought about it for a moment, then nodded.

"You said that you might be a lot of things, but you weren't a liar."

"I'm not."

"Same goes for me, Alec. I'm not lying. Especially not to you. We've gone through too much for me to start preaching something I don't believe. I know when the time comes, something will be on the other end."

"Maybe."

"I want to see you there."

Alec nodded, silent, looking up at the sky.

"We're no different, you know," I said.

"Yeah, we are," he said in a matter-of-fact way.

"No, we're not. We're all in the same boat. A leaky boat that's sinking. Going down until someone rescues us."

"Until someone judges us. If God does exist, the only thing He's going to want to do with me is send me straight down to hell."

"And that's what we deserve. That realization drove me to my knees."

"I don't particularly want to get down on my knees," Alec said.

I didn't know how to respond, wondering if I'd already said too much. The words sounded strange coming from my lips, my heart trying not to be trite or superficial or hypocritical. I just knew that if I never had another chance and if I let things pass just as I had with Carnie, I might never be able to get over that guilt.

277

I thought that this was all I could say for the moment, then I remembered the last words that I took away from Providence College, the very last words that haunted me years afterward and then finally ended up comforting me.

The last words I thought I'd ever hear from Alyssa Roberts.

I said them to Alec in the most honest, matter-of-fact way I could. "That's all I can offer you, man," I finished. "That's all I know to do."

"Yeah."

And after what could have been an awkward embrace but turned into a strong bear hug that surprised me, I said good-bye to the friend I knew as Alec.

FIFTY-ONE

May 1994

TREES AND HOUSES and cars and people and life passed by outside his window as Jake watched and wondered when he'd be able to join them. It wasn't supposed to work out like this. It wasn't supposed to end like this. There had to be more to the story, had to be something else. Somebody had to rescue him. Somebody had to come and take this gnawing pain away.

But the only one left was Bruce, who had stopped by Dunkin' Donuts to get them some coffee and breakfast and was now driving him back home from the police station, where Jake had spent the night.

"How're you feeling?" Bruce asked.

"I've felt worse."

"You look bad."

"Not as bad as my car," Jake said. "The cops said it was totaled. They said I'm lucky to be alive. That I had some guardian angels watching over me."

"Yeah, maybe you do."

Jake shook his head. "Where were they when Carnie decided to swallow a bottle of pills? That's my question."

He still felt woozy and weak from the night before. He thought of the approaching call to his parents. It didn't matter.

They would be upset, but there was nothing they could do to make things worse.

I'm already grounded, Jake thought. *And I will be the rest of my life.*

"Wait till my parents hear about this," he said.

"You gotta tell them?"

Jake laughed. "Sorta hard not to. Unless you want to drive me around all summer."

"No, thanks." Bruce finished his coffee and tossed the cup onto the floorboard. "Actually, I'm going back home myself. I'm all packed up. Ready to bolt."

In the parking lot, Bruce's car parked but still running, they said their good-byes. Simple, male good-byes. Jake opened his car door, but before getting out, Bruce stopped him.

"Jake?"

He looked over at his friend. "Yeah?"

"Think we'll be able to move on? That all this will just be— just be like some distant memory we will all slowly forget?"

Jake forced a smile. "I hope."

↠　↞

He walked into the empty apartment and felt the chill of the cool summer morning. The bedroom window was opened slightly, letting some air creep in. A fan someone had left on blew the breeze steadily, stirring the only bit of life left in the rooms. The blank walls stared at him in silence.

It was over. The people, the parties, the privileges youth allowed . . . all of it was over. May soon would be turning into June. He had graduated, and the first thing he had done was go out and get a DUI. Some people got jobs, but not Jake. He had lost two best friends in a matter of weeks. One disappeared and the other killed himself. Both left with answers Jake wanted and needed.

The apartment echoed the last four years of his reckless life. Nothing but a few bags of trash and a few lifeless posters remained. The framed picture of James Dean still hung over his bed.

He walked to the kitchen and surveyed the scene. It was

the cleanest it had been since the guys moved in. He didn't see the blinking light of the answering machine at first, and when he did, he figured it was one of the guys saying good-bye or asking for something.

Instead, it was Alyssa. The soft, sweet voice that he had longed to hear. It felt like aloe on sunburned skin.

"Hi, Jake. It's Thursday, and I just wanted to tell you—I'm so sorry to hear about Carnie. I can't say how awful I feel. I'm so sorry. And I wish I could have told you this in person, but I just didn't have the strength. So I'm doing it now. Like this. I apologize for not being stronger. But I hope you get this message.

"Everything happens for a reason, Jake. I know how clichéd and empty that might sound. Even saying it—I know how it comes across. But things do happen for a reason. Carnie's death—I don't know why it happened. But I'm sorry for it. I'm sorry for you losing your friend.

"I believe God put you in my life for a reason and a purpose. Maybe not for the one you hoped. But for other reasons, perhaps. I don't know. All I can do is pray for you, Jake. And I promise that I will keep praying for you, even after you're long gone. You know what I believe. So all I can tell you is to remember this. God loves you as much as He loves me. And wherever you go in this world, He'll still continue loving you.

"I hope you find yourself, Jake. And that you find your way. I'll never forget you or our friendship.

"I'll be praying for you. And praying our paths cross again one day."

FIFTY-TWO

July 2005

"HOW YOU FEELING?"

Bruce looked at me and grinned. "It's time to finally start smoking for medicinal purposes."

I laughed and shook my head. We had upgraded to a Holiday Inn, and sat in chairs in the lobby. Bruce's bag sat by his feet.

"So what's next?" I asked.

"I was going to ask you that same question."

"I'm meeting Alyssa for breakfast in a few minutes. After that, I'm not exactly sure."

"Yeah, me neither."

Bruce looked healthier since he'd managed to get outside and get some sun. I'd been trying to get him to eat as much as possible. Aside from his walking slowly and not being able to bend over, he didn't look like someone who had been shot in the gut less than a month ago.

"This is sorta weird," Bruce said.

"What?"

"In the end, it's just you and me again. Must be fate."

"Or the sign of a true friend."

"A true friend probably would've told you the whole truth," Bruce said.

"Yeah. But you kept me out of trouble."

"I took a bullet for you, man," he joked, sounding like a beer commercial.

A cab pulled up in front of the hotel.

"I'm not big into good-byes."

I nodded. "Me neither."

"Wherever I end up—I'll let you know."

"Sure. You've got my cell number. Among others."

"Think things will work out?"

I wasn't sure what Bruce referred to. Everything related to Brian Erwin and Alec and Carnie and Franklin? Maybe. But he might be talking about my job. Or my life.

Or Alyssa.

"Things happen for a reason," I said.

"Think so? Really?"

"I do."

"Maybe I'll see you before another ten years go by."

"Somebody's got to keep you out of trouble. And alive."

I shook Bruce's hand, and he grabbed his bag and ambled out of the hotel. I knew I would see him before too long. It wasn't a promise I was going to make to him. It was a promise I had made to myself.

→→ ←←

Alyssa was waiting for me at the Starbucks minutes away from college. I drove down the street, the windows open and the temperature a couple hours from being stuffy. On the seat beside me was my itinerary. The one-way e-ticket was for an afternoon flight.

I wasn't sure what I was going to say to her, although I'd rehearsed the conversation in my mind a hundred times. Over the last four weeks, we had spent a lot of time together. And during that time I had contemplated moving back to Illinois and making a transition in my life. My failing business could be left behind. So could the few ties I had in Colorado.

I didn't want to leave Alyssa behind. Not again.

Sometimes I wondered why God put certain people in my

life. Alec. Bruce. Carnie. Alyssa. Back when I thought life was completely random and that I held my fate and destination in my hands, I never thought about such things. But ever since God tracked me down in a shabby hotel in Kathmandu, things had never been the same. After that fateful climb in the Himalayas, I knew that something had to give.

I never thought it would be my heart.

Alec's words resonated in my head. *Sounds like a fairy tale.* And it did. Some people might hear my story and roll their eyes, thinking I'd come up with a way to appease my guilt and placate my soul. But I had nothing to do with it.

I pulled the car into the parking lot and got out. I felt anxious about the conversation I was about to have. After everything that had happened, how could I just move on and live happily ever after? That was the piece of my faith that people had a problem with. This whole business of living happily ever after in heaven with God for eternity—it sounded made up and truly unbelievable, especially in light of everything down here on earth.

Sounds like a fairy tale.

I used to think that too. All I could tell them was my story, and how I was a different person now.

I opened the door and saw Alyssa sitting in an armchair that faced another empty one. She saw me instantly and smiled, that smile reminding me of the first time I saw her a month ago in this same place.

Then I thought of the first time I ever saw her, in the dean's office at Providence. Alyssa was a different person back then, and so was I. God knew we needed to have that first fateful meeting, and that our paths would cross again somewhere down the road.

God knew we would need each other later in life. And I believed with every ounce of my being that he had allowed us to come back together. Seeing Alyssa's gaze, her sweet smile—I realized my decision had already been made.

The world loves sad endings—dark, tragic endings—but this wasn't going to be one of them.

Acknowledgments

WITH SPECIAL THANKS TO the following people:

Andy McGuire, for letting me tell this story and helping me grow as a writer.

LB Norton, for guiding me along and helping the editing process go as smoothly as it ever has.

Mom and Dad, for your never-ending encouragement and belief in me.

Cecil E. White, for your incredible gift I'll never be able to repay.

Claudia Cross, for taking a chance to work together.

Barry Smith, for your partnership, your passion, and most of all, your friendship.

Keri Tryba, for being a vital part of the AR team and so much fun to work with.

Everybody at Moody Publishers, for your continued confidence in my writing.

To all the people who put up with my antics at Trinity.

To my friends and co-workers, who should know this is a work of fiction.

And, of course, to Sharon, who knows that some of it isn't. But who stayed with me anyway.

COMING SOON FROM TRAVIS THRASHER . . .

BLINDED

Michael Grey is about to experience his very own dark night of the soul.

Michael has it all worked out: 37 years old, married, two kids, beautiful home, churchgoer, marketing director on the rise. How much of it will he risk for a seductive smile from a stranger? Alone in New York on a business trip, Michael finds out.

A simple conversation and a short phone call plunge Michael into a night out of his control. He starts by flirting with temptation and ends up fighting for his life. Michael finds himself on the run with nowhere to go, and as the night grows longer, he wonders if he will live to see the rising sun.

What could make a happily married man abandon all reason for a night with a beautiful woman? And what if the beautiful woman is not what she seems? Michael's decision might not just destroy his family. It might wreck his life. And his soul.

Blinded, the gripping new novel from Travis Thrasher, will be available in fall, 2006.

4:47 p.m.

"MIND IF I JOIN YOU?"

These are not the words you expect to hear. Not now, on a Friday midafternoon in Manhattan. Not after the two days you've had. Not after the cancelled dinner and the cancelled account. And positively, definitely, not coming from the beautiful woman in heels standing before you.

For a moment you're lost for words. You're never lost for words. But for half a second, you can't say anything.

Only half an hour ago you saw the same figure settle into her seat and order a glass of wine and cross her legs and watch the sidewalk close to Rockefeller Center. Sipping a red and people watching, just like you were doing. You looked away, first at the table in front of you, then at the half glass of Pinot Grigio, then the empty chair facing you, then the glisten of your wedding ring in the sun. But your eyes found their way back to the blonde again, sitting in front of you, her profile in full view, her eyes glancing over and easily spotting your gaze.

You were the first to look away.

And this sort of fun, harmless glancing went on for half an hour as the motion of the city blurred behind. People getting off work, tourists roaming, couples strolling. You are here because you've ordered wines from this place before. Wine is a hobby you've only picked up the last couple of years; it's harmless, but you still keep it from some of the couples you know. Drinking has a certain stigma to some of your church friends. But in a city far away from the suburbs of Chicago, nobody is going to find you. Nobody is going to care if you're on your second glass. And if you're staring at one of the hottest women you've ever seen.

It doesn't hurt to look.

But for some reason she's now standing in front of you, looking down at you, grinning, waiting for an answer.

"Sure."

That's all you say.

So this woman, perhaps in her late twenties, sits down across from you, a glass half full in her hand. For a moment she continues watching the sidewalk without feeling the need to say anything.

You have no idea how your life is about to change.

"Where are you from?" she asks after you share small talk over wine.

"I look like a tourist?"

"You don't look like a New Yorker."

"Chicago," you say, easier than saying Deerfield, Illinois.

"You don't have an accent."

"Neither do you."

"I haven't stuck around anywhere long enough to pick up an accent."

The first thing you notice are greenish-blue eyes, model eyes that would seem manufactured if they were in a magazine. Blonde hair that might be real or colored falls several inches below bare shoulders. The look she gives is confident, curious, and relaxed.

You may decide it's a dangerous look. Women might be the ones who claim to have intuitions, but you have some yourself.

"Where are you from?"

"Florida. And California."

"Which one first?" you ask.

She shines another grin. "Does it matter?"

"No."

"Florida," she answers.

A waiter comes up and before even attempting to ask the woman, she orders another glass of something called "The Thief."

"That's the name of a wine?" you ask.

She nods. You tell the waiter you'll try it.

It's the end of a long week and you didn't ask for her to be sitting there and there's nothing wrong with sharing a glass of wine with a stranger in the middle of hundreds of other strangers. A single snapshot might be strange but you have an explanation and you don't need an explanation anyway.

You're too fried to even think about anything except wondering who this woman is.

"Heading back soon?" she asks.

She has a strong voice. Nothing about this woman is weak. Her gaze doesn't waver and you keep your eyes on her and avoid looking at anything else. Or any other part of her.

"Tomorrow."

"So with all the sights to see in New York, and all the things to do, what brings you here?"

"I order wines from this place . . . Thought I'd check it out."

"First time to New York?"

"First time sitting here," you tell her.

You came here with Lisa.

Lisa is your wife just in case you need someone to remind you.

She takes a sip from her wine and you look at her lips for a second longer than you probably should.

I'm tired, you think.

Perhaps this is reasoning.

"And you're all alone?"

Now you're the one to smile.

"Am I missing something here?" you ask.

"Uncomfortable with a lot of questions?"

"I've seen stuff like this on television shows. People getting pranked."

"I just figured you might like some company. And I thought you probably wouldn't take the initiative to join me."

"And you're all alone?" you repeat her question.

"At the moment, no. Just making light conversation to pass the time."

You wonder if this is a New York thing.

"I'm Michael," you tell her, finally being friendly.

"And what does Michael do for a living?"

You smile. "Michael sells for a living."

"Sells what?"

"Does it matter?" you ask, teasing her.

"Come on. You already told me your name."

"I could've made up it up. There are thousands of Michaels."

"There are thousands of salesmen."

"So what are *you* selling?" you ask.

Her gaze doesn't waver and the grin doesn't go away. "Please."

"What?"

"A lot of women might take that as an insult."

"A lot of guys might be too stupid to ask that."

She sips her drink again and for the moment continues to watch the crowd. As if she's done, at least for the moment, with the conversation. You don't know if she's a businesswoman but she might be. Wearing a skirt and a button down shirt. Black pointy heels that look expensive. A little purse that can only carry sunglasses and a couple of credit cards.

This is the way your luck goes. A beautiful outgoing woman with that look in her eye comes and sits down at a table with you to share a glass of wine and some light banter. There is nothing more that can happen because you are a married man with two children. And Lisa might wonder what in the world you're doing in the first place with this woman talking and smiling and sharing a glass of wine.

It's harmless and you didn't do anything to prompt it and nothing else will come from it because nothing *can* come from it. And that's your luck. Because as beautiful as this woman is, she is not yours and can never be yours and all she will be is a sweet smile to look at.

And eventually the risk factor fades when the unnamed woman says she must go.

"Thanks for the chat."

"You're—welcome."

"Don't worry. I've already paid for my wine."

"It's fine," you say.

She looks at you as if she's contemplating something, sizing you up for something.

That is not a safe look. Nothing about that look is safe. It's dangerous.

"You have a pen and a business card, don't you?" she asks.

You find them and give them to her, still surprised, still stunned and wanting to know where this will lead.

She quickly writes down something and gives you back the card and the pen.

"Perhaps we can share another glass of wine later. If you're not too busy."

And she stands, and of course, you can't help but look at her. She doesn't even say goodbye and maybe that's the whole point. She's left you with a name and a phone number and now she's turned and walking away and she's leaving you with a great view you briefly lose yourself in watching.

What just happened and how did it happen to me? You're not the sort of guy who gets a Jasmine to write out her number for you.

And you're not the guy who calls that number, for whatever reason. To sample a serious vintage or to get yourself in serious trouble.

You're not that sort of man despite the fact that your plane leaves in sixteen hours and you have nothing else to do.

Because if you *were* that sort of man, there would have to be some serious reasons to do so, right? And you're a good guy. With a good family. And a good life.

You're not going to do anything with that number.

But you slide it into your shirt pocket and keep it anyway.

⤛ ⤜

6:15 p.m.

There's anonymity in New York City.

It almost feels like God can't even keep track of someone in the city, like there's too much compressed into such a small space.

You are used to Chicago, living in the suburbs and working in the city. Chicago has character; New York has crowds. Something about the faces passing you by makes you feel small and insignificant. One of the millions. Still wearing a suit you were going to wear to dinner tonight. Still wearing that new tie Lisa bought you.

The smell of the hot dog vendor makes you almost stop to buy one but you see a disaster waiting to happen smeared all over your coat. You think back to the blonde, the long legs, the phone number you still have.

There's no way.

Of course you think this. Of course you won't call it. There's some sort of catch and you're not taking it.

Maybe she's just like you. Alone in a city looking for company.

And she wants you to think this. Just like the guys you pass whowant you to spend $25 on a wallet that cost them 50¢ to make. It's part of the scenery, part of the street, part of New York.

If you're not too busy.

And you wonder how you're going to kill the night. There's nothing to do, nowhere to go, no one to see.

A man could get lost in a city like this and nobody would know. Nobody would pay him any attention. Nobody would care.

God himself might not even care.

➤➤ ◄◄

7:34 p.m.

You're waiting for someone to pick up on the other line as you sit on the edge of the made bed, the room service tray right in front of you. A wet stain from the ketchup you spilled looks like it's never going to dry. ESPN is talking about baseball, which doesn't really interest you. Baseball seasons take so long. Football seasons feel too short.

You hear your voice on the other end and decide to leave a message.

"Hey—just wanted to call. Sorry I missed you earlier. I was

out. You're probably at your parents—I'll try back in a little while. Love you."

There is a tinge of guilt you feel.

I didn't go up to that woman. I was sitting there minding my business when she came up to me.

But you didn't answer your cell phone.

I didn't feel it vibrating.

You look at the change and pen and key card on the desk next to you. Next to them sits the name and the number that seem to glow in the dark.

The room feels silent and lonely.

Jasmine.

Is that even a real name?

Your cell phone sits on the bed. Ready. Waiting.

For a minute you just stare at the name, the handwriting.

And a minute turns to ten, maybe twenty. You're not sure. You don't really know what you're thinking. You can blink and see the woman's face, her eyes on yours, her smile.

A beautiful woman is God's gift to man. She knows it and he knows it and there is nothing a man can do but admit it. He's weak and under her control.

You memorize the numbers. They're just numbers. It's just a name. A stranger passing you by, never to see you again, never to cross your path.

It's ten numbers. It could be an apartment or a condo or a hotel or a cell phone.

A ring jerks you from your trance. You pick up the hotel phone.

"Mike?"

"Yeah."

"What are you doing in your hotel room?"

"Finishing off a really bad burger."

"Sad."

"Where are you?"

"Just got back to O'hare."

"Why didn't you take me with you?"

"Just got your message. That sucks."

"Yeah."

295

"What are you going to tell Connelly?"

"The truth. What else can I say?"

"It's officially off?"

"I tried everything. They're done."

"Couldn't get a flight out?"

"Didn't even try."

"You got a night out on the town. I should be there with you."

"That could be dangerous."

"It could be fun. Look—you're in Manhattan. It's a Friday night. And you're what? Watching *Law and Order*?"

"ESPN."

"Harsh. They'll be showing the same stuff in eight hours. Go out. Do something. Anything."

"Thanks, Dad."

"I'd take you out if I was there. If you were a going out sort of guy."

"I go out. I just don't black out like you."

"Funny. Hey—I gotta get my luggage. Call me when you get back in."

"Sure."

"And Mike. Man—don't dwell on it. It wasn't your fault."

"Who said it was?"

"Connelly will."

"Yeah, right."

He laughs.

"See ya."

You hear the phone click and you just hold it in your hands. You'd like to throw it or at least bash it over someone's head. Maybe your own.

The line goes dead.

And the numbers draw you in.

You look back at the handwritten note. Very pretty handwriting.

Without thought, you dial each number.

One. After another. After another.

And then you hear the ring.

You don't really want to do this.

But you stay on. And on the fourth ring, on what should be voicemail, on what should be you hanging up and tearing up the sheet and waiting for your wife to call, you hear the same voice you were talking to earlier.

"It took you long enough," she says.

You feel a head rush and can't say anything for a minute.

"I haven't given my number to anyone else, Chicago boy."

And you suddenly realize that this might not be a con, or an indecent proposal, or anything other than a stranger like you in a strange land.

"I didn't expect to get you."

The laugh she gives is gentle and friendly. "I'm here. For now."

You can't say anything. You have no idea what to say.

"You were more talkative in person."

"Yeah."

"So I'll make this easy."

Here it comes.

"I'm heading over to Atmosphere. A great lounge. I'm sure you can find a cab to take you there."

"Yeah."

Again, you hear her laugh. Not mocking. More playful, like she finds your Neanderthal conversation amusing.

"And I'll be with several friends, so don't worry."

"About what?"

"I won't bite."

And before you can say something, she hangs up.

Again, you're left with the receiver in your hand.

Your forehead feels sweaty but the air conditioner is cranked. You go over to the windows and open the drapes, revealing a New York just ready to turn on.

Go on out, a voice tells you.

You deserve a drink.

Make something out of this abysmal failure.

She'll be with several friends.

There's nothing wrong with going out and having a conversation and enjoying yourself. Nothing at all.

You stare at the city and the motion and you feel lonely and

297

you hate being all alone. There's something about the silence, even with white noise around you, that feels hollow. That feels threatening.

You don't do well alone.

Tonight, you're not going to be alone.

More from Travis Thrasher . . .

The Second Thief
ISBN: 0-8024-1707-8

Meet Tom Ledger. Disillusioned. Bored. Willing to sell his
soul—or at least his company's most guarded secrets—to the
highest bidder. Tom has no way of knowing that within hours
of committing his first felony he'll be catapulted into a high-
stakes drama as the airplane he's on drops like a rock into a
Nebraska cornfield.

Author Travis Thrasher takes readers on a fast-paced journey
through the seamy underworld Tom encounters after the crash,
replete with espionage, terror, and murder. Tom must confront
his past and its consequences and decide his next steps.

More from Travis Thrasher . . .

Gun Lake
ISBN: 0-8024-1748-5

Five escaped convicts looking for freedom. A woman on the run from another life. A father carrying sins of the past. A broken county deputy who can become a hero. And a dangerous ringleader who will bring all their paths together.

Once again Travis Thrasher takes readers on a thrilling ride, this time through the story of escaped convicts and the people whose paths they cross. Weaving together twists of fate and fast-paced action, Gun Lake examines the consequences of evil and asks some compelling questions: Where do you turn when there is no hope left? How do you leave past mistakes behind?